CORPUS PROCESSION

GLYNN JENKINS

To Richard and Nicole Smyth,

With affection and gratitude.

AUTHOR'S NOTE

This is the third novel to feature detective George Ashley, his nephew, Tom, and the soldiers and horses of Prince Albert's Troop. The action takes place about nine months after *A Ceremonial Death* and five months after *A Meet with Murder*. Tom is still a relatively inexperienced gunner, receiving regular lessons from a military riding instructor and gradually being introduced to his ceremonial duties.

Everybody knows that Bruton is a real town and many will have heard of King's School. The school was first founded in 1519 by Bishop Fitzjames on the Feast of Corpus Christi; its Commemoration Procession and Service were held on that day until recent years, when they were moved to the first Saturday of the summer half term. The Fitzjames Dolphin continues to feature in the heraldry of King's School, even down to the naming of Arion House, the most recently established boarding house. The tale of the poet Arion riding a dolphin is told by Herodotus in his *Histories*.

Bruton also boasts a venerable hospital for the elderly, named after its founder, Hugh Sexey; it is close by the school, though not exactly opposite as it appears in this novel. Colonel Oglethorpe really did stop at Bruton on his way to take part in the Battle of Sedgemoor and the events of the Monmouth Rebellion are basically as described. Arbella Fitzjames is an invented character; she ought to have existed.

I am grateful to Staff Sergeant Ben Moore of the King's Troop RHA, for patiently describing to me many of the routines and traditions of the Horse Artillery. If I have made any errors, they are all my own. I am also indebted to Sergeant Peter Gostling for taking the picture of Gunner Adrian Clarke of B sub-section, The King's Troop RHA, which appears on the cover of this book. The picture shows Gunner Clarke riding his horse, Enchantress, as he passes out of the recruits' riding course and earns his spurs as a fully trained member of the Troop.

Some friends have allowed themselves to appear in these pages, to be affectionately portrayed and frequently lampooned: they know who they are, and all other characters are entirely fictional. Lest there should be any confusion in this matter, I ought to state that Bruton has been served by excellent community support officers, none of whom resembled CSO Sharon Flavell in any way at all.

Glynn Jenkins
Crail, Fife
January 2017

NOVELS BY GLYNN JENKINS

A Ceremonial Death

A Meet with Murder

Corpus Procession

Friendly Fire

Mediaeval Murder

All these novels feature detective George Ashley, his nephew, Tom, and Tom's comrades in Prince Albert's Troop RHA. They do not need to be read in sequence but those who choose to do so will be able to follow Tom's military career more closely.

CHAPTER ONE

REHEARSALS

Thursday morning, a week before Corpus Christi. Happy and anarchic, three hundred and fifty boys and girls are assembled on the school green. In theory, they are organising themselves into their form groups and then alphabetically into pairs; in practice, they cluster around, chatting to friends nearby or calling out to those more distant. Boys try to impress girls and girls flaunt themselves before boys. A few keen masters and mistresses attempt to impose order, here and there chivvying a form into two neat files – but as one group takes shape, another begins to waver and bulge, then bursts, scattering eager teenagers to resume former conversations and activities.

Along the side of the green, more experienced members of staff simply await the arrival of the deputy headmaster. Like their pupils, they are making the most of a rare free period, enjoying the warmth of a May sun and the pleasing sensations of a soft westerly wind. Having wandered at random over the Somerset Levels, the breeze is now making the most of its time in Bruton, exploring the course of the river, wafting along the High Street and touring around the ancient school, spreading goodwill as it travels.

Megaphone in hand, the deputy headmaster emerges from the sports hall and casts a sardonic eye over the scene; it is no more chaotic than previous years. The experience of a decade and a half has taught him to recognise the difference between deliberate bad behaviour and juvenile high spirits. The same years have taught him how to react to both. He raises the megaphone to his mouth.

1

'Right, you lot! I want you in your form groups now!'

As if by magic, it happens. The keen masters and mistresses are made aware of their own disciplinary inadequacy; they slink away and join their wiser colleagues at the edge of the green. The deputy headmaster continues: 'I know this is only a rehearsal but let's make it a good one. As you walk – nice and slowly – make sure you keep in your pairs. When we get to the church, ushers will direct you to your seats. Choir – are you ready?'

The choir prefect is acting as crucifer. He solemnly raises the processional cross and nods. The deputy headmaster lowers his megaphone and takes a radio out of his breast pocket.

'Hello Dolphins Two, Three, Four and Five – this is Dolphin One. All set at this end. How about you? Over.'

In numeric order, four affirmative crackles confirm the positions and readiness of the duty team. The megaphone comes back into play.

'Right then! Beginning with the choir and then in ascending form order! Like I said before, nice and slowly – no bunching up, and keep with your partner. Off you go!'

Led by the crucifer and two of the more sensible trebles, the procession begins to move, the square formation of the initial parade gradually unravelling into two thin, parallel columns. Off the lawn and onto a tarmac path; over the road which passes through the school, where Dolphin Two is holding up the traffic. Through the grounds beyond, past buildings devoted to maths and modern languages; closing in to squeeze across the wooden bridge over the River Brue, then widening out again, passing through the wrought iron gates which separate the school from its sister foundation, the Fitzjames Hospital.

*   *   *   *   *

2

The rehearsal taking place on the parade ground of Prince Albert's Troop is altogether smarter: hotter, too, for the cooling breeze has failed to reach North London. Underneath black fur busbies, eight ceremonially clad gunners and a trumpeter are drilling to the orders of an authoritative, exacting bombardier. They are marching and halting, turning on the spot and dressing to the right, saluting with swords, then standing rigidly to attention while the trumpeter sounds a fanfare. Every new movement creates flashes of light as their silver swords and brilliantly polished riding boots reflect and scatter the sun's rays. The gold braid on the soldiers' tunics and the red stripes down the side of their breeches add to the spectacle. George Ashley, leaning against the gate of a stable block, is impressed and entertained; the more so since he recognises his nephew, Tom, among the obedient, clockwork figures.

'He's looking very smart, Lance Bombardier Green – is it his first time in full dress?'

The lance bombardier, in shirtsleeve order and significantly cooler than the gunners on the parade ground, is also propped against the gate, enjoying the sight of other people working.

'Yes, sir – apart from fitting sessions with the regimental tailor, and then trying it on in front of the mirror, preening himself every day for the last week. Tom Two's been just as bad: I had to take a whole memory card full of pictures of him all dressed up, so he could e-mail them to his mum – and to whichever girl he's sniffing around at the moment. That's him on the trumpet, in case you hadn't realised, sir.'

Ashley *had* realised: Tom Two has very large ears, which stick out a long way. When he plays the trumpet, his face is concealed, giving the impression that the instrument has crossed itself with an African elephant.

'He tried to tuck them into his busby at first, sir, but they popped out every time he came to attention. It brought a certain novelty to the manoeuvre, but Bomber Burdett started to get annoyed.'

Bombardier Burdett is getting even more annoyed now: a

call to attention has not received the simultaneous crashing of boots against tarmac that he requires. A high-pitched, 'As you were!', miraculously compressed into a single syllable, rings out across the parade ground and the nine soldiers shuffle awkwardly back into their former positions. The bombardier punishes the moment of inattention by practising the movement repeatedly. The barracks echo alternately to commands and thuds.

'They're starting to lose concentration, I reckon, sir – the bomber's been drilling them since just after you left for your ride with Captain Raynham, and that's a good hour and a half ago. If Burdett's got any sense, he'll give them a break.'

The break comes soon. Finally satisfied with an immaculate call to attention, Bombardier Burdett nods to Tom Two. For the twentieth time that morning, Tom grasps his trumpet, extends it out in front of him, and then brings it up to his lips. But his embouchure is tired now; instead of crisp, rhythmic arpeggios and blazing flourishes, he can produce no more than a few raspberry sounds and a cascade of split notes. On either side of the trumpet, his ears turn bright red with embarrassment, while the other eight gunners try desperately and inadequately to suppress the urge to laugh. For a moment, the bombardier looks as if he is about to explode; then he chooses a more sensible course:

'All right, I get the message – time for a NAAFI break. Be back here in half an hour. Let's see if you can at least fall out smartly. Listen in!'

The prospect of a steaming mug of army tea acts as an incentive to concentration. The command is given: the gunners perform a right turn precise enough to satisfy even an irate bombardier, then they march off, breaking order after three paces. Most of them head straight for the NAAFI; the Toms turn towards Ashley and Lance Bombardier Green. Tom Two removes his busby as he walks, revealing a livid red line on his forehead and short, moist hair, glistening in the sunlight. Tom One, still carrying his sword, has to suffer a little longer.

4

'Hi, Uncle George – hi, Lance. Were you enjoying the butch ballet show?'

'Enormously – though I hadn't thought of you as performing *Swan Lake*.' Ashley suppresses a joyful vision of the gunners up on their toes, their arms entwined, prancing across the parade ground as an unlikely collection of cygnets. Tom Two observes, cynically, that *Nutcracker* is a more likely choice of ballet after the best part of two hours drilling with Bombardier Burdett.

Ashley's nephew brings the conversation back home: 'You couldn't hold my sword for a moment, could you, Uncle George?' Tom One rests the blade of his sword on his left arm and offers the hilt to Ashley, who enjoys his momentary possession of the ceremonial weapon. Unencumbered, Tom sheds his headdress with obvious relief. Cradling his busby in his left arm, he retrieves his sword, then leads the way to the NAAFI.

*   *   *   *   *

As the soldiers head for their refreshments, the school passes through the main quadrangle of the Fitzjames Hospital. The pupils have few opportunities to enter the hospital grounds, so they enjoy the moment to the full, gawping irreverently at the Tudor architecture and pointing at the painted bust of Bishop Fitzjames, whose bulging eyes stare out from a Renaissance roundel as if he is about to be sick through a porthole. By way of return, the elderly inhabitants of the hospital gather on balconies and in doorways to watch them pass. The more critical pass adverse comments on the appearance of individual pupils.

'Look at that one!' A tight-faced lady with neglected steel-wool hair. 'Hasn't had a shave in days.'

'Trousers at half mast!' Her friend agrees, though she could do with a shave herself. 'Where's his belt? And none of them has polished their shoes since the beginning of term.'

With amusement, the Master of the Hospital hears these and other comments from the balcony of his apartment. Every year, Dr Holbrooke has listened to his pensioners griping about rehearsals for the Corpus Procession; each time, a dozen geriatrics shudder to think what it will be like on the actual day; and, of course, when the day comes round, the real procession is smart and dignified. Still, he reflects, a good moan is a sign of an active mind and continued interest in life, so any complaint that is not about him or the hospital has something to commend it.

Like the students, Dr Holbrooke allows his eyes to wander around the courtyard. In one corner, a gaggle of former matrons from the school has interrupted bridge and sweet sherry to observe the annual ritual of the rehearsal. Their comments are more forgiving than those from ladies who have never had the task of smartening up adolescent boys. From the north-facing window of his new apartment, Peter Bulmer, former art master at the school, beams benignly and exchanges conversation with waspish, irascible Douglas Peachey, brilliant historian and inveterate stirrer of trouble. Peter holds a paintbrush in his hand, so has obviously lost no time in exploiting the favourable lighting of his new accommodation. Around the corner, the stairs and balcony leading to the artist's previous lodging are the only unoccupied viewpoints in the courtyard; taking advantage of the temporary vacancy, the master has had the flat decorated and the wooden stairs varnished. This latter task was completed just a few hours ago, and the varnish has yet to dry. A new occupant arrives tomorrow: the master reflects that one may run out of many things, but never out of old people.

And now the tail of the procession is passing out of the hospital. A car horn sounds from the High Street, where Dolphin Three is holding up another set of traffic. The matrons return to their vindictive rubber of bridge and another glass of sherry; the critics hobble off in search of the next good moan. The master waves to the school staff, who have tagged on to the end of the procession, and then signals to Peter Bulmer, raising a cupped palm to indicate the offer of a drier, more expensive version of the matrons' tipple. Peter beams a response and drops his brush into a jar of water. To the master's annoyance, Douglas Peachey also interprets the gesture as an invitation and scuttles across the lawn as fast as his walking stick will allow. The master groans inwardly, then retires into his apartment and extracts a third glass from the depths of a Jacobean cupboard.

* * * * *

Refreshments in the NAAFI are less civilised than the master's sherry, but just as welcome. Ashley sits at a round, plastic-topped table with the Toms and Lance Bombardier Green, drinking strong tea from enormous mugs. The Toms, like the other gunners, have loosened their tunics; underneath, their olive T-shirts are as moist as their heads.

'So, what's the occasion, Tom?'

'Guard of Honour, Uncle George. Some big-wig is visiting the barracks next Tuesday and Major Benson said it would be a good chance for us newer gunners to practise our ceremonial stuff. That's right, isn't it, Lance?'

The lance bombardier swills a mouthful of tea around before replying. Made to his exact specifications by the large lady at the counter – who has been rewarded for her efforts with two minutes of military flirtation – his beverage is a simmering, orange brew, created from two teabags, coffee whitener and innumerable heaped spoons of sugar. Green nods as he passes the potent fluid from cheek to cheek, then swallows noisily.

'It's an old soldier who served here donkey's years ago, Mr Ashley. He's just been knighted in the Birthday Honours. I'm not sure if that qualifies him for a full guard of honour but the gossip is that the Bulldog wants a favour out of him, so he's giving him the full buttering-up routine – inspection of the

7

guard, a boozy lunch in the Officers' Mess and a tour of the stables afterwards, if he can still stand upright.'

'Sounds unlikely, Lance.' Tom Two has heard all about celebrations in the Officers' Mess.

'Too true, Tom Two. And while he gets legless at the officers' expense, you and Tom One get to pose smartly on the doorstep for hours on end, thus gaining a valuable insight into the bleak mindlessness of sentry duty. It'll be easier for One – he's used to standing around vacantly.'

Tom One is about to protest, when he is struck silent by the frightening arrival of Bombardier Burdett. Both he and Tom Two know the bombardier to be a thoroughly decent person: nonetheless, it is difficult to overcome the instinctive awe which a drill instructor inspires. Ashley feels his nephew's reaction and half expects him to leap to attention in the middle of the NAAFI.

'Morning, Mr Ashley. Hi, Lance – hi, lads. Do you mind if I join you?' Ashley and Green make friendly, positive answers, and Burdett interprets the wide-eyed silence of the Toms as an affirmative. He places his tea on the table and pulls up a stool.

Unlike his nephew and Tom Two, Ashley is not intimidated by the bombardier; he does, however, hold him in great respect. Formidably intelligent, and with a particular skill for computers and electronics, Burdett could make a fortune for himself in the civilian world, designing programs and websites; but horses, the army, and Prince Albert's Troop are in his blood. His father and grandfather had served in the Troop and Burdett's only ambition has been to follow them. Ashley knows that the bombardier has successfully resisted all attempts by Captain Raynham to entice him into a desk job in the adjutant's office, though he willingly helps out when Raynham's administration gets out of hand, or when the commanding officer crashes his computer – which is almost every time he tries to use it. In addition to these extra-military duties, Burdett runs the Old Comrades' website with efficiency, and lends the quartermaster a hand with his record keeping every Friday. Not a bad catalogue of activities, Ashley muses, for one who is also a first-rate soldier, almost certainly destined to be a senior NCO. Perhaps Burdett will even be quartermaster in his own right one day, with a late commission and a transferral to the Officers' Mess. Then the Toms will leap to attention all right.

It is not the Toms that Burdett has come to see: 'I hear you're off to Bruton next week, Mr Ashley.'

Ashley is amused. Prince Albert's Troop is a small unit and news travels fast. Has the bombardier found out from the Toms and Lance Bombardier Green, or by an alternate route, via Captain Raynham and one of the gossiping Mess orderlies? He senses the Toms relaxing, now that they know that Burdett has not joined them to tell Two that he is a rotten trumpeter or to belabour One for marching out of step.

'I'm flattered, Bombardier Burdett, to know that the Troop's secret police take an interest in my movements.'

Burdett grins: 'Big Bomber is watching you, sir. We know your every movement – especially when you're solving an exciting crime.'

'Alas, there aren't too many of those just now. Dull insurance scams seem to be the order of the day. But you're quite right, of course. A friend of mine has been appointed housemaster at the boarding school in Bruton and he's invited me to their Foundation Day celebrations. I assume there's a purpose behind your inquiry?'

'There is, sir. The widow of one of our former commanding officers is moving into some sort of sheltered accommodation there – I think it's very near the school. Her husband was a bit of an old fart, apparently, if you'll excuse the expression, sir, but the senior NCOs here remember his lady very fondly. She was the sort who'd always go and visit a gunner who ended up in hospital – and she was very good to the soldiers' wives as well. So we wondered, sir, if you'd be kind enough to call on her and take her a copy of our new book. You've seen it, presumably?'

'I certainly have, Bombardier Burdett – I have my own

copy, signed by Tom Two and with my nephew's thumb print underneath.' The book is a pictorial record of life in the Troop, the pictures taken over the course of a year by a leading society photographer. It is a pleasing and glossy amalgam of horses, soldiers and artillery, which is selling quickly. The Toms, in truth, have shown only minor interest in the volume, since the pictures were all taken before they arrived at the barracks. In contrast, Lance Bombardier Green has managed to worm his way onto every other page, and regards the whole undertaking as a personal hagiography. He grins broadly now: 'It's very good, sir, isn't it?'

'It is, Lance Bombardier – especially the one of you mucking out your horse on a cold December morning.'

'Well, that was after quite a heavy night sir – and he didn't get my best profile. Personally, I prefer the one of me saluting the Queen.'

'It's her favourite as well, Lance.' Tom Two relaxes enough to enter the conversation.

'I bet she's got a copy on her sideboard.' Tom One joins in the fun. 'People probably ask her, "Is that you, Ma'am, with Lance Bombardier Green?".'

Green sniffs, haughtily: 'You're only jealous.'

'Anyway, sir,' Bombardier Burdett returns to the point, 'all the chaps who were here in her time have signed a copy, and we'd be very grateful if you could deliver it. We could just send it, of course, but the personal touch will be much better.'

'It'll be a pleasure, Bombardier Burdett. I look forward to meeting Mrs…?'

'Compton, sir – Mrs Mary Compton. Incidentally, sir, by way of returning the favour, a retired sergeant from the Troop runs a stable about five miles from Bruton – wonderful hacking country all around. I'll send him an e-mail and fix you up with a ride, if you like.'

Ashley looks dubious: 'It sounds good, but I wasn't planning to take riding kit with me. I'm going by train, so I need to travel fairly lightly.'

10

The rapid turning of cogs in Burdett's mind is clear for all to see. 'Have you booked your ticket yet, sir? No? That's good – just leave it with me and I'll sort something out.' Burdett brings the matter to an enigmatic close. Standing up, he addresses his miniature army: 'Listen in, everyone – playtime over. I want you on the square in five minutes, ready for a final run-through.'

The gunners react as instantly as they would to a command on the parade ground itself. Dregs of tea are swallowed standing up, tunics are re-buttoned and nine pairs of hands reach out for headdresses and swords. Burdett places his own busby on his head, adjusts the chinstrap, and turns once more towards Ashley.

'I'll be in touch, sir.'

CHAPTER TWO

TRAVELLING TO BRUTON

The following Tuesday, Ashley found himself bouncing down the motorway in an aged, indestructible army Land Rover. At the wheel, booted, spurred and wearing his khaki service tunic, sat Lance Bombardier Green, driving with an appropriately cavalier approach to speed limits and highway codes. Behind them, in a muddled heap – the result of successive London roundabouts taken too quickly – were Ashley's luggage, Green's bulging kit-bag and half a dozen military saddles.

'Bomber Burdett and I have done a shifty, sir,' Green yelled happily: 'If I deliver the saddles to Larkhill Camp on Salisbury Plain, it counts as a day on duty rather than the first day of my leave – and what's more, I get the use of this old crate until I go back to barracks next week. Not a bad deal, is it?'

'It sounds good to me, Lance Bombardier. I wondered why you were still in uniform – I suppose Captain Raynham might not have been convinced if he'd seen you drive out of barracks in jeans and a sweat shirt?'

Green agreed: 'I think he might have had a few choice words to say, sir, as he reached for the book of regulations. Besides, the Bulldog likes us to look smart and equestrian when we go over to the regular Artillery – it puts them in touch with a bit of glamour, and makes them realise that there's more to life than playing with giant pea-shooters. The Troop runs a small stable at the camp – hence the delivery of the saddles. Then, of course, there's another advantage to being in uniform...' Green grinned even more widely than usual.

'Yes, Lance Bombardier?'

'Well, sir, I reckon when Wendy from Warminster sees me in this outfit, her knickers will hit the ground with a clang. After a regulation two-three pause, she'll be smothering me with kisses and rushing me upstairs to her bedroom.'

Ashley resisted the temptation to point out that, with her underwear around her ankles, the lady might find mobility a problem. 'And does, er, Wendy, have a proven track record with the military?'

This time, Green blushed as well as grinned. 'Strictly speaking, sir, I don't know – I haven't actually met her yet.' He paused for effect: 'The internet's a wonderful thing, isn't it, sir? "Warminster Wendy", twenty-two, GSOH, NS…'

Ashley knew enough about acronyms to work out that Wendy enjoyed a laugh but didn't smoke. Green continued: 'TLM, DPAS…'

'Sorry, Lance Bombardier, you've lost me there.'

'Tits like melons, doggy position a speciality, sir. Actually, I made those two bits up, but you never know your luck. Anyway, she's looking for "handsome, kind, attentive graduate for long-term relationship" – and that's me down to the ground, apart from the "kind, attentive graduate" bit.'

'And how much leave do you have, Lance Bombardier?'

'A week, sir – and that's long term by my standards. Whoops – here's our turning!'

Wendy from Warminster returned to the obscurity of the World Wide Web as the Land Rover lurched across two lanes of traffic and sped up the exit lane to the A303.

'Sorry about that sir. Still, no harm done.'

Ashley opened his eyes and allowed the colour to return to his knuckles. He decided to turn the conversation to less distracting topics: if Green driving could be controlled by his brains rather than his loins, they might reach Bruton unscathed.

'Tom's doing his Guard of Honour today, isn't he?'

'That's right, sir.' Green checked his wristwatch and the Land Rover swerved to the left. 'They'll have done the fun bit by now – he'll either be in the guardroom drinking lager, or on sentry-go wishing that he hadn't had that second can just before his stag began. At a guess, I'd say he's discovered the origin of the expression, "All down one leg and a boot full".'

*　*　*　*　*

The lance bombardier's assessment of Tom's predicament – drawing on vivid personal memories – is accurate. The unfortunate gunner stands at the entrance to the Officers' Mess, wiggling his toes inside his riding boots, clenching his buttocks and gripping the hilt of his sword as tightly as his uncle has gripped the seat of the Land Rover. His condition is accentuated by the sounds of the party within: corks pop loudly from bottles, and a violently gushing soda siphon stands next to an open window. Every topped-up whisky represents physical and psychological torment to Tom.

Out of the corner of his eye he can see Tom Two, posted at the barrack gates. For the first forty minutes of his guard, Two had relieved monotony by stamping to attention, turning to the right or the left and marching up and down the pavement, before returning to his original position. Now, he too is motionless and Tom One easily diagnoses the same discomfort affecting his friend.

It must be at least five minutes since he last allowed himself to glance in the other direction and stare through an open window at the quartermaster's clock. No – the minute hand has barely moved. Has the clock stopped? Has the quartermaster guessed Tom's situation and maliciously put the hands back by five minutes when he wasn't looking?

Tom decides to take his mind off the uncomfortable present by recalling the immediate past. The Guard of Honour had gone well and surprisingly quickly, considering how many hours of practice had gone into it. The gunners had marched, turned and presented arms to the satisfaction of Bombardier Burdett; Tom Two had blasted away at his fanfare as if it were something out of the Book of Revelations; the commanding officer had nodded approval. Sir Andrew Esmond had turned out to be a genial old boy, with hairy ears, eyebrows and nostrils. He was delighted to be invited back to the barracks and had spoken to each of the gunners in turn as he passed along the line. To Tom Two, he confided that he had also been a trumpeter in the days of his national service: 'Though I was never good enough to be given that call to play.'

A trumpeter on national service: that meant he had been an enlisted soldier, like them. This raised the importance of the event in the minds of the guard, who now felt that Sir Andrew was as much their guest as the officers'. Afterwards, in the guardroom, Bombardier Burdett had wondered whether he should ask the former gunner to join his Guard of Honour for a drink ('If he can still stand, by the time they've finished with him'); it was agreed that this was a fine idea. Over that fatal second can of lager, the Toms had invented titles for themselves and their comrades, to be adopted when they, too, were advanced by a grateful government. They had got as far as His Shiftiness, Lord Scott and Lord Two of the Failed Fanfare, when Bombardier Burdett had called them to duty and marched them to their posts, without so much as a halt and a right turn as they passed the guardroom lavatory.

But now the quartermaster's minute hand has finally condescended to move. At the same time, Tom hears the antique grandfather clock in the Mess making arthritic preparations for the Westminster chimes. As the Mess clock strikes the hour, the reassuring sound of marching boots is heard, each step bringing Tom's relief closer. The boots contain Gunners Sorrell and Vernon: when Bombardier Burdett follows the new guard around the corner, Tom brings himself to attention. Two pints of lager, fresh from the kidneys, slosh around his bladder; he grips his sword even more tightly.

'New guard – halt! New guard will advance – left turn!'

There is a gap between Gunners Sorrell and Vernon. On the Bombardier's next command, Tom moves to fill the space and Gunner Vernon advances to take up Tom's former position. A similar routine takes place at the gate as Tom Two changes place with Gunner Sorrell. When Bombardier Burdett barks out the command, 'Old guard! By the front – quick march!' he is only issuing the standard order. To the Toms, it is poetry.

*　*　*　*　*

As the Toms relieved themselves copiously and thankfully in adjacent cubicles, a barman pumped two pints of beer into handled glasses for Ashley and Lance Bombardier Green. Inevitably, the pub was owned by an old Patty, leading Ashley to speculate that ex-members of Prince Albert's Troop were like rats and that you were never more than a few yards from one. This thought brought to the front of his mind a second speculation, which had been niggling him subconsciously for a few days. He raised the matter with Green as they shared a generous plate of sandwiches.

'Lance Bombardier, if a former member of the Troop runs a stable a few miles from Bruton, why didn't Bombardier Burdett just send him a copy of the new book and ask him to deliver it to Mrs Compton?'

Green gave a grin in which bread and beef featured prominently. He swallowed, and washed his food down with a mouthful of beer.

'My guess, sir, is that the bomber regards Sergeant Jones as too uncouth for a sweet old lady like Mrs Compton. Jonesy was a great chap, but he was at the horse-poo-and-straw end of the scale, rather than at the pomp-dash-and-panache end. Burdett probably thinks that poor old Mrs Compton would have to put newspaper down for him to stand on, and open the windows afterwards to let out the smell. Then there's the little matter of Jonesy's language – he doesn't know many words, sir, and the one he uses most isn't very nice, if you see what I mean.'

Ashley got the idea. He had a vision of a frail gentlewoman collapsing on the sofa as the former sergeant fired off a burst of Anglo-Saxon from his emplacement on the centre spread of the *Daily Mail*.

'So I'm an altogether safer candidate for the diplomatic visit.'

'That's about it, sir – Jonesy's best left to his mucking-out, and cleaning docks with his middle finger. Mind you, his yard will be absolutely pukka, so you'll get a good ride on a first-rate horse if you take up Burdett's offer. He got his sergeant's stripes on the strength of his stable management – I learned a lot from him. Do you want that last sandwich, sir?'

Ashley generously surrendered his claim with a wave of the hand and spent the next two minutes contemplating the lance bombardier as he consumed the final, substantial slices of bread and the last wedge of pink beef. He had known the soldier for almost a year now and from the very first, Green's openness, honesty and humour had appealed to him. Green knew when to poke fun and when to be respectful; to those placed under him, he knew how to encourage and how to criticise positively, leaving his subordinates both grateful and loyal. Ashley knew that his nephew and Tom Two regarded Green as half mentor, half hero. This attitude was shared by the orphaned, homeless Gunner Sorrell, who had adopted his lance bombardier as a sort of honorary parent. Green took his paternal duties seriously, though he regarded them with characteristic amusement.

'How is Gunner Sorrell going to cope without you for a week, Lance Bombardier?'

'He'll be all right, sir. I've left food out for him, and the Toms will change his litter tray when it starts to fill up. Seriously, though, he's been a bit less of the doe-eyed limpet since his chum Keith joined us. Do you remember him sir? Cadet Vernon?'

After a moment's thought, Ashley recalled an undernourished cadet with crooked teeth, who had shared work experience with Toms One and Two. Keith Vernon, who had never been on a horse before, had turned out to be the best rider of the group; only his age had prevented him signing up

17

for the Troop when the three-week course had ended. Ashley nodded remembrance.

'Well, sir, Sorrell has appointed himself Vernon's guardian – he's teaching him everything from stable routines to seven-card stud. They've even started getting into trouble together, which is probably a good sign – they may as well get it out of the system early.'

On the whole, Ashley agreed. Tom One, after all, had spent most of his early teenage years getting himself into hot water: after that, he had embraced the discipline of the army gratefully. Now, fitter than ever before, with a sense of self-worth, and with colleagues who would remain friends for life, Tom had found his niche. Ashley rather envied him, though he knew that, as far as he was concerned, the military life was best experienced at second hand.

It was time to continue their journey. By half past two, they had delivered the saddles to a grateful staff sergeant at Larkhill Camp and, shortly after three o'clock, Green dropped Ashley and his luggage at the door of Old House, King's School, Bruton. The lance bombardier parped on the horn and waved cheerfully as he turned the Land Rover round and headed in the direction of Warminster.

CHAPTER THREE

OLD HOUSE

Ashley had known Colin Clifford since university; for two terms, they had lived in the splendour of the faux-mediaeval keep of Durham Castle before moving out to less grand but more comfortable accommodation in the city. For the last eight years, Colin had taught mathematics at King's School; now, he combined a reduced teaching timetable with responsibility for the fifty boys who boarded in Old House.

As the Land Rover had driven into Bruton, Ashley had seen expansive cricket fields dotted with boys clad in white, running, bowling, or frozen in anticipation of the batsman's next strike. Lounging on the steps of pavilions, or simply lying on the grass, other boys occupied themselves with hardening their bats, adjusting pads or checking the course of the game in the score book. A handful of girls, dressed for tennis, had insinuated themselves into the scene and provided alternative entertainment for a few unoccupied youths. The boarding house, therefore, was deserted. Colin Clifford led Ashley through an adolescent debris of discarded books, training shoes and pencil cases until they reached the civilised haven of the housemaster's quarters. Colin shared the private side with a Canadian wife and a wayward daughter. At the time of Ashley's arrival, he also shared it with Douglas Peachey, who had called for tea and showed no sign of leaving; Colin went through the introductions with a definite grudging undertone, then disappeared to make a fresh pot.

'Colin tells me that you are an historian as well?' Douglas Peachey was an aggressive inquisitor. 'What period?'

Ashley was taken aback: it was a question he had last been asked about fifteen years ago.

'The Wars of the Roses – I wrote my undergraduate dissertation on the events leading up to the restoration of Henry VI.'

'Ah, really? The *readeption*, of course. Fascinating century, the fifteenth, absolutely fascinating.' With this compliment, the retired master dismissed Ashley's area of interest and got down to the much more important subject of his own speciality. 'Now, I spend all my time on another restoration – the Stuarts. The late seventeenth century is a terribly underrated period. Everyone bangs on about the Civil War – as if there was only one – but they just write off the reign of Charles II as a bawdy knees-up and of course, there's much more to it than that. And as for the reign following...'

By this time, Peachey was in full swing. He talked of Popish plots and Rye House plots, of secret treaties and the legitimacy or otherwise of Charles the Second's liaison with Lucy Walters. When he started on the intrigues of the Country Party, Ashley allowed his mind to wander: would Colin Clifford bring in a much-needed gin with the tea? Or was he holding back on the alcohol until this old bore had departed? Was Lance Bombardier Green even now ranging the artillery of his charm against the fragile defences of Castle Wendy? Had Tom finished his guard duty and, if so, what was he up to?

Colin returned with fresh tea and no gin.

'Mr Ashley and I have been having a most interesting discussion about the later Stuarts,' announced Peachey, with heroic disregard for the truth. Colin compounded his sin of temporary teetotalism by setting the monologue rolling again: 'Well, of course, George, Bruton has quite a lot of late Stuart history of its own. That's right, isn't it, Douglas?'

It was, as Ashley discovered at length. The Monmouth rebels, it seemed, had come within eight miles of Bruton; Colonel Oglethorpe of James II's Life Guards had actually planned his campaign in the master's lodgings at the Fitzjames

20

Hospital. And then – Peachey announced a new phase of his lecture with a contented sigh – the famous courtesan, Arbella Fitzjames had her country house just a few miles away…

Ashley stared into the depths of his teacup, hoping that the grouts would foretell an imminent Peachey-free future. In truth, he might well have found the subject interesting had it been delivered at half the speed and with some attempt to involve the listener more actively. As it was, the colourful life of Arbella Fitzjames shot from one disgraceful episode to another with great rapidity and no regard to chronology. Ashley passed the time by staring around the housemaster's panelled drawing room: a pair of signed oars above the fireplace testified to Colin's athletic past as captain of the Castle Eight at Durham; his team and college photographs hung alongside newer school pictures, including a recent one of Colin and his wife seated among the boys of Old House. There were earlier pictures of the boarding house as well: surely that wasn't a younger version of Douglas Peachey, thinner, but just as red-faced, posing as housemaster? What headmaster would be mad enough to appoint him to a boarding house?

Mercifully, in the very middle of a confusing anecdote from Pepys' diary, Peachey froze, looked at his watch and announced that he must go. 'A pupil will be waiting for me. Enchanting conversation, Mr Ashley – I hope we can continue it on another occasion.'

Colin Clifford showed him out, returning with a large jug of gin and tonic. He poured two glasses, drank deeply from one of them, and sank into an easy chair.

'I'm sorry, George – when Douglas gets onto his hobby horse, he can bore for England. I saw you staring around the walls – did you work out that he used to be housemaster here?'

'I did – but I found it hard to believe. Mind you, I only spotted him in three photographs.'

'That's right, he didn't last very long. My predecessor had to pick up the pieces afterwards. In fairness, Douglas was quite an inspirational teacher if he had clever pupils – and, as you heard, he still takes on some private ones. He always had the scholarship set – a lot of his pupils went on to Oxford or Cambridge. He wasn't so good with the less bright.'

Ashley could imagine: 'My nephew had a few teachers like that – they put him off education completely.' He drank more gin and wondered once again what Tom was up to. 'If anyone needed teachers who could inspire the less academic pupil, it was Tom. But then again, it all seems to have worked out for the best.'

*   *   *   *   *

Oddly enough, as Ashley and Colin Clifford began to discuss Prince Albert's Troop, Tom and his friends were talking about school – a recent experience for many of them, especially the Toms and little Keith Vernon.

The adjutant had visited the guardroom just before the four o'clock change-over. The Toms, wisely emptying their bladders in preparation, had overheard his conversation with Bombardier Burdett from their cubicles. Captain Raynham liked the idea of Sir Andrew meeting the guard informally but, sadly, it would have to wait for another occasion: three Mess orderlies had just carried him upstairs to bed, where he seemed likely to remain for some time. 'In fact, Bombardier Burdett, I came over to tell you that we can probably wind up the guard now, rather than keep them hanging around. If you do a parade at four o'clock rather than a change-over, I'll get a junior officer over to inspect and fall them out. After that, we just need Gunner Marsh to sound Officers into Dinner and the Last Post.'

So, instead of a dull hour on duty, the Toms had marched out with their comrades, stood to attention while Lieutenant Dawson cast a glazed and uncritical eye over them and had then been dismissed. Bombardier Burdett decided that the crate of beer he had bought for Sir Andrew's visit might just as well be drunk anyway, so the guard had retired to the harness room, where most out-of-hours, illegal parties were held. They hung their tunics on saddle brackets, allowed their braces to hang from their waists and made a teetering pyramid of their busbies. The room took on the appearance of the regimental tailor's stores.

'So, Keith, how was your first experience of ceremonial glamour?'

Gunner Vernon, squatting on an upturned bucket, smiled through snaggled teeth. 'Just like Sorrell said – fifty percent polishing, fifty percent just standing around and ten percent busting for the loo.'

'That adds up to a hundred and ten percent,' Tom Two was probably the only gunner present able to deal with such complicated mathematics. His addition was helped by the need to remain sober for the last two trumpet calls of the evening.

Keith justified himself: 'I was only quoting.'

'And anyway, Prince Albert's Troop always gives one hundred and ten percent.' Tom One swigged patriotically from his bottle of beer and clicked his spurs together for emphasis. 'So the arithmetic is sound for all military purposes.'

'Ballistics?' Bombardier Burdett was unconvinced by the Thomist philosophy.

'Absolutely, Bomber – when the riding master goes ballistic, he certainly gives a hundred and ten percent.'

Burdett sighed, 'Just remind us, Tom One – what sort of school did you go to?'

Tom beamed: 'It was posh and expensive, Bomber – that's why I don't know anything.'

*   *   *   *   *

Refreshed, Clifford and Ashley decided to head towards the playing fields and catch the final overs of an inter-house match. On the way, and beginning in Old House itself, Clifford pointed out various sights and gave a history of the school, briefer and more interesting than history as taught by Douglas

Peachey. The foundation was monastic. Bishop Fitzjames had built Old House, the first school building, in the grounds of the abbey in 1519. At the same time, on land specially purchased, he had erected a hospital for the elderly-but-Godly of Bruton.

'Let me guess – at the Reformation, the school closed, but the hospital continued because it wasn't part of the monastery.'

'Correct. The school as originally established only lasted about twenty years. Edward VI re-founded it in 1550, hence, "The King's School".'

Colin opened a door and Ashley found himself standing in Bishop Fitzjames' schoolroom. A richer school would probably have turned the room into a museum, but it now served as the common room for the Old House boys. Table tennis, a television and squashy sofas clashed incongruously with Tudor panelling and Victorian engravings of Holbein portraits. In the ceiling corners, carved coats of arms alternated the royal lions and *fleur de lis* of Edward VI with shields bearing an extraordinary fish-like creature. Ashley worked out that the large-mouthed, moustachioed monster with pop eyes must be the emblem of Bishop Fitzjames. What it actually was, however, defeated him.

'A dogfish?' Surely, heraldry had never stooped that low?

'Believe it or not, it's a dolphin – or at least, a mediaeval Bruton monk's idea of one.'

'He must have led a very sheltered life – or copied a picture from a rather ill-informed bestiary.'

Colin agreed. 'Both, probably. According to Douglas Peachey, the dolphin symbolised social love, which seems particularly appropriate now that we've gone co-educational. There are dolphins all over the church too – you'll see them on Thursday.'

They left Old House and walked towards the cricket fields.

'Tell me about Thursday's service, Colin.'

'It's very straightforward, really. The school's foundation charter was signed on the feast of Corpus Christi, so every year on the Thursday after Trinity Sunday we process solemnly into church, commemorate our Founders and Benefactors…'

'Bounders and Malefactors,' Ashley repeated a joke that probably pre-dated the school.

'Precisely – and then we party for the rest of the day. Champagne on the lawn, hampers from Waitrose, which is as posh as it gets around here, and then the half-term exeat begins. It's a very pleasant day, as long as the sermon isn't too dull and the choir stays in tune. This is our match, by the way – how are we doing, Rory?'

A blond boy with red stains on his white trousers looked up from the scorebook.

'We need twenty runs off the last three overs, sir.' He handed the book to his housemaster, who decoded the arcane patterns effortlessly, as a conductor reads an orchestral score. Looking over his friend's shoulder, Ashley recalled that there had once been a time when he could have done the same.

'David Masters seems to have bowled well.'

'It was a fluke, sir. The first chap hit the stumps with his bat and the second one tripped over his shoelace before he reached the crease. The third one was good though – the batsman hit a real cow shot and James Begg caught him out. And talking of cow shots, sir…'

There had been a sharp cracking sound and now a ball flew into the air like a doomed space shuttle. Ashley, Clifford, and the boy called Rory watched its climb gradually decelerate and then followed its inevitable plunge into the cupped hands of an opposition fielder. The boys of the opposing house roared approval, and Rory tightened the straps on his pads.

'If you'll excuse me sir, I think I'm in.'

Thirty seconds later he was back.

'Sorry about that, sir – sun in my eyes. I think the wind must have been in the wrong direction, too.'

Colin was stoic; there were things in life more important than cricket.

'Perhaps we should return to that jug of gin, George.'

After the Last Post, Tom Two did his best to make up for lost alcoholic time but he was still relatively sober when he and Tom One, still in their ceremonial uniforms, finally lurched up the stairs of their accommodation block. He opened the door of the third floor room which they shared and Tom One fell in. Storing their busbies on the top shelf of the wardrobe was easy enough: unbuttoning their tunics was more problematic, and replacing their swords in their scabbards was downright impossible, even for Tom Two. Tom One removed a layer of skin from his thumb, yelped with pain and gave up the attempt. He laid the sword on his desk, then collapsed backwards onto his bed.

'I say, Two?'

Two rested his sword next to his comrade's. 'Yes, One?'

'Do you know of any regulation that says we have to take our spurs off before going to bed? I don't think I can manage.'

Tom One proved his point by sitting up and stretching his arms out to grip an ankle. The right angle of his body remained constant as he fell back again and his legs rose into the air. He held the pose for a moment, then returned to the horizontal.

'See what I mean?'

Tom Two, still just about in control of his limbs, unlatched his own spurs, then crossed the room and removed Tom One's. A pair of sharp tugs removed the boots as well.

'And that's where friendship stops, One – you're on your own as far as your breeches go.'

'In that case,' slurred Tom One, 'I shall sleep in ceremonial style.'

He closed his eyes and began to snore loudly.

CHAPTER FOUR

ARION ASTRIDE THE DOLPHIN

Ten o'clock on Wednesday morning. A brutal combination of sitting trot and a steel-framed army saddle is knocking Tom One's hangover out of him. Outwardly, he looks as smart as the other gunners, riding in formation over the scrubland; inwardly, he feels like a nauseous punch ball, and he wishes that Tom Two would stop sounding those stupid commands on that bloody trumpet. Every note sends a harpoon through his eardrums; worse, his horse reacts to the calls, causing an agonising interaction between the parts of the saddle which are hardest and the parts of Tom which are softest. Still, as long as the instructor doesn't decide to practise dismounting by backward somersault, he thinks he will survive.

*　　*　　*　　*　　*

In more civilised circumstances, Ashley was taking tea with Mary Compton. The process of moving from a six-bedroom manor house to a tiny apartment in the Fitzjames Hospital had been a long and difficult one, and Mary was clearly pleased to be settled at last; pleased too, with her new surroundings, which were as elegant as their occupant.

'I'm glad you waited until today, Mr Ashley. Yesterday, I was feeling very tired, and half the pictures were still leaning against the skirting board – and then Peter Bulmer called in and helped me to hang the rest, so all the jobs are done now. And thank you for bringing me the book – I really appreciate it.'

The book lay open on a table next to her chair. She leafed

slowly through the bright pages, recognising in some of the senior non-commissioned officers the keen, high-flying gunners of many years ago. 'And who is that handsome lance bombardier saluting the Queen?'

Ashley resolved not to pass this question on to Green, lest he should burst out of his uniform with inflated pride. Mary's gentle reminiscences required very little of his attention and he cast his eye around the room, as he had done in Colin Clifford's study the previous day. Mary, more sensitive to her audience than Douglas Peachey, looked up from the book and followed his gaze.

'Of course, it was hard work, but I really rather enjoyed the task of choosing which furniture to keep and selecting the possessions that I couldn't bear to be without. There were some nice pieces that just wouldn't fit in, which was a shame, but on the whole I'm very pleased with my new home.'

Ashley nodded agreement. Everything in the room contributed to a well-proportioned and tasteful whole, from the tilt-top mahogany table, gleaming with beeswax, to the velvet upholstery of the Victorian slipper chair in which Mary Compton was seated. Ancient floorboards were visible between expensive oriental rugs; on top of a thin-legged Regency sideboard, silver-framed photographs traced the progress of Colonel Compton's military career, and his sword hung above the fireplace. On a small writing desk, the letters of the day were held firmly in place by a large *millefiori* paperweight of Murano glass, and the walls were hung with landscapes, military scenes and family portraits. One of these commanded Ashley's immediate attention, as much for its damaged condition as for the obvious excellence of the artist's technique.

A lady, with luxuriant hair in the style of the seventeenth century, stared wantonly from the canvas. Her lips were pouting between heavily rouged cheeks; her eyebrows arched expectantly and thick eyelashes seemed to resemble the fronds of a carnivorous plant, poised in readiness to entrap the victim of the day.

28

And that was it. A head, the hint of a bare shoulder, half an inscription in the top right hand corner, and no more. To add to the mystery, the inscription – just a few letters – was handled so clumsily, that it could not possibly have been painted by the master who had so brilliantly captured the lasciviousness of his subject. Above the lettering, an equally incompetent sequence of brushstrokes formed no more than a fragment of some larger drawing. Ashley found himself torn between an admiration of the main portrait and an urge to turn his powers of detection on the conflicting messages that the picture was transmitting. Mary Compton looked up from a photograph of soldiers jumping fences with their arms folded (Lance Bombardier Green was third in line).

'I see you've noticed wicked Aunt Arbella. She was exercising her charms on Peter Bulmer yesterday – he was quite excited about her.'

Ashley could see why: he stood up and moved across the room for a closer inspection.

'Am I right in thinking that wicked aunt has been cut down at some point in her history?'

'That's quite right. I'm afraid my great-grandmother thought that morals were more important than art. According to my mother, Aunt Arbella – she wasn't an aunt at all of course, more like a distant cousin many times removed – well, she was originally almost naked, and sitting astride a dolphin, of all things, like Arion in the legend.'

Ashley pondered the information. Many strands of it seemed oddly familiar. Mary continued: 'Well, great-grandmother was the sort of woman to cover up the legs of the piano, so she wasn't going to allow Arbella to disport herself all over the drawing room. I'm sorry to say that she chopped off all the bits she found offensive and re-framed the rest – then she didn't like the result, so stuck her up in the attic, which she could have done in the first place, without having to vandalise her.'

Mary sounded quite indignant. Ashley pictured a

bombazine-clad matron with a tight bun and an impregnable bosom, slicing away at the masterpiece; he hoped the old bag had cut herself in the process.

'I suppose it's too much to hope that the rest survives somewhere?'

'I think it fairly unlikely. Mother thought that she burnt the pieces, though that was just a guess. It was mother who rescued the picture from the attic, after the old lady died. We spent many evenings making up stories about Arbella's life, though from what I can gather, our imaginations fell far short of reality...'

Mary continued reminiscing. Listening with rather less than half an ear, Ashley continued to examine the mutilated picture. What was the clumsy fragment in the corner? Perhaps it formed part of a family crest; there was no outline of a shield, but the indecipherable drawing might be part of some supporting heraldic device. In that case the few letters would be the beginning of a motto – Latin or English? There was a wobbly D, a curly E that might just about be a B (but that seemed less likely), and the first stroke of a letter that could have been almost anything. Short of removing the picture from its frame, there was no way of being certain. Ashley shrugged and turned back to Arbella herself. Why was the name familiar to him? As he had told Douglas Peachey, the seventeenth century was not his period.

It was the thought of the retired historian that jogged Ashley's memory. Of course – Peachey had waffled on only yesterday about Arbella Fitzjames and her escapades in the post-restoration Stuart court. To his annoyance, Ashley was unable to recall a single anecdote, so efficient had he been at blocking out the old man's irritating and digressive account of the courtesan's progress. Was she a mistress of Charles II? Or were her talents "unconfined", like the courtly harlot in the poem by Pope? Perhaps she had been at the centre of the intrigues to depose or restore James II, depending on what side of the protestant/catholic divide she found herself...

30

Ashley abandoned the fruitless speculation, and tried to guess who might have painted the portrait. His detecting career had brought him into contact with a good deal of art and he had built up an extensive, if erratic, body of knowledge. Arbella must have appeared on the courtly scene far too late to be painted by van Dyck. In the second half of the seventeenth century, the artistic world in England was dominated by two painters: Godfrey Kneller, whose workshop mass-produced full-length portraits of society ladies; and the less prolific, but infinitely finer…

'Peter Lely.' Mary Compton pre-empted Ashley's guess. 'My mother said that it was one of his last paintings, though I don't know where she got her information. Of course, the damage renders it valueless, except as a curio but, on the whole, that's a relief. Otherwise, I'd spend all my time worrying about it being stolen. More tea, Mr Ashley? And you must tell me about your nephew – how is he getting on in the Troop?'

*　　*　　*　　*　　*

Tom is getting on by staring into the depths of a lavatory. Seven backward somersaults and then a brisk trot back to the barracks have had a predictable effect on the fermented contents of his stomach. He retches for the fourth time, then sits back, stabbing his buttocks with his spurs.

'Ow!'

'You've only yourself to blame.' Tom Two, clear-headed and sanctimonious, passes over another handful of lavatory paper. 'Did you realise that, if only there was a W in "Armitage Shanks", you could rearrange the letters to make something really obscene?'

'Thanks for that information, Two – my life is enriched by the knowledge.' Tom wipes his mouth and contemplates the seething contents of the porcelain bowl. 'I think I'm done.'

'Jolly good. Vernon said he'd groom your horse if you cleaned his saddle later, and Sorrell's doing the same for me, so we're off the hook for a while. Shall I make some tea?'

Back in their room, Two boils water while One, his spurs removed, sits cross-legged on his bed. He contemplates his crumpled ceremonial breeches and the blood-stained tip of his sword: 'I think it must have been something I ate.'

'That's right, One – after all, there was nothing wrong with those eight cans of beer, so it can't have been anything to do with them. Anyway, better out than in, as they say in the Household Cavalry. Here, drink this.'

Two mugs of tea later, Tom One feels as though he has rejoined the human race. 'Thanks, Two, you're a hero.'

'No problem, One – you'd do the same for me. If you hand your sword over, I'll sort out the gory details.'

Tom Two gets to work with an oily cloth, caressing the steel blade gently and methodically. Ten minutes later, pleased with the result, he returns the sword to its scabbard with a satisfying clang. 'And the good news is, it's Wednesday – sports afternoon. What shall we do, One? Nothing too strenuous, I presume?'

'How about making daisy chains in the park?'

'It could bring about a relapse. On the other hand, if we treat Sorrell and Vernon to this week's dose of sex and violence at the cinema, they might overlook those saddles. What do you think?'

Tom One contemplates an idle afternoon in front of a wide screen. 'Do you think Vernon's a bit young for the violence?'

'Buy him enough popcorn and he won't even notice – he'll just look up for the dirty bits.'

'Sounds good to me, as long as he doesn't get the popcorn stuck in those teeth.'

*   *   *   *   *

Ashley stood on the newly varnished balcony of Mary Compton's apartment, pondering his next move. Gin and Canadian conversation with Colin Clifford's wife were available

32

back at Old House, or he could wander up to the High Street and explore the town. He could even telephone ex-Sergeant Jones, if he felt energetic enough, and arrange a ride through the local countryside.

Any decision was postponed by the sight of Colin Clifford entering the courtyard in the company of a thin boy with greasy hair and an explosive complexion. Colin waved a greeting and Ashley descended the stairs to join him.

'It's matron's day off,' Colin explained, 'so I'm using a free period to deliver William to the medical centre for his appointment. I thought I'd look in on the way to see how you were getting on.'

The medical centre (or the 'San', as the boy William called it) stood outside the school grounds, next door to the Fitzjames Hospital. Presided over by a nurse, generous of figure and alcoholic distribution, the building was a picturesque muddle of combined cottages set in a walled garden. Sister Barnfield trundled indoors with the eruptive William, leaving Colin and Ashley seated on a bench in a sunny corner, refreshing themselves from a pair of well-filled glasses.

'Did you enjoy your visit to Mary Compton?'

'Very much. Have you met her, Colin?'

Clifford nodded. 'A few times, at school plays and concerts. Her husband was an Old Boy of the school, and always took a great interest in anything going on here. He even founded a scholarship. A big one too, fifty percent.'

Ashley was impressed; having contributed to his nephew's school fees, he had a good idea of how large a sum was necessary to establish even a minor award.

'That was very generous of him.'

'Well, there were no children to the marriage, so perhaps it was his way of fulfilling his paternal instincts. We award every five years, to the most able son of a serving officer in the Artillery. The colonel followed the progress of his scholars very closely.'

Ashley was getting a different picture of Colonel Compton

from the one given by Bombardier Burdett. He had imagined a rather aloof figure, stuffy, disciplined and every bit as exacting as the bombardier himself, only with significantly more authority. The silver-framed photographs in Mary Compton's apartment had emphasised rather than contradicted Burdett's unflattering estimation of the former commanding officer. Ashley remarked on the apparent contradiction and Colin laughed at the soldier's description of the colonel as 'an old fart'.

'I think your bombardier was half way to being accurate – Compton certainly could be a pompous ass when he was feeling grumpy, but there was a kind side to him as well, which perhaps those serving under him didn't see very often.'

Ashley nodded. 'And Burdett must have been relying on reports from older soldiers – his father, perhaps – because he's too young to remember back to Compton's time. I ought to add that Mary Compton is remembered very fondly by the senior troops.'

'I imagine she would be. There was talk of her setting up another scholarship, now that the estate has all been sold, but I haven't heard anything about it recently. Perhaps there wasn't enough cash. Had you worked out that she was a Fitzjames by birth?'

'Sort of – I'd realised that there was a connection, but not that it was that direct. Have you seen the portrait of the enchantress Arbella?'

'The woman Douglas Peachey was droning on about last night? No, I haven't and I'll tell you something you'll enjoy, George – I bet you Peachey hasn't seen it either. The Comptons lived about ten miles from here and it only tended to be headmasters who were invited over – that was the pompous side of old Compton coming out. Peachey was always trying to scrounge an invitation and you can be sure that we'd have heard if he'd ever been successful. Do you think he even knows that the picture exists?'

Ashley drained his glass and spoke with emphasis; 'Well,

let's not tell him – it would be a shame if poor Mary had him banging on the door every five minutes, making a nuisance of himself.'

Colin agreed: 'Unless, of course, I ever need a trump card during an after-dinner conversation. It would give me great pleasure to silence him with a bit of history he didn't know.'

The door to the medical centre opened and William emerged, his face glowing like a Belisha beacon, and a plump, sisterly arm around his shoulder.

'One nitric acid and cleansing lotion treatment completed.' Sister Barnfield brought her patient over to the sunny bench. 'And I'm sure William is capable of finding his own way back to the house if you two gentlemen would like your glasses topped up?'

It seemed like a good idea. Clifford calculated that he could persuade a reluctant post-luncheon class across the *pons asinorum* on two gins, and Ashley consigned a canter across the local countryside to another afternoon. As William departed in the direction of an exciting half hour in front of the mirror, a second nurse entered through the garden gate. Sister Barnfield managed to beam with her entire body.

'And here's Sister Jamieson come to relieve me.'

She reached into a window, drew out a bottle and another glass, and joined her guests on the bench.

CHAPTER FIVE

PREPARATIONS FOR CORPUS

The Toms would have understood and appreciated the hectic preparations in Old House. As they work their methodical way through four saddles and bridles in the harness room (sex and violence in the cinema having been regarded as an inadequate bribe by an ungrateful Sorrell and Vernon), fifty schoolboys are frantically tidying, cleaning and polishing. Naturally, this requires maximum movement and volume. Shirts are inspected for whiteness and creases are coaxed out of crumpled school ties; suits and jackets are noisily reclaimed from the dry-cleaning hanger and, everywhere, shoe polish is being applied with extravagant enthusiasm to scuffed toecaps and neglected uppers. A barber has taken up residence in Colin Clifford's study, where clippers and scissors are being employed with all the sensitivity of a tomahawk. In the showers, sensible juniors wash their newly shorn hair, knowing that the seniors will be in full-time occupation in the morning and that the best they will be able to hope for is a quick splash in the dormitory sink. Experienced sixth formers, in their shared rooms, conceal posters of silicon-enhanced blondes beneath pictures of aeroplanes and fast cars, aware that the chances of a maternal visitation are high.

On the private side, Diana Clifford presides over an ironing board and a small group of unfortunates who have forgotten to have their uniforms pressed. She exacts revenge on them by steaming trouser creases into tramlines and by assigning kitchen duties to those around her: two boys assemble a tottering column of sandwiches for tomorrow's picnic; a third dubiously prods the shrivelled remains of what was once a promising risotto; the eruptive William, whose natural development will probably be arrested by the experience, arranges flowers, jabbing mimosa and carnations randomly into green oasis. At the sink, in aprons too large for them, three dwarf-like specimens with high voices work their way through the house collection of wine glasses; half a bottle of washing up liquid and no rinsing ensures that the school chardonnay will taste even soapier than usual.

'Will this do, Mrs Clifford?'

'It's perfect, William.' Diana sprays starch liberally on the trouser seat of an especially unloved pupil before glancing at the anarchic floral arrangement. 'Everyone will assume that the florist has had a nervous breakdown, but that's an unimportant detail. If you'd like to take them into the common room and put them on the pedestal in front of the patch where the rain got in, that would be lovely.'

'Okay, Mrs Clifford.' William disappears behind his creation, which walks, as if unaided, towards the door: 'I'll try not to drop them.'

'Oh, I shouldn't worry too much. And if you see my husband on the way, you might tell him his dinner has turned into a graveyard – which is appropriate, given that his wife is working her way to a skeleton.'

*   *   *   *   *

Around a bridge table, the retired matrons sit with particular rigidity, apprehensive, like duchesses of the *Ancien Régime*, of any sudden movement that might damage the brittle curves of their newly shampooed-and-set hair. In an attempt to recapture her swinging sixties, Avril, the oldest, has had a blue rinse; sitting at cards, she looks like a patch of sky peeping out between three rain-filled *cumulonimbi*.

'One club. Is there any more sherry, Jasmine, dear?'

'There's another bottle in the sideboard. Whichever of us

is dummy can get it in a minute. One spade.'

'One no trump. I thought we might have seen Mary Compton in the hairdresser's this afternoon.'

'She probably goes somewhere *far* grander, Mavis. Wells, I should think – and by taxi. Come on Irene, it's your bid.'

'I was just thinking that Mary Compton might be the sort of person who doesn't think it necessary to have her hair done for Corpus. Just a hat, I dare say – straw, with flowers, like donkeys used to wear. No special effort of any kind. Pass, by the way.'

The other matrons make clicking noises with their tongues, expressing a disapproval that is enhanced by the implied class distinction. Jasmine, the matron with one spade, makes hers with special emphasis, to include frustration at her partner's spinelessness: surely she must have a few decent cards behind the knobbly knuckles and fake jewellery?

'Two hearts. Douglas Peachey trimmed his moustache this morning. He cut himself.'

'A few years ago, he shaved it off altogether. He looked very feminine without it, I thought.'

Jasmine rebids her suit in a voice which suggests repercussions against her partner if support is not forthcoming: 'Two spades. And if you ask me, Douglas doesn't look that masculine, even *with* a moustache.'

'Pass.'

'Your turn again, Irene.'

Irene chooses the coward's way out and bids three spades. Three passes and a heart lead later she lays down a hand deficient in trumps and republican in its lack of court cards. Avoiding the steely glare of her partner, she heads for the sideboard.

*   *   *   *   *

Unaware of the vicious dissection of his facial and personal deficiencies, Douglas Peachey is teaching a private pupil.

38

Today's part of the syllabus concentrates on the Franco-Prussian War, so Douglas is giving a well-ordered recital of facts, rather than flitting chaotically from one story to another, as he had done with Ashley the previous day. His student, sallow and gangly, like a plant deprived of light, takes down notes on the Spanish succession, the follies of Napoleon III and the disastrous influence of Eugenie.

'She should have stuck to buying shoes, sir, shouldn't she?'

Peachey chuckles. 'You could say that about a lot of women, James – but don't put it in an essay. And in fairness to her, she *was* Spanish herself. The French called her *"l'Espagnole"*, just as they used to call Marie Antoinette *"l'Austrienne"*.'

'So it wasn't a compliment then, sir?'

'It was *not*.' Peachey contemplates a digression on the consistent awfulness of the French over the centuries; but the examination is shortly after the half-term exeat and James needs the highest grade. He steers the lesson back: 'And do you see how her arguments played into Bismarck's hands?'

'Yes sir – because he wanted the war, but wanted Napoleon to start it, isn't that right?'

'Absolutely. It's a theme which recurs throughout history. So often in fact, that you wonder anyone falls for it. But then,' Peachey pauses, admiringly, 'Bismarck was a *master* of manipulation…'

*   *   *   *   *

'I think we're done, One.'

Tom continued the poetic theme: 'We're through, Two.'

He rolled his polishing cloth into a tight ball and projected it across the harness room. It hit a wall, unravelled, and fell limply onto a pile of saddle blankets which, as Tom Two remarked, was no bad idea. He flopped down on the same pile, pulling the top blanket around his bare torso, and threw Tom One's cloth back to its owner: 'Here, catch.'

39

The heap of blankets was too small to accommodate a second person. Tom One caught his cloth, arranged it carefully over one of the saddles and swung himself into the seat. Reaching out, he retrieved his green army sweater from a work surface and draped it over his shoulders. It itched against his flesh, but it was warm.

'What do we do now, Big Chief Sitting Bull?'

Two shrugged beneath his brown woollen load and adopted an appropriate accent: 'Braves could go NAAFI and drink firewater with white men. We play darts and revenge ourselves on gunners who eat our popcorn with forked tongue and then make us clean saddles anyway. On the other hand,' he lapsed back into ordinary English, 'we'd have to shower and get back into civvies and by the time we'd done that there'd only be fifteen minutes to chucking-out time.'

'Let's not bother.' They had already changed to go to the cinema, and climbed back into uniform to clean the saddles and bridles. 'Anyway, I could do with a night off the booze, to be honest.'

'Your uncle would be ashamed to hear you say that.'

'Yes, but Uncle George doesn't have to get up at six-thirty tomorrow morning and transport horse poo from one side of the barracks to the other. I'll tell you what ...'

'Yes?'

'We could ring Sorrell and Vernon and get them to come over here. We can rub their noses against some seriously gleaming tack and they can bring some drink across.'

Tom Two produced a mobile from the depths of his blankets and returned to his impression of a Red Indian: 'Me send smoke signal. Pow-wow at Dead Man's Harness Room. They bring peace offering of beer, fags and cola.'

He tapped out a more comprehensible version of the message and texted it to Sorrell.

*   *   *   *   *

The Franco-Prussian War has gone on for a long time: 'Far too long, in fact, for such a brief conflict. Good night, James.'

'Good night, sir – and thank you.'

Ghost-like, the thin, pale youth crosses the darkened courtyard and heads towards the gates to the High Street. It is even later than he had realised: heavy iron bolts have been pushed into place, guarding the elderly inhabitants of the hospital from intruders. James hesitates: should he return to Douglas Peachey so that the old man can replace them after his departure? Then again, is Peachey actually capable of replacing them, unwieldy as they are? The alternative is to knock on the master's door – but no light shines from any of Dr Holbrooke's windows. Perhaps he has already gone to bed.

Deciding that the youth of Bruton present no real danger to the hospital and its occupants, James tugs the bolts across, lets himself out and simply pulls the door shut behind him. The street is quiet; on a Wednesday night, the pubs are rarely full and any drinkers are docile. Pondering his lesson, James heads through the town and home to bed.

Snug in his hospital flat, Douglas Peachey pours himself a glass of Madeira and settles down to a chapter of Clarendon's *History of the Rebellion*.

* * * * *

'It's no good pretending to be asleep, One – I can hear you grinning.'

'Only because your ears are so large.'

'No – it's because the smug waves you're sending out have found the natural frequency of the room. If they get any more intense, the window will shatter.'

Tom One rolls over and peers at the Tom Two-shaped black lump in the opposite bed. He knows that his friend is as pleased as he is.

'It was good, wasn't it, Two?'

'Good? It was sublime! Perfect justice is seen to be done

41

and the Toms come up smelling of roses.'

'As opposed to Sorrell and Vernon, who are going to be smelling of saddle soap and polish for the next couple of days.'

'My heart bleeds…'

Sorrell and Vernon had brought beer, cigarettes, cola – and a pack of cards. Being the only entirely sober person present, Tom One had steadily transferred the cash of the other three soldiers from their pockets to his upturned service cap. Foolishly, Sorrell and Vernon had sought to make good their losses by increasing their stakes and by taking chances on hands that should have been discarded. Vernon bit his lop-sided incisors ever deeper into his lower lip and Sorrell looked more and more like an animal dazzled by headlights: circumstances which made successful bluffing impossible. As Tom Two said, shovelling another pile of cash towards his roommate, it was appropriate that Sorrell and Vernon should lose their shirts to Tom One, who wasn't wearing one.

At the end of the evening, the two younger soldiers had gratefully accepted Tom One's offer: to refund their losses provided they polished his boots, saddle and bridle for the next couple of days: 'And Two's, of course,' he added, when they seemed overly eager, as if they had got off lightly.

Back in their room, Tom had handed back his friend's rather smaller losses: 'That's for looking after me earlier, Two.'

'You're a star, One. Correction, you're a bloody supernova.'

'I'm not sure what that is, but it sounds good.'

A triumphal, well-lathered shower had removed the dark, streaky evidence of labour from their faces and bodies, and now they lie in the semi-darkness, chatting in subdued voices.

'How do you think the lance bomber is getting on?'

'Well, if everything has gone according to plan, Wendy from Warminster is probably arranging herself comfortably under a hundred and seventy pounds of military heavy breathing and squelching. If the wind's in the right direction, we'll probably hear her climax. What about your uncle?'

'I don't think he's with them.'

'Idiot.'

'I know – and I hope that was a clean sock you just threw at me, because it got me in the face. At a guess, I'd say Uncle George is just staggering up to bed after the usual boozy evening.'

*   *   *   *   *

In fact, Ashley, like the Toms, is lying awake, contemplating the day. He has been kept busy, meeting people, seeing the town and exploring the school and hospital. Tea with the headmaster, his wife and a few demob-happy staff merged neatly into pre-prandial drinks with Dr Holbrooke, Master of the Hospital. At Dr Holbrooke's he had been introduced to several people, including the genial Peter Bulmer, and had renewed his acquaintance with Douglas Peachey. Peter Bulmer had talked of his latest picture and of the favourable lighting of his new apartment; Douglas Peachey had been agreeably restrained on his favourite subject and had left early to teach a boy from the town. Throughout, Dr Holbrooke had kept champagne flowing; this was obviously to celebrate the forthcoming Corpus Procession and service, but the tactful doctor had given Ashley the impression that the party was entirely in his honour. Back at Old House, Diana Clifford's desiccated risotto had been coaxed back to life with half a bottle of school chardonnay, and the rest of the evening had passed pleasantly with a mixture of chess, gossip, and wine from a vintner in Castle Cary.

Sophisticated people in civilised surroundings; intelligent conversations and amusing anecdotes. So why does Ashley feel uncomfortable? Is it the risotto? Perhaps the Arborio rice is scheming its way to a mass break-out from his stomach and indigestion is affecting his mind? Or is it his detective's instinct, hunching away where no hunch is required? There is no crime to be solved, no clues to hunt.

And yet...

Ashley gradually loses consciousness. Arbella Fitzjames dances with the headmaster; Peter Bulmer captures her on canvas as she straddles Colin Clifford, who has turned into a dolphin; Diana Clifford sings old lumberjack songs as she floats alongside them on a raft of solidified risotto.

CHAPTER SIX

CORPUS

And now Corpus Christi has arrived. The school flag is raised by a grumpy custodian; set on a soft blue background, a golden dolphin appears to be swimming against a current, for the breeze sets it in constant motion yet it makes no progress. Above it, a royal crown bears heraldic witness to the school's re-foundation. In a side chapel of the church, the vicar hastily celebrates Holy Communion while he can still call the building his own; amongst elaborate flower arrangements and stacks of imported chairs, he and two elderly ladies keep the religious show on the road.

The school busies itself with inspections, carnations and house photographs. The Old House matron returns from her day off, wafting back just in time to take up a serene and relaxed pose on the front row of the photographer's stand. Diana Clifford grinds her teeth and is immortalised looking as though she is chewing tobacco.

In the Fitzjames Hospital, four canisters of hairspray are expended on the elaborate architecture rising out of the skulls of the retired matrons; they are now bomb-proof, but highly flammable. Two of them smoke cigarettes, oblivious to the risk of spontaneous combustion. The matron of the blue rinse builds up a layer of blusher over a solidified crust of foundation cream, ensuring a temporary victory over the aging processes of eighty years and a bottle of sherry a day. Mary Compton adjusts a flower in her straw hat and tries it on in front of the looking glass; Douglas Peachey combs his moustache, making sure that yesterday's scar is concealed.

By ten o'clock the cricket field is covered in cars. Imperious women exchange greetings and commands over the roofs of sleek and silvery motors; less embarrassing mothers hold their tongues and nervously adjust their straps in the reflection of the passenger seat window. Fathers manhandle hampers and rugs to pre-arranged picnic spots, which have to be bagged before the procession and service begin.

A quarter past ten. The parade on the school green is everything the deputy head could wish for: the choir, smart in their royal scarlet robes; the form groups in neat columns, wearing carnations in house colours; the staff, looking impressive in an array of academic hoods over flowing black gowns. Ashley, watching from a distance, imagines Bombardier Burdett striding to the front and calling the school to attention before sending the pupils off to invade France – or Shepton Mallet, if they turn the wrong way at the end of the High Street.

The reality is much more civilian. The deputy head simply nods to the choir, who gather up the music folders that they have been dangling. The choir prefect raises the processional cross aloft and sets off at the pace of a slow march.

The Corpus Procession has begun.

*　　*　　*　　*　　*

Ashley watched the procession as it crossed the road and headed towards the Fitzjames Hospital; then he took a shorter route to the church. A senior boy directed him to a seat in the north aisle and he squeezed himself between a lady in an unyielding frock and a gentleman in a blazer with military buttons, fastened over a green and orange striped tie. After a few minutes of polite conversation on either side, he gazed around the building, admiring what he could see of the carved wooden vaulting in the nave, decorated with angels and elaborate bosses. There were plenty of dolphins as well, swimming round corbels, ornamenting the screen and generally getting in the way of the saints in the clerestory. Given that most of the Apostles were fishermen, Ashley considered this rash behaviour, especially since the carver was obviously another craftsman who had never seen a dolphin and had created something scaly and hairy, that might well have popped out of the Sea of Galilee.

Above the north door, there was a different piece of heraldic work to be admired: an enormous carving of the royal arms. The Stuart Lion took up one quarter, and a spectacularly well-endowed unicorn acted as one of the supporters, so Ashley worked out that the arms dated from after the Union of the Crowns in 1603. Douglas Peachey would probably have been able to tell him exactly which Stuart monarch the arms represented: and whether the monarch had slept with Arbella Fitzjames. Ashley decided that there was a lot to be said for ignorance, and resolved not to bother asking.

Parents and important looking guests trickled steadily in. At ten to eleven the hospital residents arrived and were ushered to special pews at the front of the nave. Like Ashley, they had watched the procession, and then they had made their way to church in two minibuses. Ashley ticked off the faces he knew; not Mary Compton, who was already sitting with the headmaster's party, but there was Dr Holbrooke, making a dignified approach to his seat, Douglas Peachey, self-importantly greeting familiar faces, and the matrons, tottering beneath minarets of hair and looking as though they might fall over backwards. Peter Bulmer was not among the party. Perhaps he was elsewhere in the church.

Just before eleven o'clock, the organ prelude reached its final cadence. There was silence in the church, so that the chimes of the four quarters from the tower clock were clearly audible inside the building. Then, as the hour itself was struck, the crucifer and choir made their entry through the great west door. Simultaneously, the organ exploded with chord after chord of triumphal fanfare and the congregation, impelled to its feet, experienced the thrill that attends the transformation from spectator into participant.

47

The choir was in no hurry. Their steady pace established a solemnity which seemed to pass around the pews. Mothers who had planned to smile and wave at passing sons and daughters instead looked ahead, clasping their orders of service in readiness; fathers, like the military specimen next to Ashley, were practically standing to attention. Even the retired matrons pulled themselves up to what was left of their full height, so that their steely hair peeped above the general level of the Fitzjames residents.

Around a lectern, the choir divided, then drew together again to mount the chancel steps in their well-rehearsed pairs. Behind them, third formers set the pattern for the rest of the procession, turning off before the choir screen to seats reserved in the nave and the aisles. Once the choir had filled the chancel stalls, the organ – just when it seemed that it could play no louder – came to a heart-stopping moment of silence. Then the first line of the opening hymn, imperative in bare octaves, ushered in one of the loudest confined sounds that Ashley had ever heard. Some schools do not sing. This one did – and parents and guests followed their example. Successive forms took up the hymn as they passed through the west door and moved into the nave, so that throughout its verses it grew ever louder and louder, until the final verse hailed the Redeemer who had died, with such intensity that it was impossible not to be moved. Ashley, who had taken his place cynically, assuming that the service was something that had to be endured before the drinks could begin, was almost frightened by the violent thumping of his heart against his ribcage, brought on by the passionate reverberation of voices, old and young, against ancient stone. He thought of Saint Augustine, praying twice by singing, and of the Psalmist who sang a new song, praising the Lord in the beauty of holiness. Not for the first time in his adult life, he sensed a power outside of himself that could be first comprehended only through instinct rather than intellect: he shrank from it and was rather relieved when the hymn reached its conclusion.

48

There were lessons, prayers and anthems; a sermon bumbled along, pleasant and undemanding, as if the preacher was picking theological blackberries from the hedgerows of a quietly religious country lane. There was a commemoration of the founders and benefactors, in which Fitzjameses throughout the centuries took their place. Ashley pricked up his ears, but the wanton Arbella failed to gain a mention among the patrons of education. Perhaps she had other things to do with her time.

And then there was the final hymn – every bit as impressive as the first, but less over-awing, because its power was anticipated. The choir and congregation crossed the verge of Jordan with all guns blazing and ended, probably safe and certainly militant, on Canaan's side. A blessing, rising above the echoes of the last verse, and some massive fugue by Bach, brought the service to its close. Out marched the choir and clergy; following them, the school reversed its former order, beginning with the staff, then the senior pupils and ending, anti-climactically, with the two smallest third formers. Then the north and south doors of the church opened and the congregation made its exit as best it could. Though nearest the north door, Ashley found himself caught up in a flow towards the huge Gothic arch at the west end. Resistance was useless; relegated to the status of liturgical jetsam, he allowed himself to be washed up in the churchyard among a crowd of newly liberated pupils, questing parents, and staff who, like himself, were desperate for a drink.

One of these, mercifully, was Colin Clifford. He grabbed Ashley by the arm and steered a path through the living and dead of Bruton. Years of careful practice had enabled him to perfect the art of exchanging cheerful greetings with parents without actually stopping so, sooner than Ashley would have thought possible, the two found themselves on the Old House lawn, standing in front of a table laden with full wine glasses. Ignoring these, Clifford reached under the tablecloth, withdrew an expensive *Chablis* from an ice bucket and poured for himself and Ashley.

'My God, that feels better.' He returned the bottle to its hiding place. 'The parents will be along in a minute. I've primed the spotty William to top us up any time our glasses look low. If parents ask, he's to tell them it's a special diabetic wine.'

'Very resourceful.' Ashley sipped from his glass and smiled approvingly; exclusivity made the wine taste even better. 'What's in the deal for William?'

'I don't tell his mother that he hasn't been taking his vitamin supplements. As you've probably guessed, William exists mainly on a diet of takeaway pizza – which is why he's started to look like one. He seems to regard anything else as unwholesome, particularly if it arrives in the form of pills from his mother.'

Parents began to arrive. Clifford adopted an all-purpose smile and began to circulate. Ashley entertained himself by watching the pained expressions of fathers who had headed hopefully towards the drinks table, only to discover that the school wine was obviously obtained through a special deal with the paraffin man. Most of them, sensibly, decided that a second glass would take the taste away, and by the third, they had stopped caring. Sixth formers, furtively hanging around the table, consumed illicit glasses with every sign of enjoyment.

'Can I top you up, sir?' William had deftly side-stepped two fathers and a house tutor on the way over to Ashley. His palm carefully concealed the label on the bottle.

'Thank you, William. Did you enjoy the service?'

'I didn't really notice it, sir. I was stuck behind a pillar, so I could doze off without being seen. The procession was good though, wasn't it? And an old lady at the front of the traffic queue got seriously stroppy – she was tooting her horn and shouting out of the window. A motorcycle policeman had to go over and tell her to shut up. We hoped he was going to arrest her – but he didn't.'

William's story ended with a distinct feeling of disappointment. The tale of a pensioner being man-handled to the ground and handcuffed would have been immortalised in schoolboy folklore. Ashley sympathised, and remarked that a well-deserved and neatly executed arrest could be a very exciting sight.

'Have you seen many, sir?'

'A fair few, William. For sheer entertainment value, nothing will ever beat the mounted policeman galloping after a streaker in Hyde Park; on the other hand, the arrest of a murderer is more dramatic, though it's not usually very enjoyable.'

'Wow!' William looked as though he disagreed with the last part of Ashley's observation. 'Which are you, sir – a policeman or a private detective?'

'The latter - but don't get too excited, William. For every interesting crime, there are twenty dull ones.'

'Sounds like lessons, sir.'

'*Just* like lessons, William, with lots of notes to take and homework to do – not to mention clients who don't pay up on time and those who kick up a fuss if what you find out isn't what they wanted.'

'And are you here to find something out, sir?'

Ashley was amused by the directness of the question. 'If I were, this conversation wouldn't have taken place. No, William – I'm purely here for a lazy few days.'

'Well I hope you get them, sir. If you'll excuse me, Mr Clifford is shooting desperate looks in my direction, so I'd better refill his glass before he dishes the dirt on me to my mother. Shall I top you up before I go?'

After a few more minutes, the reception began to break up; families headed in the direction of the cricket fields or the ornamental gardens in front of the science block, where rugs and hampers were waiting to be put to use. When only a few stragglers were outstaying their welcome, Diana Clifford enlisted Ashley to assist with their own luncheon, carrying food and plates to a quiet spot by the river, not far from the gates that led to the Fitzjames Hospital.

'Amelia was meant to be helping me, but she's managed to scrounge an invitation to have lunch with the latest boy.'

51

'You don't sound too happy, Diana.' Ashley placed a pile of sandwiches on a large gingham cloth.

'Oh, I'll be happy enough if she's still with the same boy by the time lunch ends. She's at a difficult age – and probably will be until she retires. Now, George, if you'd be so kind as to uncork that bottle, the sound should bring my husband scuttling over.'

*   *   *   *   *

Two hours later, Ashley was casting a benign eye over the remains of luncheon. There was some warmish *Chablis* still to be drunk, or a chicken leg to gnaw on, if he didn't mind getting his fingers sticky, and there were still signs of life in the sandwich pile. In contrast, Diana Clifford's trifle, which was beginning to melt, looked distinctly unhealthy. The colour had seeped out of the hundreds and thousands, so that the layer of cream looked like a chromatography experiment that had gone wrong. A large bowl of strawberries was proving a much more popular pudding.

Their party had expanded, as outdoor meals tend to; the chaplain, who had been doing valuable pastoral work wandering from party to party and scrounging drinks, decided to settle down with them; then Amelia had arrived with a blond-haired, embarrassed boy. Ashley set himself the detecting task of discovering whether this was indeed the boy that she had started with and established within ten seconds that he was not. Amelia laughed, and gave a frighteningly direct answer to his indirect question; the boy blushed and Diana Clifford adopted her chewing tobacco expression once more.

'Rory's family had to go quite early to catch a plane, Mr Ashley. Stephen lives in Bruton, so he's in no hurry.' Amelia carefully selected the largest strawberry from the bowl, dipped it in cream and bit it in half. Ashley rather admired the way in which she had waved goodbye to a parting lover and then fixed herself up with something more local for the half term holiday.

Arbella Fitzjames would have approved.

Perhaps it was the thought of Amelia's illustrious role model that made Ashley turn his eyes to the gates of the hospital. Framed by them, Sister Barnfield was approaching as fast as her stumpy legs and an over-tight uniform would permit. Looking around, she registered the presence of Colin Clifford and the chaplain; she also noticed that Amelia and the blond boy were busy feeding each other strawberries and were unlikely to listen to what she had to say. She crossed the bridge over the river and headed towards them. Pausing to get her breath back, she leaned over the picnic cloth at a dangerous angle. Ashley briefly wondered whether any food would survive the impact if she lost her balance, then discarded the thought when it became clear from the nurse's expression that she had serious news to deliver.

'I don't want anyone to panic – I've already called an ambulance. We need to get a message to Dr Holbrooke.'

Colin answered. 'That's easily done, Sister – he'll be at the headmaster's luncheon, with all the other hospital people. We can send Stephen over.'

Hearing his name, Stephen looked up, a strawberry half way in his mouth, like a baby's dummy. Not wishing to be overheard by him, Sister Barnfield leaned forward still further, so that her centre of gravity was directly over the trifle. She delivered her news in a stage whisper.

'It's Peter Bulmer – I've found him dead in the hospital courtyard.'

CHAPTER SEVEN

THE PASSING OF A PAINTER

A small, ill-matched group had assembled in the courtyard of the Fitzjames Hospital. Two ambulance men were covering Peter Bulmer's body with a blanket; in a moment, they would lift it onto a stretcher and carry him out to the High Street, where their vehicle was parked. In the absence of a policeman, a community support officer wrote notes into a small book. She was clad in an unnecessary, cumbersome protective vest and was clearly enjoying her temporary importance. Standing on her left, Sister Barnfield delivered her information in a low and confidential voice. Dr Holbrooke was at the centre of a solemn huddle which included the school chaplain and Colin Clifford. Ashley stood by himself, as near to the body as decency would allow.

Peter lay at the foot of the stairs leading to Mary Compton's flat: the apartment which, until ten days before, had been his. Before the blanket covered him, Ashley had observed the dark red matting of blood and hair on the back of his head and the slight discolouration of those parts of the body which had been nearest the ground. As the ambulance men raised him, a dark stain was revealed on the paving stones, where his head had been. His legs hung loose at the knees as his body left the ground: *rigor mortis* had not yet set in, though the stiffness of hands and face suggested that the process would begin soon. Sister Barnfield would have knowledge of this; maybe she could even give a rough estimate of the time of death.

They watched Peter's journey to the ambulance. The driver had brought the rear of the vehicle right up to the gates of the

Hospital, thus disappointing the huddle of townsfolk who had been attracted by the harbinger of tragedy. They heard, rather than saw, the stretcher being loaded into the back, and were forced to rely on speculation as the doors slammed shut and the ambulance drove up the High Street. Dr Holbrooke closed the gates, neatly avoiding the gaze of his curious audience.

'I'll be off too, Dr Holbrooke.' The CSO had finished her note-taking. 'There'll have to be a post-mortem, of course, and I'll write up a report – but it all seems very straightforward.'

Ashley heard as far as that, then allowed his mind to wander. It did indeed seem very straightforward. Peter Bulmer, absent from the service, for any one of a hundred good reasons, had forgetfully wandered up the stairs to his old flat. Realising his mistake, he had swivelled round, lost his balance and fallen, crashing his frail skull on the stone below. Why look any further, when the solution was simple and obvious? And yet...

The instinct which had kept Ashley awake the previous night was playing up again. He wanted to run after the woman from the community support unit, to grab her by the shoulder and point out the suspicious circumstances: except that there were none. There was nothing at all to suggest that what they had seen was anything other than an accident; not even a tragic one, for Peter was a very elderly man and could hardly have been expected to last many more years. Anybody who wanted him dead could simply have waited.

So Ashley controlled his urge, and heard himself accepting, automatically, Dr Holbrooke's offer of tea. Sister Barnfield returned to the medical centre, which was otherwise unsupervised, and Clifford and Ashley retired to the hospital's guest room, where they sat on uncomfortable Jacobean chairs among wood panelling and bad portraits of Dr Holbrooke's predecessors. Most of these appeared to have devoted themselves to over-indulgence on a large scale; the general tendency was to fit the frame rather tightly, though a couple of ascetic looking clergyman testified to more austere periods in the hospital's history.

Dr Holbrook brought in a tray of tea things and laid it on a heavy oak table.

'The other residents won't be back for an hour or so. The headmaster's lunch goes on for ages – for quite a long time after he's left, usually. When they return, I'll bring them in here and break the news.'

'How will they take it?' Colin was picturing himself having to announce a death to his boarding house.

'Stoically. We're a community of elderly people, after all – death visits every couple of months on average, sometimes more often. They'll be solemn for twenty-four hours – partly because they're thinking about their own mortality – and then they'll get back on with things. Oh, and they'll enjoy the funeral, of course.' The master smiled as he handed Ashley a strong cup of tea: 'We do funerals very well here.'

Ashley drank thoughtfully, then asked, 'Why wasn't Peter at the service? I saw the hospital party arrive, but he wasn't with them. I wondered at the time if he was sitting elsewhere in the church: but, clearly, he wasn't.'

The master shook his head. 'That's right – Peter excused himself at the last minute. He said that he wasn't feeling very well'

'Dizzy?'

'If he was, he didn't say. Perhaps you know, Mr Ashley, that we all watch the procession passing through the hospital, then a couple of school minibuses take us to the church, so that we arrive shortly before the service begins. We were just getting onto the buses, when Peter made his excuses. A few minutes before, he said how much he had enjoyed the procession, and I know he'd been looking forward to the service.'

Ashley took in the information. 'Were you worried about him?'

The master shrugged. 'If I worried every time a resident had an ache or pain, I'd live a very stressful life. We have a nurse who visits every other day and a medical doctor who holds a surgery in this room on Mondays. As well as that, there is an emergency button in every apartment, which is wired through to the school medical centre. Help is never far away, if you're taken ill.'

'It all sounds very thorough.'

'The system's evolved over the years. It's pretty good now – we don't have to trouble the emergency services very often. I suppose...' Dr Holbrooke paused, putting his thoughts into chronological sequence. Ashley and Clifford waited expectantly.

'Well, my guess is that poor Peter went to lie down for a while, then took a walk when he felt better – and returned to the wrong flat. I think you know that he lived there until a short while ago. Half way up the stairs, he realised his mistake, turned round, and lost his balance.'

And his life, thought Ashley. The master's reasoning was perfectly sound: indeed, it was the same as the sequence that Ashley had come up with, almost the moment he saw the body.

So, why was it wrong?

There were plenty of other questions that Ashley would have liked to ask, but they would have made his suspicions clear, so he kept them back. He didn't want to give his thoughts away just yet; nor did he want to look an idiot, if Peter's death really was an accident. The three men continued to drink tea in an awkward half-silence, making disjointed and dull observations, just to fill out the time before the tea was finished and they could separate.

*   *   *   *   *

Conversation was flowing rather better in North London. Horses had been fed, stable routines completed, and now the Toms were lounging in their shared room, bootless, and with their braces hanging loose around their breeches, killing time before the evening meal. Tom Two sat cross-legged on the desk, methodically peeling a large orange, while One brewed tea of a cheap and potent brand unknown to Dr Holbrooke.

With them, up to their elbows in the Toms' discarded riding boots, Gunners Vernon and Sorrell were paying off their debts to society.

'You're doing well, chaps – salivate, then activate, that's the secret, isn't it, One?'

'That's right – shoot out your froth, then bull with the cloth. Don't forget the spur straps – they were part of the bargain.'

Sorrell and Vernon responded obscenely and accepted steaming mugs of tea. Vernon swallowed a good mouthful, then asked, 'What are we going to do tonight?' He added, quickly, 'Not cards.'

Tom Two suggested, innocently, that there was an opera on at Covent Garden, and then they agreed to play darts in the NAAFI – the stakes being pints of beer only. Tom Two was a notoriously inaccurate darts player ('In spite of the stabilizers on either side of his skull'), so Sorrell and Vernon at least had a cheap night's drinking to look forward to.

Sorrell took an interlude between Tom Two's left and right boots. 'So, One, what's your uncle up to in Somerset then?'

'No idea.' Tom One shrugged. 'He said it was just a holiday, but Uncle George can be a shifty sod when he's on a case. Mind you, Somerset's not exactly the crime centre of the universe, is it?'

'I don't know.' Tom Two swallowed the last segment of his orange. 'He could be unmasking incest in Shepton Mallet.'

'That's not a crime, it's a custom. More tea, anyone?'

*   *   *   *   *

'Another gin, George?'

'Thanks.' Ashley interrupted his torpor to hold out his glass. 'Sorry, Colin – I've been bad company for the last hour.'

'That's all right - I've been discreetly catching up on my paperwork, in case you hadn't noticed.'

They were in the housemaster's study, Clifford sitting at his desk and Ashley lolling in an armchair. The haphazard piles of unmarked homework, parental letters and bulletins from the Director of Studies looked no smaller, but they had been rearranged slightly, so Ashley took his friend's word for it that the time had not been wasted. He decided to waste some now.

'Colin, tell me about Peter Bulmer.'

Clifford rested his pen and sat back in the chair. 'He was a nice old boy, of course – you saw that when you met him.'

'Any enemies?'

'None that I know of. I dare say you can't live in an enclosed community without rubbing a few people up the wrong way now and again, but I haven't heard of anything. He taught at King's – and very well – for about thirty years, retired ten years ago, and moved into the Fitzjames Hospital when his wife died.'

'Which was?'

'About the turn of the century, I think.'

Ashley digested the information before continuing. 'And what's the process for moving into the Fitzjames? I don't really understand how it works – who qualifies, for example?'

Clifford wasn't completely sure of all the rules himself, but he filled the detective in with what he knew.

'In the first place, you have to be a long-standing resident of Bruton, though I'm not sure if an exact number of years is specified. When it was founded, I imagine that it was taken for granted that most people would have spent their entire lives in the town – but that certainly isn't a requirement now. There's an exception as well – Bishop Fitzjames specified that members of his family have a right to retire there, which is how Mary Compton qualified.'

'Presumably it must have been crawling with Fitzjameses over the years?'

This had not occurred to Clifford. He tried to remember other members of the family, but failed. 'I don't think so – they were a fairly rich family in their day, so probably they didn't need anywhere to retire to. Perhaps the foundation is more

59

specific about the line of descent than I know of – the Bishop didn't have any children, of course, because he was pre-Reformation, but he had a brother. Maybe one has to be in the direct line of descent from him. Douglas Peachey would know.'

'I bet he would. Let's move on – you don't have to be poor, do you?'

'No, it's not an almshouse any more – the residents pay a proper rent. I think the ex-matrons find things a little tight, but most of the people there seem comfortable. Peter sold quite a large house when he moved in, so with the income from that and his pension, I think he was reasonably well off. Not rich, of course, but all right.'

This was an interesting possibility. 'I suppose we don't know where the money will go now?'

'Sorry – I can't help you there. There were no children, but Peter spoke of a sister and a couple of nieces, I think. He had visits about twice a year. I never met them, so I can't tell you any more than that.'

Ashley took some more time to file these facts away. 'Let's go back to the Fitzjames Hospital – last question, I promise you. Is it a popular retirement home?'

Clifford nodded emphatically. 'Very – there's quite a queue for places. I'm told that there were one or two noses out of joint when Mary Compton got her flat, because she didn't have to join a waiting list.'

'Really?' Ashley was interested enough to break his promise. 'I suppose you don't know who the next in the queue would be?'

'Sorry, no. Holbrooke will know, of course, and a lot of people will probably have worked it out, but the gossip hasn't reached me. You can probably guess who the main source for that sort of speculative information is.'

Ashley could. Much as he hated the idea, he was going to have to spend some time with Douglas Peachey. This unpleasant thought was interrupted by the telephone. Clifford answered, listened with surprise and amusement and then passed the receiver to Ashley.

'Do you know somebody called "the Lance Bomber",
George?'

Green's irrepressibly cheerful voice assaulted Ashley's left
eardrum. 'Hello, sir – I gather you've got a body on your
hands?'

'News travels fast, Lance Bombardier – you're
extraordinarily well informed.'

'Local news channel, sir – which is about as exciting as
Warminster gets. There was an item about your celebrations
being upset by a tragic death – and I figured that any tragic
death within five miles of you must have some mysterious
circumstances attached to it. If you need an assistant, I'd be
happy to come over.'

For the first time that evening, Ashley began to feel
cheerful. Regardless of any detecting skills, Green was
unfailingly good company. With the authorities apparently
satisfied that Peter's death was just an accident, the two of them
could probably spend an interesting and unimpeded few days
gathering information and following up ideas. Cupping a hand
over the mouthpiece, he asked Clifford if it would be possible
for Green to stay. There was no problem: 'As long as he doesn't
mind sleeping in a boy's bed.'

Ashley relayed this to Green, who immediately wanted to
know where the boy was going to be at the time: 'Remember
sir, you're talking to the Horse Artillery here, not the
Household Cavalry.'

'I'm in no danger of forgetting that, Lance Bombardier. It's
quite all right, the boys are all on holiday. Which reminds me,
what about Warminster?'

'Don't worry sir, I'll get her to chuck me this evening –
we're going out for a meal, so it shouldn't be difficult. Then I
can be with you first thing tomorrow.'

'That's excellent news, Lance Bombardier Green – the
sooner the better.'

CHAPTER EIGHT

THE BOTTOM OF THE STAIRS

Ashley discovered the hard way that the phrase, "first thing in the morning" was open to different interpretations. His own idea was somewhere about half past eight, when civilised people were contemplating the day to come in the company of eggs, bacon and a pot of tea. To Lance Bombardier Green, as to any mounted soldier, the term signified something altogether earlier. He barged into the middle of Ashley's mildly erotic dream, bearing two large mugs, one of which he rested noisily on the bedside table.

'Morning sir – one lance bombardier reporting for duty.'

Gruesome reality forced itself upon Ashley's consciousness. Staring into the half-darkness through bleary eyes, he watched Green vault onto a chest of drawers, where he sat, alternating his actions between slurping tea and dandling his legs. Suppressing the unworthy hope that the soldier would attempt both tasks simultaneously and topple off, Ashley hauled himself into a sitting position and contemplated the simmering brew next to him.

'I thought you might like some tea, sir. Blow away the cobwebs.'

"Like" was not exactly the word. Ashley had allowed Green to make tea for him on several occasions and had invariably suffered from the effect of a week's worth of tannin and sugar hitting his system all in one go. On the other hand, the second part of Green's statement might well be true. He held his breath and took a large mouthful.

'There you are, sir.' Green obviously regarded bulging

eyeballs as a symptom of revival. 'A couple of mugs of that and a gunner can muck out a whole stable without feeling any pain.'

'That's good, Lance Bombardier, because if I have a second mug, I may well have to muck out the bed. What time is it, by the way?'

'Half past five, sir.'

'Oh, God…' Ashley fell back onto his pillow and stared at the ceiling, hoping it would collapse on him and put him out of his misery. Half past five in the morning was like liver failure: you rather hoped that you'd get through life without actually experiencing it.

Green began to realise that he might be on the early side of welcome. 'I could come back later, if you like, sir.'

Ashley was resigned: 'No, don't worry – I'm awake now. Just give me a moment to check that everything's in working order.'

'Well, sir, judging by that bulge in the middle of the duvet, you're doing all right – in fact, I'd definitely consider applying the safety catch, if I was you.'

Ashley looked down the length of the bed. 'Sadly, Lance Bombardier, that's my knee – I'm only a civilian, remember? I don't pretend to compete with your military thirteen-pounder.'

The soldier gave a broad grin. 'Don't worry, sir – I'm told there's a lot of fun to be had with a pop gun.'

Ashley rolled onto his side and reached for more tea. Like school wine, the second mouthful wasn't quite as bad as the first. It occurred to him that Green, even in mufti, and at five-thirty in the morning, still looked immaculately smart. He was sure, though, that the soldier would be unable to return any compliment. For a moment, he returned to his dreams, imagining himself on a parade ground, unshaven and with hair sticking out in all directions, while Green (promoted to sergeant major for the occasion) contemplated his most unlikely recruit and improvised a virtuosic cadenza of criticism, complete with variations on a four-lettered theme.

'Do I look a complete mess, Lance Bombardier?'

63

'Well, sir, it's not exactly pretty – and you do look as if you were conceived when your mother took the bog brush to bed – but after three days with Wendy from Warminster I'm not inclined to be fussy.'

'I'm glad to hear it – chuck me a comb and I'll do my best to repair the damage while you tell me about the great romance.'

Green looked around for a comb. None being within convenient distance of his perch, he reached into his pocket and threw his own over.

'I don't mind if you don't, sir. And Warminster Wendy was a bit of a washout – she had some very unpleasant personal habits.'

'Such as?'

'Chastity, for one. She could hold hands for England, but anything between the neck and the knees was strictly out of bounds. One move from me and it was down with the portcullis and up with the drawbridge.'

'And your artillery was unable to penetrate the fortifications?'

'You couldn't have put it better, sir. Credit where it's due, though – she chucked me beautifully last night. I made a coarse suggestion over the crispy duck, she sulked all the way through her chop-suey, and shortly after the lychees arrived, she gave me the heave-ho. Actually,' he added, reflectively, 'I think the lychees might have acted as a catalyst. Anyway, sir, I spent last night in the back of the Land Rover wrapped in a horse blanket. It wasn't comfortable, but at least my kit bag didn't reject my advances.'

Having finished his narrative, Green swallowed the last of his tea in a single gulp. 'Anyway, sir, what about this dead body? What are we going to do – re-enact the crime like we did back at the barracks last year?'

Ashley was now halfway to becoming human again. He had nothing better to suggest and it occurred to him that if they went over to the hospital straight away, they could probably do their work unobserved. 'That is a very good idea, Lance Bombardier – give me a moment to stick a pair of trousers over my pyjamas and we'll do it now. I'll brief you as we go over.'

They left the house via the back door ('If I'd known it was unlocked, sir, I wouldn't have climbed through a window.') and headed towards the river. At the bridge linking the school to the hospital grounds, Ashley halted.

'Right, first things first. Yesterday, at about twenty to eleven, the whole school processed over this bridge and through the hospital grounds on their way to church. They do it every year, and it's a big local event.'

'Like Trooping the Colour, sir?'

'Precisely. All the residents of the hospital turned out to watch, including Peter Bulmer, the man who's dead. After the procession, the hospital people climbed into minibuses and went to the church as well – but not Bulmer. He said he wasn't feeling well.'

'So he was left alone back here, sir – I get the idea.'

'Good. The last thing you need to know before we go into the hospital is that from about half past twelve until three o'clock, I was part of a picnic party just there.' Ashley pointed to a spot about ten yards away. 'I'd swear to it that nobody entered the hospital through these gates during that time.'

'Are there other entrances, sir?'

'One to the High Street – and I think there's probably a connection through to the school's medical centre, which is next door. I need to check up on those.'

They walked through the gates and into the hospital courtyard. As Ashley had foreseen, it was deserted. Curtains were drawn across windows and only Bishop Fitzjames observed them, disapprovingly, from his roundel on the south wall. Ashley dropped his voice to a whisper as they crossed the courtyard diagonally and stood at the foot of the wooden steps leading to Mary Compton's balcony.

'Now this is where the body was found. Someone's had a go at cleaning up the bloodstain, but you can still see the mark.

65

That was where the back of his head was, with his feet towards the steps. Until a fortnight ago, he lived in the flat at the top.' Ashley outlined the theory that Peter had climbed the stairs by mistake and lost his balance.

'Would that be enough to kill him, sir? People have falls all the time and they break bones, but they don't usually die, do they?'

'It must depend on how one falls. Have you taken a tumble, Lance Bombardier?'

'Off a horse, about a trillion times, sir. Only once down stairs, though. I was a brand-new gunner and forgot that I was wearing spurs – I bounced all the way down on my backside, and then had to ride my horse for two hours. It wasn't my best day.'

'I can imagine. Now you must have fallen facing forwards. How did you land?'

Green looked thoughtful, then climbed up the first few steps and relived his descent in slow motion. 'I was going quite fast, sir, and caught my right spur on a step – so my leg folded underneath me. Then my other leg shot out in front and I slid down like that, sir.' He froze in a position rather like a Cossack dancer, complete with raised arms, then moved to the bottom of the stairs and took up his final pose. His left leg was still outstretched with his right leg twisted underneath. His spine extended over the three lower steps, with his head resting on the fourth. He had clearly been very lucky not to break his right leg: nonetheless, his position in no way resembled Peter Bulmer's. Peter had been on his back with a good few inches between his feet and the lowest step. Ashley pointed this out to Green, who looked thoughtfully from the stairs to the flagstone.

'When you fall off a horse, sir, you nearly always fall forwards. You might land on your back, but that's because you've done a somersault in mid-air, or you've rolled up into a ball and that's how you've unwound yourself. I don't see how either of those would fit falling downstairs.'

Neither did Ashley. They tried several experiments: falling in the process of ascending and descending the stairs, or while turning round half way up. Green ended up in a number of awkward poses, but never the same one as Peter Bulmer's. They rested, sitting together on the second step, contemplating the dark patch six feet away.

'I reckon they'd have to fire him from a cannon to get him that far from the stairs, sir.'

It was an exaggeration, but Ashley could see what he meant. It was as though Peter Bulmer had flown, not very gracefully, from the staircase to his final resting position. After a few minutes, Ashley had another idea, and they checked the banisters in case there were signs of Peter's attempts to save himself from falling; but the fresh varnish was undisturbed by any obvious scratches or other marks.

'Besides,' observed Ashley, 'if he had made a grab for the rails, he would very likely have broken a wrist or arm in the process, and I didn't see any sign of that. He was lying fairly awkwardly, but not in that way.'

Green resumed his seat on the second stair. Ashley leaned against the rail, stroking his stubbly chin.

'So, sir, have we shut the door completely on the possibility of it being an accident?'

Ashley shrugged. 'I suppose it's just possible that he had a dizzy spell as he climbed the lowest step, and just fell backwards – but as far as I could see, the skull was quite badly broken. I don't believe a simple fall from practically no height could have created enough force to do that, even given that old bones are fragile and that he landed on solid stone. Apart from that...'

'It's murder, sir, isn't it?'

Ashley nodded, grimly. 'It is, Lance Bombardier. I can't prove it – but I'm sure of it.'

Their conclusions received confirmation from an unexpected source. Mary Compton opened her front door and contemplated the ill-matched pair at the foot of her stairs. Even in his surprise at being caught like a trespassing schoolboy,

Ashley noticed that she looked poised and regal in her silk kimono and satin slippers. He expected a reprimand for disturbing her sleep; so, too, did Green, who instinctively sprang to attention.

Instead, Mary said: 'You don't think it was an accident, do you? Neither do I – and I'll show you why.'

*   *   *   *   *

'I love sausages.' Tom Two speared a regulation army banger and contemplated it for a few seconds, before biting off a large chunk.

'I know you do.' Tom One twirled a mushroom in the broken yolk of his fried egg. 'It keeps me awake at night, sometimes.'

'Don't be vulgar, One.'

Tom One gave a yellow and black smile. 'Sorry, Two.'

They busied themselves with breakfast. Around them, a hundred soldiers, dressed variously in riding kit, barrack dress or combats, did the same. A couple of tables away, Vernon and Sorrell seemed to be engaged in a competition to see who could eat the most toast. Like the Toms, they were dressed for riding: open necked khaki shirts were tucked into breeches, which were held up with green and cherry stable belts; breeches, in their turn tapered into polished riding boots. Their inverted hard hats rested on the table beside them, wobbling as the gunners buttered and marmaladed their way through their meal. The four of them were detailed for an early jumping lesson in the indoor riding school.

Jumping lessons could be terrifying or exhilarating, triumphant or humiliating – and they were always exhausting. Once in a while, aided by a good-natured horse, you sailed elegantly over the fences, progressed around the school in that most elusive of gaits, the collected canter, and felt yourself to be a horseman of Olympian standard. Then there were the other occasions, when you lolloped from jump to jump, leapfrogged over the bars like a badly sprung jack-in-the-box, and finally parted company with your saddle, ending up clinging on to the horse's neck with a passion normally reserved for favourite dogs and ladies of easy virtue. Tom Two, the most intelligent of the four, was easily the least confident over fences; in contrast, Vernon, whose brain was almost as under-developed as his body, sat on a horse naturally and gracefully, following its movements with an instinctive skill. Somewhere between the two, Tom One and Sorrell accepted occasional equestrian ups and frequent equestrian downs as an occupational hazard. As Tom One said, practising for a jumping lesson was easy – all you had to do was to stand at the top of the stairs and lean forward.

* * * * *

'You're the smart soldier in the book, aren't you?' Mary Compton shook hands with Green as he reached the balcony.

Green glowed with barely suppressed vanity. Ashley was convinced that the lance bombardier grew by two inches, and he wondered what would happen if the extremes of his grin met round the back of his skull, as seemed imminent. Perhaps he would end up looking like a breakfast egg, with the top sliced off? Then you could dip your bread in his brains, which were bound to be runny, rather than hard boiled.

Green confirmed his identity and established that Mary Compton, whom he addressed as 'ma'am', held the rank of dowager commanding officer.

Introductions over, they followed Mary indoors and into her sitting room. It was just as elegant as it had been the previous day.

But the portrait of Arbella Fitzjames was missing.

CHAPTER NINE

BROKEN FRAMES

'Don't move! Stay exactly as you are!'

It is an unnecessary command. Tom One lies, as if staked out, on the dusty floor of the riding school. A dull, aching sensation fills his whole body and his collapsed lungs try desperately and unsuccessfully to re-inflate themselves. In this painful and breathless limbo, he is surprised at how calm he feels and how acute his perceptions seem to be. He observes Sergeant Miller standing astride him, a booted foot on either side of Tom's motionless torso. From this angle, the riding instructor looks like a Renaissance study in perspective: his head is miles off and diminutive; the red stripes down the sides of his breeches apparently extend upwards for several yards, and his boots are of the seven-league variety, enormous in all dimensions. He bends over and the perspective changes: as he moves, Tom's lungs manage to take in a desperate gasp of air and suddenly his ribcage and arms are juddering frantically, as a succession of spasmodic, panting breaths follows. The movement increases his pain and his eyes fill with moisture, blurring his vision. Sergeant Miller, so sharp in outline a moment ago, is now a vague and ill-defined presence. His voice, however, is clear.

'Keep calm Tom – get your wind back. When you feel able, start to take longer and slower breaths.'

It takes time: the body has set up a pattern and it is hard to slow the motions to a regular pace but, gradually, the cycle of inhalation and expulsion becomes steadier. As the process normalises itself, Tom hears the sergeant yelling instructions to

Tom Two; although he cannot see what is happening, he becomes aware of Two dismounting, handing over his reins to Sorrell, and then striding rapidly to the far end of the school, where Tom One's panic-stricken horse is prancing and snorting. The noises of fear subside and Tom knows that his friend has caught and steadied the animal. Their shadows pass over him as Tom Two returns the horse to the worried group assembled at the far end of the riding school.

Tom blinks several times and the instructor begins to come back into focus. 'What happened, Sergeant Miller?' On other occasions, falling had been a surprisingly slow process: you felt yourself sliding forwards down the horse's neck and had time to curl yourself into a ball, so that you just rolled a couple of times on the ground before coming to a halt. This time, he has no knowledge of anything that has taken place between the time he was executing a well-balanced jump and the agonising moment of impact when all his vertebrae seemed to slam simultaneously against the ground.

The sergeant is reassuring: 'Don't worry – there was nothing you could have done. Some idiot outside must have knocked something over – didn't you hear the crash?'

'No, Sergeant, I didn't hear anything.'

'It happened just as your near foreleg touched the ground after the jump. The horse spooked at it and bucked before landing – you were still in the jumping position, so you didn't stand a chance. None of us could have stayed on in those circumstances.'

This information comes as a relief. On instructions from Sergeant Miller, Tom clenches and unclenches his fists, and wriggles his toes inside his riding boots.

'Okay, you've passed your functions test. Now listen carefully – we're going to get you on your feet, but we're going to do it in easy stages, with no sudden movements. Got that?'

'Yes, Sergeant.'

The instructor lowers himself to his knees, taking care to keep his legs clear of Tom's ribs. Tom feels one hand slide

71

under his neck, taking the weight of his head and preventing it falling back to the ground.

'How does that feel?'

'Fine, Sergeant, just fine.'

'Good lad. I'm going to keep that hand where it is and slide the other under your back – that might hurt quite a bit. When I've done that, I want you to put your arms around my waist. If you can't reach far enough round to join your hands together, hang on to my belt. Then I can lift you up into a sitting position. All right?'

Tom gasps with pain as the hand passes under the arch of his back and then moves up to the hollow between his shoulder blades. Sergeant Miller is practically on top of him now; no more than a few inches separate their faces and bodies, but nowhere has any weight been placed on the junior soldier. Tom feels the reassuring strength of his instructor around him and stretches his arms around Miller's body, grasping the sergeant's belt tightly.

'Now, let me do all the work – you just keep your back straight and hang on tightly. Don't let go, even when I've got you sitting up. Understand? Good – after three…'

On the count, Sergeant Miller slowly raises his own back to an upright position, and Tom is brought with him, pressing himself against the sergeant's chest. The movement causes his body to shudder again; he grips more firmly on the belt until his palms and fingers hurt.

'Don't fight it – just relax and it'll stop in its own time.' The words are spoken softly and directly into Tom's ear: Tom can feel the sergeant's breath as the sounds are formed. His heart feels like a rubber ball, bouncing around inside his ribcage; he is sure Sergeant Miller must feel it punching against him. The pain has caused his eyes to fill again and this time blinking fails to restore his vision.

Tom has no idea how long the position is held. A few moments? A quarter of an hour? As before, the trembling slows, and his heartbeat returns to normal.

'If I take my hand from the back of your head, Tom, can you support it by yourself?' Again, Tom feels the words as well as hearing them.

'I think so, Sergeant.'

Now the sergeant's hands lock together under Tom's shoulder blades. Acting on instructions, Tom hunches up his knees, and moves his arms up to the instructor's neck. Miller changes his own position back to a crouch, ready to rise and move back, so that Tom's legs will move naturally into place. Once more he counts to three and Tom is lifted aloft. Gingerly, he allows his weight to be supported by his legs, moving his feet slightly apart for better balance.

'Don't let go just yet – hold on until you're sure you're going to be all right. Back okay?'

'I think so, Sergeant – it's a dull ache, not a sharp pain.'

'That's good. When you're ready, just drop your arms to your side.'

Tom does so, and Miller, still gently supporting him under the shoulders, steps back slightly, so that they are now simply facing each other.

'Thanks, Sergeant Miller.'

'No problem, Tom – well done.' Miller lowers his voice, so that only Tom can hear his words: 'Before we rejoin the others, what do you want to do? I can take you over to the medic right away, if that's what you want.'

It must have been a bad fall: Tom has never been given this option before. His reply brings back an awareness of all the pain in his body, but it is the only reply worth making.

'No, Sergeant – I want to get back on and finish the lesson, if you think I'm up to it.'

'Good lad.' Sergeant Miller takes Tom's right hand and shakes it; this hurts, but the gesture of approval is worth the pain. Then the sergeant drops his hands and they slowly return to the ride.

*   *   *   *   *

73

Possibilities and theories whirled around Ashley's mind, colliding with each other and contradicting themselves at the rate of about three inconsistencies a second. After a while, he decided to fall back on some routine questions in the hope of bringing some order to his thoughts. Borrowing a pen and some writing paper from Mary's bureau, he sat down and took notes as he established some basic facts.

'When did you get back last night, Mrs Compton?'

'Fairly late: the headmaster's wife had invited me for a quiet supper after all the celebrations were over. The headmaster walked me back home at about half past ten so I must have been here by a quarter to eleven.'

'And the picture was gone then?'

'I don't know for certain – I didn't come into the sitting room. I went to the kitchen for a glass of water, then got ready for bed. I didn't hear anything in the night.'

'So you discovered it missing first thing this morning?'

'That's right. I woke up at about a quarter past six…'

Ashley and Green exchanged guilty glances: they had begun their experiments at about that time. Mary continued: 'So I made myself some coffee and came in here. I didn't notice the picture was gone until I'd put the tray down, which I think was probably just as well. Then, of course, I sat down and began to worry about how it might have fitted in with poor Peter's death.'

Ashley was worrying about that as well. 'When did you hear the news about Peter?'

'When I was at supper with the headmaster. Dr Holbrooke rang to tell us after he'd broken the news to all the other residents. I was ready to come away at once, but the headmaster's wife wouldn't hear of it. There were quite a few lights on when I got back, but I didn't think it would be right to knock on a door and ask for more information – I'm very new here, as you know.'

Ashley nodded and jotted down a few more notes. Mary Compton's last remark gave a jolt to his imagination.

'Mrs Compton, how many people have visited you since your arrival? In other words, who knew of the existence of the portrait?'

Mary took time to consider. Green used the pause to suggest that he, 'Might make some tea, ma'am?' Innocently, Mary accepted the offer with a smile and a nod, and Ashley made a silent resolution to interpose his body, if necessary, between the dignified old lady and the lance bombardier's hell-brew. As Green busied himself noisily in the kitchen, Mary Compton rehearsed her list of visitors.

'There was Dr Holbrooke, naturally, and his wife. They first called when everything was a complete muddle and Arbella was just leaning against the skirting board – but they've called several times since then, so they must have seen her, though they didn't mention her. Peter Bulmer, of course, was very interested, because he knew straight away who had painted her...' Mary paused, respectfully. Ashley wondered if she too had worked out that the most likely thief was already dead.

The sounds of ceramic and metallic crashes came from the kitchen. It sounded as though Green, surprised by a caddy containing leaf tea rather than bags, had sprayed the whole lot over the floor. Mercifully, proximity to a commanding officer by marriage curbed any natural soldierly instinct in the direction of invective and obscenity; instead, there were only the sounds of footsteps, and a deferential head peered round the door to inquire after the whereabouts of a dustpan and brush. Mary directed Green to the cupboard next to the washing machine and continued her recollections.

'The retired matrons called, all together, which was a bit exhausting, I'm afraid. They snooped around dreadfully, so they must have seen the picture, but I don't think they knew what it was – they seemed more interested in the fact that I don't have a television and play a weak no trump when I'm not vulnerable.'

By the time Mary had recollected all her visitors, Ashley had added to his list the headmaster and his wife, the school chaplain and Sister Barnfield. News, naturally, travelled: while Ashley was wondering who might have heard about the portrait from one of these visitors, Lance Bombardier Green entered with a surprisingly elegant salver on which silver and bone china were neatly arranged. An opened carton of milk struck the only jarring note in the ensemble. Presumably, Mary Compton possessed no chipped mugs, plastic trays or boxes of sugar lumps, otherwise Green would certainly have included them.

'I had to guess how much tea to use, ma'am – I'm not used to the fancy stuff.' The silver spout produced an arc of perfectly brewed Darjeeling, which Green contemplated with disappointment: 'It's a bit runny.'

'It will do very nicely, Lance Bombardier.' Ashley passed the cup to Mary before Green could pour its contents back into the pot. 'I'll have one just like it.'

'If that's what you want, sir.' Green sounded unconvinced. 'I'll wait for it to brew for another hour or so before I pour mine.'

Mary took pity on the soldier: it was easy to see why she had been popular with the ranks.

'If you want some really strong tea, Lance Bombardier Green, I keep an emergency supply of tea bags in the cupboard under the sink.'

'Thank you, ma'am.' Green scuttled out. A few moments later he returned with a handful of bags, which he popped triumphantly into the teapot. After a good stir a thick, black fluid appeared; Green added milk to produce his favoured orange colour and applied himself to dissolving as much sugar as possible into it.

'By the way, ma'am, if you want, I'll sort out that firewood under the sink for you. It's all a bit of a mess at the moment.'

Mary looked confused. 'Firewood, Lance Bombardier?'

'All that kindling, ma'am. Someone's just shoved it in there any old how – nails and splinters sticking out. You'll do yourself a nasty, if you handle it carelessly.'

Ashley observed the puzzled expression on Mary's face; he

linked it in his mind with an earlier reflection, that walking off with a picture is a tricky and inconvenient business. He went into the kitchen, opened the cupboard under the sink, and stared at the broken remains of Arbella's frame.

*   *   *   *   *

Tom One is being groomed, like a horse. He had tried to insist that he could look after himself, but an attempt to comb his hair had been accompanied by the sensation of forked lightning striking his back. He now sits on the edge of his bed, taking his orders from Tom Two, who has cast himself as barber, shower room attendant, and nurse.

For the rest of the lesson, Sergeant Miller had continued to display his nearly human side, even giving Tom a leg-up to help him remount. As a ride, they had walked their horses around the school, while the instructor had lowered the fence until the centre of the crossed poles was barely nine inches off the ground. They had jumped this as a ride, rather than individually. Tom had been third in line; all he had to do was to keep behind Vernon and Sorrell and look after his balance. Afterwards, Miller had taken him to the medical officer, who prodded about insensitively and pronounced him alive.

'Are you on stable routines over the weekend?'

'No, sir.'

'That's good – take it easy and get some rest. I'm taking you off all duties for the rest of the day. That's not time off, it's time for lying on your bed. Who's your roommate?'

'Two – er, Gunner Marsh, sir.'

'Can he be detailed to look after him, Sergeant Miller?'

'I'll see to it, sir.'

So Tom Two has patted his friend's sweaty hair dry and organised a more or less accurate parting down the middle.

'There you go, One – would sir like something for the weekend? We've had a consignment of the extra small just delivered.'

'And you know where you can stick them, Two.'

'Ingrate.' Methodically, Two continues his work, unbuttoning and peeling off Tom One's dirty shirt, wiping him down with a flannel and gently drying him, before taking a rugby top from the wardrobe: 'Give me your right arm – now the left – there you are.' He pops it over Tom's head and unravels it over his body. Then he stands back to inspect his work so far.

'You're going to have to keep your boots on for a bit, One – tugging them off might be painful.'

Tom One agreed. 'I think my whole leg might come off at the same time.'

'I'll wipe the muck off them and take the spurs off, then I'll get you lying down.'

Two minutes later, Tom is resting under a blanket, having been guided into a horizontal position by his friend. Tom Two sits on the edge of the bed, looking down at him.

'Is that all right, One?'

'It's great – thanks, Two.'

'No problem. Vernon's going to get you some food from the NAAFI when they get a break and Sorrell offered to bring along his dandy brush and hoof pick and give you a blanket bath. I told him not to forget a curry comb, because you've got a lot of dandruff down there.'

Tom One laughs and regrets it as his spine registers its objection to the movement. He gives a yelp of pain.

'Oh – sorry, One, that was my fault. Look - why don't you try and get some sleep? Once you've nodded off, I'll take my shower and get our stuff down to the laundry room.'

There is not long to wait; sleep comes quickly to Tom's tired and bruised body. Softly, so as not to disturb his friend, Tom Two eases himself up from the bed. He strips off his uniform, grabs a green army towel from his bed, and heads in the direction of the washroom.

CHAPTER TEN

ARBELLA FITZJAMES

Washed, shaved and in clean clothes, Ashley sat in the shade of an enormous copper beech tree on Old House lawn. Welcoming her guests back from the hospital, Diana Clifford had prepared a late Canadian breakfast of pancakes and maple syrup, which he and Green were consuming in an approximate ratio of one to four. Every so often Amelia Clifford, oozing availability, brought out reinforcements and fresh supplies of tea, each time sending out strong and not-very-subliminal signals of desire in the lance bombardier's direction. To Ashley's relief, Green's sexual antenna was non-operational and there was no apparent response to Amelia's messages.

'After all, sir,' Green drizzled syrup onto the latest arrival, as his host's daughter wiggled seductively back to the house, 'one woman is very much like another – but these pancakes are something special.' He paused before sinking his teeth into the rolled-up delicacy: 'And, talking of women, I didn't think much of that policewoman, or whatever she was, who came to Mrs Compton's place.'

Ashley was cynical in his reply: 'She's a community support officer, Lance Bombardier. In a small town like this, the CSO is the first legal port of call – and some of them are about as much use as the Home Guard would have been had we ever been invaded. But we had to start by contacting her – she'll send in a report and, with any luck, somebody more able will take charge.'

'And what about us, sir – where do we go from here?'

Ashley sat back in his chair and contemplated the leaves

and branches above him. 'That, as they say, Lance Bombardier, is the million-dollar question. Let's talk a bit about detecting in general and see if that gives us some ideas.'

'Sounds good, sir – go on.'

'All right, suppose for a moment we had a very simple crime on our hands. A clumsy burglar, who doesn't really know what he's doing, breaks into a house. We'll call it Mary Compton's house – flat, rather – just to make it relevant, but it could be any place. Well, our burglar steals anything that looks valuable and that he can carry. If he has a van, he'll take electrical goods, because he knows he can pass them on at a car boot sale. In the process, he leaves all sorts of clues behind – footprints, fingerprints, threads from his clothes, a bit of blood even, if you're lucky.'

'I get the idea, sir.'

'Good. Now, in that case, all you have to do is collect the information and it should lead you directly to your criminal – he might just as well have signed a letter saying, "I, Joe Bloggs, of 47a, Acacia Avenue visited these premises today and pinched everything in sight; I shall be available for arrest during normal working hours." Crimes like that happen all the time, but they don't often come my way, because the police can sort them out very quickly, if they have the resources.'

Ashley paused, and drank some tea before continuing. 'Then there are the crimes, much more interesting ones, where the information left is less precise. Unless our art thief has left his prints all over the broken frame – and I'd be prepared to lay money, Lance Bombardier, that the only paw marks found on them are yours, Mary Compton's and Peter Bulmer's – well, as I say, unless he's done that, our evidence is much vaguer. At this point – the point we're at now – we need to do two things: we have to find out more information somehow, and to start forming theories. Those are two very distinct operations and we mustn't muddle them up.'

Green nodded. 'I think I know what you mean, sir – we had to do quite a lot on correct procedures on my JNCO course, and they put all sorts of hypothetical situations in front of us.'

'Good – we're on the same wavelength then. Now the problem with coming up with theories is that, when you find some good ones, you fall in love with them. That means that, if you're not careful, any information you subsequently obtain, you try to make fit your theory rather than the other way around.

'Take our bossy community support officer. Mercifully, it's not her job to theorise – she just passes information up the line. Nonetheless, yesterday, she was sure that Peter Bulmer's death was an accident. If she wants to cling on to that idea, she has to conclude that the two episodes are separate incidents, linked only by an incidental proximity of time and location. The picture was stolen – the thief disappeared – Peter Bulmer came along, fell down the stairs and died.'

Green was as unimpressed as Ashley intended him to be. 'Sounds like a pretty crummy theory to me, sir.'

'And to me – but that problem can crop up in more subtle ways and we have to guard against it all the time.'

'Understood, sir. And do you have any better theories?'

'Several. How about this one: the thief has entered the flat specifically to steal the picture. He knows that the hospital residents will be in church between eleven and twelve o'clock, so he has the best part of an hour to take the picture out of the frame and roll it up. He hides the broken pieces of the frame in the cupboard under the sink and goes to leave the flat – and sees Peter half way up the stairs. He rushes past Peter, pushing him back with such force that the old man flies through the air and is killed when his head strikes the flagstone at the bottom. The thief then makes his exit as quickly as possible, leaving Peter to be found about three hours later.'

Green pondered the scenario over a pancake. 'I like that one, sir. It explains how the old boy was some way from the stairs.'

'I like it too, Lance Bombardier, but that doesn't mean it's correct. Here's another possibility: Peter Bulmer – the only person, remember, who is known to have recognised the picture as the work of a great artist – is himself the thief. He excuses himself from the service specifically to steal the picture, but loses his balance as he makes his way downstairs and kills himself. The first person to find him guesses that the picture is valuable and makes off with it – a simple crime of opportunity, just like taking a handbag from a car when the window has been left open.'

Another pancake's worth of thought followed. 'I'm not sure I like that one as much, sir.'

'No – the coincidence is a more awkward one, and we're back where we started when it comes to explaining the position of the body. On the other hand, the first theory doesn't take into consideration Peter's knowledge of the picture – he just happens to find himself in the wrong place and turns our thief into an accidental killer. I could come up with another half-dozen situations, probably; all with their strong points and flaws. Conclusion?'

This time, Green didn't need a pancake: 'We need to gather more information, sir.'

'Spot on. The police will scour around for fingerprints – they'll need to take ours at some point – and they can do that sort of thing far better than us, so we'll let them get on with it. We'll try and explore aspects of the case that might not occur to them.'

'Such as, sir?'

'In the first place, I'm going to find out everything I can about that seventeenth-century slapper, Arbella Fitzjames. That will involve visiting a particularly rancid specimen of humanity called Douglas Peachey, but I'll try the library first. That'll take up the couple of hours before luncheon, and I can call on Peachey afterwards if I need to – he might be quite harmless if I catch him in the middle of his afternoon nap.'

'And what about me, sir – anything I can do?'

Ashley gave the smug look of one who is about to stitch up his friend. 'There's a task, Lance Bombardier, that the police would be *very* bad at, and I wouldn't be much better. You, however, will perform it brilliantly…' He paused for theatrical effect.

'I want you to give a middle-aged and overweight nurse the biggest thrill she's had for thirty years.'

∗   ∗   ∗   ∗   ∗

Sister Barnfield was preparing her midday meal when Green arrived; she wielded a large, antique chemist's pestle in a determined manner, pulverising garlic, pine nuts and basil leaves in a stone bowl.

Suppressing the thought that it was no wonder Sister Barnfield was still single, if she treated her men like she handled the pestle, Green explained that he had woken with a bad head and that Colin Clifford had sent him over. Sister Barfield took him through to her surgery, fussed around him and issued painkillers; distrusting pills, Green slipped them into his pocket while the sister was busy entering the details in her ledger. Then they returned to the kitchen and Green got down to work.

'I bet you're a really good cook, Sister, aren't you?'

The nurse glowed serenely as she steeped the pesto in olive oil. 'Well, I do like my food, Lance Bombardier – as you can see.'

'Well, good on you, Sister. My mum's a well-built lady, and she's a fantastic cook – my dad reckons he's the happiest man in the country.' In fact, Mrs Green was a tiny woman who subsisted on celery and whose husband preferred ration packs to his wife's cooking; but that was neither here nor there. For added effect, Green invented two brothers who had married girls of equal voluptuousness: 'So it's like a tradition in our family, Sister – no stick insects allowed. When my younger brother got married, you could practically hear the pew ends splitting as his bride processed down the aisle. Lovely girl, she is, too,' he added, realising that this last piece of corroborative information might not be taken too well.

83

Sister Barnfield finished her pesto by stirring in a mound of Parmesan, then tried a spoonful by way of testing the mixture. She passed a second spoonful to Green, who privately thought that garlic was foreign muck and that herbs were for cissies.

'Fantastic, Sister! A dollop of that on the side of your plate will really perk up your pie and chips.'

Things had started well, he thought.

*   *   *   *   *

In the Old Library, Ashley was having fun of a more academic variety. Like many schools, King's had two libraries: a sparkling modern building which housed computers and shiny textbooks with unbroken spines; and the original library, with dusty volumes, portraits of headmasters, and Victorian desks with names carved into them by decades of bored pupils. Although he might need the computers later, Ashley had started his research in the Old Library, to which Colin Clifford had a key. On a desk in front of him lay bound copies of Pepys' and Evelyn's diaries; Bishop Burnett's *History of His Own Times* and Aubrey's *Brief Lives*. Guessing that the last source would be the most entertaining, Ashley had started there. Sure enough, Arbella Fitzjames emerged rather larger than life from the page:

> *When brought to court, this lady conceiv'd such a passion for the Duke of Monmouth — which she later attempted to revive on his coming into the Western Counties — that she was thought by some to be in danger of losing her reason; and by others of losing her virtue, albeit that the Duke had eyes for none other than Lady Wentworth. (Mem. Find out from Sir Anthony in which year this was.)*
>
> *Thinking to gain by audacity what charm had failed to win, she appeared in a masque as Arion, riding a dolphin — this being, according to Dr Ashmole, her family emblem (check). So shock'd was the Queen that Arbella was sent from the court, though not before the King had caused Sir Peter Lely to paint her likeness in*

84

the same manner. I had it from Sir Anthony that Sir Peter did consider it one of the best pictures that he ever made: also, that Mr Cooper did most ingeniously take a miniature off the same, he dying not long after.

When the Duke rebell'd, this lady was so convinc'd that he would be King and in such hopes that she would be either mistress or (if the Duke could be rid of his wife) Queen that she caused to be built a triumphal arch at her family home in Somerset, ready to welcome him, with banners and a dolphin rampant (Mem. Upon which, Col Oglethorpe of His Majesties Life Guards did make a very fine joke, but too coarse to be written here). Upon the Duke's suffering on Tower Hill, she did indeed part with her senses and died not long after – Sir Anthony says from a pox but Dr Ashmole who knew her says not. Her arch, being but of wood, burnt down. Sir Anthony says the house is now almost ruinous, this being a matter of great regret, for it was very fine.

Ashley began to see why Peachey was so fond of the late seventeenth century; during his own special period, the only sources of gossip were the Paston letters, of an almost unbearable tediousness. An age in which scandal had become an art form, and a legitimate subject for amateur scholars like Aubrey, must have suited Peachey down to the ground.

Arbella received a snooty mention from Evelyn and a walk-on role in Burnett's *History*. Sadly, she appeared too late on the courtly scene to be mentioned by Pepys, who would certainly have had some ripe anecdotes in the manner of Aubrey – unless his wife had intervened in time.

Ashley lingered in the library a little longer. He read several accounts of the short, turbulent life of the Duke of Monmouth, and looked up Lely and Cooper in a dictionary of art. Then he prowled up and down the room, trying to fit his new information around the known facts.

Surely the only person who would want to steal the portrait of Arbella would be Douglas Peachey? But did he know of its existence? And how could he have stolen it when he was at the church service and the headmaster's entertainment afterwards? Unless it was taken from the flat later, and the theft and Peter Bulmer's death really were two unrelated incidents. Ashley disliked this idea intensely because it meant that the community support officer would have been right all along – nonetheless, he would have to give it proper consideration.

Something else occurred to him: suppose Mary Compton was wrong about the picture's value? Perhaps pictures by Lely commanded so high a price that even a badly damaged one would fetch – well, what? Surely no more than a few thousand on the black market: scarcely enough to be worth the risk and the trouble.

Ashley knew that he was speculating outside of his field of knowledge; he had no idea of the price the stolen picture might command.

But he knew someone who would.

After a moment's more thought, he took out his mobile and called his nephew.

CHAPTER ELEVEN

TOM'S TASK

'Hello? Hi, Mr Ashley, sir – no, it's Tom Two here. Tom One's fast asleep – he had a bit of a prang this morning… Don't worry, sir, it's all right, but it was very nasty at the time. It was like that moment in the film, when you start to believe that a man can fly… Yes, sir, right over the horse's head – he landed on his back, a long way off… He's been ordered to rest for today, but I reckon he'll be up and about tomorrow. Okay, sir, I'll get him to call you when he wakes up.'

Tom Two turned off the mobile and went back into his room, which he had left so that he could take the call without disturbing his comrade. Tom One's bedside table now held a large bottle of cola, several packets of crisps and a squashed pasty, which Vernon appeared to have tucked under his armpit to keep it warm during the journey from the NAAFI to the bedside. There was also a "get well" card, with One's rank and name printed laboriously and awkwardly on the envelope. Tom himself remained cocooned in his blanket and was producing gentle snuffling sounds, like a contented piglet. Tom Two quite enjoyed the sound during the day, but he hoped that One would be able to sleep on his side when night came.

It was strange to be taken off duties, and rather dull. Having been told to look after his roommate, Two felt unable to leave him for long, but he also felt that he had exhausted the time-passing resources of the room. Kit had been cleaned, shirts had been ironed and limitless cups of tea had been consumed, but both television and trumpet practice were out of the question while Tom One slept. There was a small collection of paperbacks on a shelf and a rather larger collection of magazines in a desk drawer; their subject matter alternated between equitation and titillation, neither of which appealed to Tom Two in his present mood.

He stared out of the window, over the parade ground and to the buildings beyond. For more than six months now, this strange kingdom, part bastion, part stable and – as it sometimes seemed – part monastery, had been his life. The parade ground had echoed to the sound of his trumpet, and the pounding of his and a hundred other pairs of boots had mingled with the natural harmonies of the barracks: the jangling of soft steel traces and harnesses; the clattering of hoofs on concrete; the eternal campanology of the forge, beating out the old shoes and ringing in the new. It seemed to him the best of symphonies, for the rhythms of real lives and the age-old melodies of tradition and service combined into one equal music. Tom Two gazed down with a sense of belonging; whether his time with the Troop was to be long or short, he knew that this would always be a spiritual home. When he left, he would take a part of it with him, and he would leave a part of himself behind.

A good deal of this feeling, he knew, was connected to the bruised soldier underneath the army blanket. The Troop without Tom One would be no more than a half-existence; they had joined together, progressed together and, occasionally, got themselves into trouble together. Nursing his comrade this morning had been a natural duty, and Tom Two would have been mortified if the task had been assigned to anyone else.

His thoughts came to an abrupt conclusion. Tom One gave the gelatinous grunt of one who has just swallowed the contents of his sinuses; he choked, and woke up. Two, called back to duty, raised him to a sitting position so that he could clear his chest. A coughing fit, painful and productive, followed.

When it was over, Two arranged the pillows from both beds so that Tom One could sit back. Then, using a pair of boot hooks as tongs, he picked up his friend's full handkerchief and deposited it in the bin.

'It's another of those occasions, One, when friendship can go no further. I'll buy you a new hanky – but I'm not rinsing that one out.'

'Fair enough, Two.' Tom One rubbed his eyes and looked around the room, registering the food and the card. 'Was I asleep long?'

'Best part of three hours. How's the back now?'

'Like a steak after it's been tenderised, I should think. If you want to smear some paté over me, I'll turn into *Tournedos Rossini*, like Uncle George gave us at his club that evening.'

Tom Two considered the culinary possibilities: 'A couple of minutes, either side, on a high heat?'

'That's right – just like a cavalryman's love life.'

It didn't bear thinking about, Two decided. He changed the subject: 'Vernon and Sorrell brought the food and the card. I think Vernon must have played truant the day they were taught joined-up handwriting. And your uncle rang – I told him about you getting binned this morning. Hope you don't mind.'

'No problem.' Tom One ripped the card from its the envelope and studied the cartoon of a fat pony galloping gleefully away from a scene of equestrian disaster. Inside, Sorrell and Vernon had signed themselves "Ben" and "Keith". There was no further message: Tom received the strong impression that both gunners had shot their bolts as far as literature was concerned. 'Did Uncle George leave a message?'

'No – I said I'd get you to return the call when you woke up. Do you want to do it now?'

'May as well.' Tom reached for his mobile and scrolled down the addresses for his uncle's number. After a pause, he heard Ashley's voice: 'Hello – is that you Tom? How are you feeling?'

'Hi, Uncle George, I'm fine. A bit beaten-up, but I'll live. Nothing's broken – I've got to rest today, but I want to be up and about tomorrow if I can.'

'Glad to hear it – do you fancy being up and about doing some detective work?'

Tom did: he had helped – and hindered – his uncle on a couple of occasions and had thoroughly enjoyed the furtive world of sleuthing. 'That'd be great, Uncle George – I'm not on duty this weekend. Neither's Tom Two – shall I get him in on the act?'

'I was going to suggest it – it's going to need some brains.'

'Thanks Uncle George.'

'My pleasure. Do you have a pencil and paper to hand?'

Tom smoothed out Vernon's crumpled envelope and Tom Two threw a pencil across the room. 'Okay, Uncle George.'

'Good - now listen carefully…'

*   *   *   *   *

Ashley gave a final piece of advice before bidding his nephew farewell: 'And in *no* circumstances, Tom, should you allow Mr Robbins to sell you a picture.'

'Do you think he'll try?'

'Is the Pope Catholic?'

'All right – I get the idea, Uncle George.'

They exchanged farewells and hung up. Ashley was once more under the tree on Old House lawn. He had in front of him the notes he had taken in the library and a few other jottings. One set was headed, "Possible Chronologies"; the other, "Things to do". There was also an open Ordnance Survey map of the area and a pint of beer, both thoughtfully provided by Colin Clifford. An empty glass and a second bottle awaited the return of Lance Bombardier Green.

With a feeling of distaste, Ashley took up his list of things to do: at the top, he had written in capital letters, INTERVIEW DOUGLAS PEACHEY. This was a task from which he instinctively shrank. The thought of sifting through Peachey's malicious and digressive monologues for a few grains of real information was a depressing one. Still, it had to be done: revising his earlier plan, Ashley guessed that if he timed his visit for about six o'clock, he might at least be given a drink to go with his boredom. Also – a bright idea occurred to him – he could get Green to ring Peachey's doorbell after an hour and drag him away on some fabricated piece of urgent business.

The thought of being rescued by Her Majesty's Armed Forces made Ashley smile in a particularly welcoming manner when Green, despising the gate, vaulted over the garden fence and strode towards him. On his face was the triumphant leer of conquest.

'Did she sing, Lance Bombardier?' asked Ashley, thinking of the fat lady at the end of the opera.

'Like a canary on steroids, sir. I got the tour of the medical centre, complete with oh-so-convenient door through to the hospital; I had her vivid description of finding the body and how long she thought it had been dead; and I got neat little thumbnail sketches of all the people we've talked about, including details of friends, relations and local feuds. What's more, sir, I don't think she so much as suspected that I was trying to get information out of her.'

Ashley poured out the second bottle of beer and handed it to his new assistant. 'So, poor Sister Barnfield succumbed, unsuspectingly, to your military charms.'

'She did, sir,' Green took a long draught from his glass. 'By the time I'd finished, her cheeks were glowing pink and there were little wet patches all over her uniform. Fortunately, I could run faster than her, otherwise she'd be practising her CPR techniques on me now – at one end or the other. Incidentally, sir, I ought to spend a few minutes writing all this stuff down before I forget it.'

Ashley passed him some paper and a pen, which the soldier held in a grip that rivalled Sister Barnfield's technique with her pestle.

'Keep them brief,' Ashley advised. 'Notes are much better as an aid to the memory than as exact transcriptions – unless you're a policeman taking a statement, when you have to be completely accurate. For our purposes, the shorter the better. You can always clarify them when I read them.'

'Short and to the point it is, sir.' Green received the instruction with obvious pleasure and settled himself down to write. Judging that the soldier would prefer not to be observed while engaged in this unnatural intellectual activity, Ashley picked up the Ordnance Survey map and opened it out like a broadsheet newspaper.

Bruton lay centrally, about five miles north of the A303 and equidistant from Wincanton and Shepton Mallet. It was tucked into a corner of Somerset: the border with Wiltshire was only a few miles to the east, and Dorset was just a little further off to the south. Somewhere, in that little segment, Arbella Fitzjames had lived and had built her triumphal folly. Presumably, Mary Compton would be able to point out exactly where: if not, Douglas Peachey could doubtless give an eight-figure grid reference from memory. This, however, would be less satisfactory; Ashley had a whim to see whatever might be left of the place, but he would rather pay his visit without Peachey's knowledge.

The hunt for the Fitzjames house proving fruitless, Ashley searched for place names associated with the Duke of Monmouth's rebellion. The Duke, he knew, had been within eight miles of Bruton itself: there was Frome, up in the north-east of the map, where the rebel forces had reversed their march towards London and turned instead to Bristol; a little further to the north lay Norton St. Philip, where Monmouth's untrained rustics had actually won a skirmish against the forces of the crown. After that, the rebels had continued their westward movement; Ashley guessed that the debacle of Sedgemoor had taken place somewhere beyond the left margin of his map.

He speculated on the Duke of Monmouth's intentions. If circumstances had been different and his way to London unimpeded, would he have visited Arbella during his progress? And, if so, would she have succeeded where she had failed before? Could she have persuaded him to turn his affections towards her? Divorcing his unloved Duchess would certainly

92

have been a priority for Monmouth, had his campaign been successful. How close had England been to having a Queen Arbella? At university, Ashley remembered, his lecturers had been scathing of books which explored alternative versions of history; their writers, he was told, were playing games, rather than engaging with real scholarship. Since then, even serious historians had enjoyed these speculations, sometimes gaining valuable insights into the minds of historical figures and of whole nations. Would an understanding of the fruitless ambition of Arbella help him to track down her thief? Only, he concluded, if the thief was Douglas Peachey – and he hadn't needed to read half a dozen history books to get that far.

Lance Bombardier Green threw down his pen with a clatter and drank freely from his glass.

'I think that's about it, sir – it's all the important bits.'

Ashley took up the sheets of paper and read from Green's precise and angular script, in which all the letters seemed to be standing to attention:

1. There is a door leading directly from the medical centre to the hospital.
2. It is never locked. The school has an arrangement with the hospital and Sister is paid a retainer to act as a first responder in the event of an emergency.
3. There were no visitors to the medical centre on the day that Mr Bulmer died. Sister was expecting this and spent a lazy day.
4. She estimates that Mr Bulmer had been dead for 3-4 hours when she found him. She thinks his death was an accident.
5. Sister Barnfield dislikes the retired matrons, the serving matrons and Douglas Peachey.
6. She is slightly scared of Dr Holbrooke, the headmaster and Mary Compton.
7. She likes Peter Bulmer (dead), Colin Clifford and the headmaster's wife.

8. And she is madly in love with Lance Bombardier Green.

It was, Ashley thought, an admirably concise summary. Green had a few supplementary remarks to make as Ashley read down the list:

'Reference serial three, sir, she says that no one is ever ill on Corpus day. She told me that she was asleep during the time of the service, and that her mobile was by the bed in case there was an emergency.'

'So, anyone could have gone through the medical centre without her knowing – assuming she's speaking the truth, of course.'

'That's right, sir. Her bedroom – I didn't actually go in it, thank God – is up a floor and along, so it would have been easy to sneak through that way, if you knew about it. And reference serial four, sir...'

This had been the sentence that immediately caught Ashley's eye. 'Yes, Lance Bombardier?'

'I reckon she was just saying it in that polite way that people have, sir. I didn't push the point, because I didn't want to break cover, but I'm pretty sure she knows it was more than just an accident.'

Ashley nodded. 'Of all the people we have to deal with, she's the one who's most likely to have worked it out.'

'And what about you, sir? What's with the map?' Green rose from his seat at the garden table and looked over Ashley's shoulder. He used his pencil to point out Bruton. 'That's us there, isn't it, sir?'

'That's right. Somewhere around here...,' Ashley indicated the right-hand corner of Somerset, 'our lady of little virtue had her country house. I don't think there'll be much left of it, but I'd still quite like to see what there is.'

'Well I tell you what, sir,' the lance bombardier put his pencil to use once more and pointed to a village called Penselwood. 'I reckon that clump of buildings there must be

Jonesy's stable. When you've found out exactly where the old house is, and if it's not too far off, why don't we combine business with pleasure and hack out to it?'

Ashley contemplated the prospect with pleasure. It was a practical suggestion as well, for the roads of the area looked to be few and narrow. A horse was probably the most efficient way of getting about.

'That, Lance Bombardier Green, is the best idea I've heard since Mr Clifford suggested bringing out some beer. Let's do it.'

'I'll get it organised for tomorrow morning, sir. And talking of good ideas, here comes Mr Clifford with another round of brainwaves.'

CHAPTER TWELVE

AFTERNOON ACTIVITIES

Human beings are resilient – or callous, depending on how one looks at it. After any excitement, normality reasserts itself remarkably quickly. In the barracks, Tom's friends got on with their duties and in Bruton, the matrons got on with their bridge, playing for lower stakes than usual, as a sign of respect.

Having been up since early morning, Ashley and Lance Bombardier Green took accidental siestas. Following a late luncheon, they carried their tea up to Ashley's room to sort out their notes and to plan ahead: and promptly fell asleep, Green in an armchair and Ashley on the bed. The notes, on their separate sheets of paper, fell from Ashley's languid hand and scattered over the carpet.

In these positions (Green looking like Marat in his bath and Ashley resembling a freshly-poisoned Chatterton) they were discovered by Amelia Clifford, who came to tell them that the police had arrived. With heroic self-restraint, she resisted the temptation to enter the lance bombardier's dreams and contented herself with shaking his shoulder gently.

'It's the police, Mr Green. They want to see you.'

'What? But I only made the suggestion so she'd chuck me.'

'It's about the stolen picture. They're down in my father's study.'

'Oh, right…'

Detective Sergeant Archdale turned out to be a middle-aged West Countryman, down to earth and sensible. His uniformed constable contented himself with being silent and muscular. The two stood up when Ashley and Green entered the study; the older men shook hands while Green eyed the policemen suspiciously.

'Hello, gentlemen – we're sorry to trouble you.'

'Not at all, Sergeant – we were expecting a visit. Are you here because of the picture, or because of the death?'

The sergeant smiled: 'I think in a day or two, sir, they'll work out that a death and a theft within twenty feet of each other make up an industrial-sized coincidence, and then they'll get an inspector out from Yeovil – just to make a nuisance of himself, probably. Constable Telfer and I are here about the theft, for the moment, sir. It was you, I understand, who contacted us.'

'That's right, Sergeant. Lance Bombardier Green and I were trying to work out how a man could have fallen down the stairs and landed as Peter Bulmer did, when Mrs Compton saw us. About half an hour earlier, she'd realised the picture was missing. I telephoned on her behalf.'

'That's exactly what she said, sir. It seems there was a valuable paperweight stolen as well.'

'Really?' This was news to Ashley. 'Do you know when Mrs Compton noticed it was missing?'

'It was while we were there, sir, just a few minutes ago. Constable Telfer was checking her bureau for prints and a draught blew some papers off; that's when she picked up on it. She was going to ring you to let you know, but I said we were coming over and could pass the information on.'

'Thanks very much.' Ashley was intrigued. The paperweight was valuable and could easily be slipped into a pocket but it made an odd coupling with the portrait. He put the information to the back of his mind, for later examination. 'And what can we do for you now, Sergeant?'

'There are two things, sir, if you don't mind. One is to take the fingerprints of both of you, so that we can eliminate some of the ones we've found. After which,' the sergeant checked his notes, anxious to be accurate, 'we can let Lance Bombardier Green go. The other thing, of course, sir, is to ask you about

97

any ideas you might have concerning the theft – and so forth.'

Ashley understood the nuance of the policeman's final clause: clearly, Sergeant Archdale was happy to go beyond his brief when he considered it appropriate.

The process of fingerprinting was familiar to Ashley, though he had only rarely had to submit to it himself. He was entertained by Green's surprise when Constable Telfer insisted on guiding each finger in turn to the inkpad, pressing it down with a rotating movement to ensure that the top joint was fully coated.

'I can do it myself, you know,' he said, petulantly.

'Sorry, sir – it's the regulation.' The constable carefully transferred the oily coating on Green's little finger to an official card, using the same swivelling motion. When he lifted Green's hand, a prune-like blotch became visible.

A resentful frown clouded Green's brow; he disliked the passive indignity of his situation and he loathed being called "Sir". Ashley defended the policeman: 'He's right, Lance Bombardier – you'll just have to do as you're told.'

Another finger was manipulated into the inkpad. 'So I'm supposed to just lie back and enjoy it, sir, is that right?'

'Well, now you know what it's like to be on the receiving end of that command for once. Unlike Wendy from Warminster, I suggest you obey the order.'

Amused, Green visibly cheered up. By the time Constable Telfer began on his other hand, he had started to enjoy the experience and expressed a worry that his feet might have come into contact with some of Mary Compton's furniture.

'You're sure you don't want to do my toes as well, Constable?'

'No thank you, sir. We have to do lip prints sometimes, though.'

Green assumed this involved the constable holding him by the ears, then plunging his face into the ink and rocking his head from side to side. 'I'll pass on that one – I might have handled that picture frame but I didn't snog it.'

When the constable had finished his business, Sergeant Archdale sent him off to see Dr Holbrooke. Ashley suggested that Green went over to the hospital with him.

'If Mrs Compton has just had her flat checked for fingerprints, she'll have a hell of a mess to clean up. That's right, isn't it Sergeant?'

'I'm afraid so, sir – it's horrible stuff to get off.'

Green was quite happy to undertake 'a bit of spit and elbow' for a commanding officer's wife. While he and Ashley washed the ink from their hands in the bathroom, he asked, 'Presumably there's something you want me to do while I'm there, sir?'

Ashley nodded. 'In the first place, make friends with the constable on the way over: I think we're going to be seeing more of those two, so we may as well get on.'

'Fair enough, sir.' Green arranged his towel so that Diana Clifford wouldn't see the black stains. 'What else?'

'Keep your ear to the ground. People will call on Mrs Compton while you're there – they always do after a police visit. Naturally, they'll pretend they've come to help, but most of them will be there out of curiosity. The picture and Peter Bulmer will be the only two topics of conversation, so you might learn something that we can follow up later.'

'I get the idea, sir – while they talk, my lugs are flapping like Tom Two's in a high wind.'

'I couldn't have put it better, Lance Bombardier.'

As Green and Constable Telfer headed for the hospital, Ashley and Sergeant Archdale settled down into armchairs and exchanged ideas and information.

'Frankly, sir, I think the fingerprints will be a waste of time. You don't go into a house to steal a picture and then leave your marks over everything else. This wasn't the sort of job where the thief was rummaging through drawers for what he might find.'

Ashley agreed: 'Which is why I'm intrigued by the paperweight, Sergeant Archdale. If the thief came specifically to take the picture, why steal the paperweight as well? I've put that badly: what I mean is, why *only* the paperweight? There are a dozen other bits and bobs in Mrs Compton's drawing room which would fetch quite a nice price at an antique fair.'

The sergeant clicked his fingers as he thought. 'I think I see what you mean, sir – perhaps it just caught his eye, though. He's in the room – he's taken the portrait out of its frame and dumped the wood – he looks round to check he hasn't left anything, sees the paperweight and thinks, "That's nice, I'll have that." That's my guess, sir.'

It was a good guess too; Ashley could easily visualise the scene and follow the thought process. Nonetheless, there was still something about it that he didn't like and he said so. Sergeant Archdale nodded.

'I know what you mean, sir – it's an irritating little detail, isn't it? And they're sometimes the ones that help us solve a crime – or get us wandering up the garden path for ages after a false lead.'

This was another thought process that was easy to follow: both men had experienced the frustration of following the wrong trail. 'And, as we know, Sergeant, following it is the only way of finding out that it *is* wrong.'

'That's very true, sir.'

They exchanged ideas and information. Ashley told the policeman what he knew of the history of the portrait.

'So, it's of historical interest, even if it's not very valuable, you think, sir?'

'To the right person, Sergeant. I'll be completely honest and admit that I would love to pin the theft on a ghastly old bore called Douglas Peachey.'

The sergeant laughed, interrupting before Ashley could develop his theme: 'You don't need to tell me about *him*, sir. He's always calling the Wincanton station to complain about some trivial thing, or getting on his high horse about the police today, when he's read an article in a newspaper. His main theme is that Bruton ought to have its own police station like it used to. It's a fair point, but there just isn't the money any more, as I'm sure you'll understand, sir.'

Ashley smiled ironically. 'Which is why Bruton is left in the capable hands of a community support officer, I suppose?'

He was rewarded with a loud snort from the sergeant: 'Yes, sir – and let's not talk about *her*.'

Ashley reverted to Douglas Peachey, observing that if the theft took place at about the same time as Peter Bulmer died, then Peachey – with everybody else from the hospital – was in church.

'As I gather, sir – along with most of the great and good from the town. I've got a list of all the prominent locals who get invitations, if you want to see it.'

Ashley shook his head. 'I don't think the names would mean much to me at the moment, Sergeant. I know it's possible that the theft was an outside job...'

'Likely, even, I'd say sir, in the circumstances.'

Once again, there was a good deal of common sense in the sergeant's reply. Ashley wondered aloud whether a small town like Bruton would have a resident with sufficient knowledge of art to appreciate the historical interest of the picture.

'Don't underestimate some of these old crocks, sir: Bruton's a popular place to retire to, and some of them have had very distinguished careers. There are some surprisingly knowledgeable people around here.'

Ashley smiled: 'I am put in my place, Sergeant – my apologies.'

The Sergeant smiled as well: 'None needed, sir. Look, I've got to keep my eyes open to see if anyone tries to sell the picture. While I'm about it, I can find out who the arty people and historians are locally and then I'll get back to you, if you like.'

'That would be kind of you, Sergeant Archdale.' In return, Ashley promised to pass on any information he might obtain, including anything his nephew might discover in London. By now, they both felt that they had talked enough about the theft.

'So, Sergeant, shall we discuss the accident?'

Sergeant Archdale raised an eyebrow.

'No sir, I've got a much better idea – let's talk about the *murder*.'

*　*　*　*　*

'Five diamonds.'

'Jasmine, don't be ridiculous – you can't open five diamonds after I've passed.'

'Well, I don't see why not – we're only playing for tenpence a hundred. At that price, pre-emptives come cheap.'

'Five diamonds isn't pre-emptive, it's predestination – we're doomed.'

'So what? It stops them getting the rubber.'

Irene, whose blue rinse was sagging, allowed Mavis of the North and Jasmine, sitting South, to continue a little longer and then said, smugly, 'Double.'

Bidding standards had undoubtedly declined as a result of playing for lower stakes: on the other hand, opportunities for savage analysis of one's partner had multiplied, so the rubber was just as enjoyable in its own way. As Jasmine's contract imitated the *Mary Rose*, Mavis walked to the other side of the room and drummed her fingernails on the window ledge. Just as the final trick was conceded, Constable Telfer and Lance Bombardier Green arrived in the courtyard; news of their arrival took temporary precedence over vituperation.

'The police constable is back again – and he's got that young man with him.'

The other matrons abandoned the card table and crowded round the leaded window.

'I wonder what's happened to the other one?'

'The other one with the policeman, or the other one with the other one?'

'I'm sorry, Irene, you'll have to grapple with that sentence again if you expect an answer.'

'Look! They're separating!'

The matrons, their souls shredded by curiosity, watched as Constable Telfer headed towards the master's accommodation and Green climbed the stairs on the opposite side of the courtyard. A minute later, both men were out of sight. For the matrons, there was a pensive, anticlimactic interlude before Irene said: 'You know, I think we've been very remiss in not calling on poor Mary Compton. After that theft, she must be feeling very low.'

'She'd appreciate a helping hand, I'm sure.'

'A sympathetic ear.'

'I always think at times like this, it's important for communities to come together.'

A visiting resolution was passed, then refined by Jasmine. 'I think it might be a little much for her if we all went at once.'

'How do you mean, dear?'

'I mean,' Jasmine clarified her intentions, 'That I need to tell the master about a faulty light bulb in my bathroom.'

Mavis instantly remembered a leaking radiator.

'So, girls – back here in half an hour?'

The tottering posse set off in pursuit. Dividing in the courtyard, Avril and Irene followed the trail of the lance bombardier; Jasmine and Mavis sought to head off Constable Telfer in the master's drawing room.

CHAPTER THIRTEEN

A DIFFERENT KIND OF HISTORY

The clock in Colin Clifford's study seemed determined to win the prize for the World's Fastest Minute Hand. It twirled around the face, skimming past Roman numerals, intent on reaching half past six as quickly as possible.

This was the time Ashley had finally settled on for his visit to Douglas Peachey. Successive postponements had taken place at intervals of a quarter of an hour since five forty-five: one more, and Ashley was in danger of clashing with the old man's dinner. Worse, he might be invited to share it. Ashley's resolve was stiffened by an unpleasant vision of Peachey talking with his mouth full, shooting food across the table and up into his moustache.

In the ten minutes that remained, he decided, there was time for another gin.

'And another beer for you, Lance Bombardier?'

'I wouldn't say no, sir – it's thirsty work being mentally undressed by two old biddies, who haven't had it since the days of the Blitz. Telfer reckoned he practically had to fight the other pair off with his truncheon – though, come to think of it, that might have inflamed them all the more. Thank you, sir.' Green accepted a new can and pulled the ring vigorously.

'It sounds as though you've forged an alliance with the constable, then?'

'That's right, sir. It turns out that he's found disappointment in Warminster as well, so we had something in common. He reckons we must have picked the only two unavailable girls in the whole town – the council will probably put blue plaques on their houses, one day.' Green paused for a long draught of beer, then concluded, 'Telfer says he tends to stick to Wincanton now, but apparently Yeovil's good if you like it dirty, sir.'

Ashley expressed a preference for cleanliness, before moving the conversation on: 'How did Mrs Compton seem?'

'She was fine, sir – glad of a hand with getting all that muck off. The matrons helped too, but mainly so they could poke into cupboards and drawers while they cleaned them. They're probably working out the value of her china and glass as we speak – Mrs Compton's got some nice stuff, hasn't she?'

'She has, Lance Bombardier – which is why the theft of the paperweight continues to niggle me. Even granting that the thief might not want to take any of the breakable pieces, there were still half a dozen valuable objects he could have slipped into a pocket or a small bag.'

'I know the ones, sir – the police had gone over them really carefully for prints, but didn't find any. There was that little box thing with fiddly bits all over it.'

'That's right – the snuffbox. And the candlesticks are Georgian silver.'

'They were dusted all right, sir. Mrs Compton cleaned all that sort of thing herself. In fact, after the matrons arrived, I was mainly the tea boy.'

Ashley pictured the pursed lips of the matrons as they took their first tentative sips of Green's trademark orange tea. He was enjoying a supplementary vision of them soaking their dentures in some powerful solvent, when the clock struck the half hour. He stood up, swallowed the last of his gin, and announced his departure in a resigned voice.

'Anything you want me to do while you're gone, sir?'

'In the first place, if I'm not back by half past seven, I want you to come and rescue me. Before then, perhaps you could fix up tomorrow's ride; I'll find out where the old house was and when I get back, we can spend some time working out a good route.'

105

'Okay, sir – best of luck.'

'I need it, Lance Bombardier, I need it.'

* * * * *

The browny-yellowish bruises which were developing all over Tom One's back proved to be quite a tourist attraction. Soldiers who called in on the way to supper admired their size and extent, then spread the word in the cookhouse. There wasn't actually a queue outside the Toms' accommodation, but the room itself was permanently crowded as comrades came, saw and congregated.

The positive side of these reconnaissance missions was that most gunners brought beer as a companion to curiosity, so a pleasing party atmosphere was developing. Tom One gave up lifting and lowering his rugby shirt and just removed it altogether, sitting bareback and mottled astride a hard chair. Now that the bruises had developed, the pain had lessened, so he was mobile and cheerful, enjoying being the centre of attention.

Diverse opinions were expressed. Gunner Scott thought the bruises made Tom look like a tortoiseshell cat; Gunner Chadwick maintained that he resembled a tarnished trumpet and recommended remedial work with Brasso and an oily cloth. A baby giraffe and a slug with jaundice were the suggestions of Gunners Carlton and Gillham, the latter adding that half a pound of salt should induce entertaining death spasms. Finally, the medical officer appeared and announced that Tom looked like someone who needed to be left in peace. The soldiers melted away in the direction of Friday evening entertainments.

The medical officer brought pills and cream rather than beer, and pointed out that parties were fun, but rest was therapeutic.

'If you want to be up and about tomorrow, take it easy tonight.'

'Understood, sir.'

'The painkillers are in case you need them to get through the night. I'm not going to say they can't be taken with alcohol, because I know that you'll just drink the booze and ignore the pills – but they mustn't be taken with *too much* alcohol. Do you get my idea?'

Tom glanced at the substantial pile of cans on the desk. 'Yes, sir.'

'Good. If you feel up to it, report for a check-up first thing in the morning. If I haven't seen you by nine, I'll come up here. No, don't get up...' Tom Two was already standing to attention and One was rising from his chair in preparation for the officer's departure: 'I'd rather you rested that back than braced it for my benefit. Thank you, Gunner Marsh, carry on.'

'Thank you, sir.' Tom Two waited until the door was closed and the footsteps along the corridor had grown faint before adding, 'We must remember to invite Captain Killjoy next time we have a party, One. He really helps the flow, doesn't he?'

'Yes – the flow towards the exit.' Tom One's eyes travelled to the refreshments on the desk; then they rested on the officer's collection of pills. 'I suppose I'd better play safe. I don't want to jeopardise Uncle George's mission just for a couple of cans of beer.'

In a spirit of camaraderie, Tom Two denied himself a further can. He tidied the collection into a wardrobe, where it was out of sight, and dumped the empty cans into the bin. Tom One retrieved his rugby shirt and put it on, before returning to his bed and leaning back against the pillows.

'Brief me about tomorrow, One – what exactly are we supposed to be doing?' Two sat himself on the desk and rested his feet on the hard chair that Tom One had just occupied.

Tom One took up the envelope on which he had scrawled as many notes as would fit. 'We're going to the Portobello Road to see someone called Joshua Robbins.'

'Friend of your uncle's?'

'Contact, rather than friend, I think. Uncle George says Robbins owes him about a million favours...'

'Meaning your uncle's kept him out of prison from time to time. What sort of dodgy dealer is he?'

'Art, apparently. I've got to check up on the value of pictures by some chap called...' Tom One took time to scrutinise the name, 'Peter Lely – and another one called Samuel Cooper.' He passed the envelope across to Two: 'Do you want to have a look at it while I obey orders and try and get some more sleep?'

Tom Two took the paper and studied it from at least eight different angles before he felt that he fully understood the tasks ahead of them. More methodical than Tom One, he decided to write out the detective's instructions neatly and in a logical order. By the time he had finished, the tortoiseshell cat, the tarnished trumpet, the giraffe and the slug had transformed themselves once more into the contented piglet. Two felt able to retrieve a can of beer from the wardrobe without loosening the bonds of friendship.

*   *   *   *   *

Ashley's instinct for irony told him that he was well punished for all his prevarication: the absence of Douglas Peachey from his flat in the hospital was a possibility the detective had not considered. Who, after all, would want to invite him out?

Perhaps he had just gone for a walk, or had called on an acquaintance who was steadfastly refusing to offer alcohol, in the hope of soon being rid of him. Ashley considered various possibilities, nearly all of which concluded with Peachey's return in the near future. It was worth hanging around for a few minutes; now that he was here, he might as well get the interview over with.

There was a bench near Peachey's front door, so Ashley sat himself down and looked around the courtyard. Opposite, Peter Bulmer's flat had its curtains drawn; between them and the window, a glass jar with a paintbrush bore poignant testimony to the dead man's occupation. Higher up, and facing in a different direction, Mary Compton's sitting room window displayed flowers between crimson curtains. Other flats showed signs of life within; it was quite likely that Peachey was in one of them, gathering or disseminating gossip.

Ashley heard the gate to the High Street open. He had almost stood up, ready to greet Peachey, when he realised that the footsteps he could hear were far too fast to belong to an elderly man. A moment later, a pale youth came into view.

He was tall and thin; like Tom One, Ashley thought. But there was no closer resemblance; Tom's body was upright and muscular, the result of nearly a year of military service and a sporting career at school. This new figure had rounded shoulders and his head stooped, as though he was embarrassed by his height. His clothes were cheap and uncoordinated, and his brown hair was badly cut. The weight of a large briefcase did nothing to enhance his posture.

The boy walked around one side of the grassed courtyard, then turned onto the path which led to Peachey's flat. Since he had to walk past Ashley to get there, he smiled an awkward greeting and spoke with a surprisingly polished accent.

'Hello, sir – are you waiting to see Mr Peachey?'

'I am. Do you by any chance know where he would be?'

'No, sir, I don't. I've come for a history lesson – it's meant to start at a quarter to seven, so he shouldn't be too long. He's very prompt, normally.'

Ashley recalled the retired master rushing off from their meeting three days earlier. Presumably this was the pupil he had to meet? The tall boy confirmed this.

'That's right, sir. My name's James – James Oakley.' Ashley stood to shake hands and introduced himself. Then they both sat, at opposite ends of the bench.

'And are you studying the history of the late seventeenth century, James?' Ashley asked the question with a wry smile: it produced a laugh from James.

109

'No, sir, but I dare say I'll get some thrown in anyway. I've got my A-level in two weeks, sir, and Mr Peachey is giving me extra coaching on the Franco-Prussian war. Next week we're revising the English Reformation.' James added, needlessly, 'I'm not a King's pupil, sir, I go to the sixth-form college in Yeovil. My mother thinks some extra lessons outside school will increase my chances of an A grade and I need an A to get into Oxford.'

There were plenty of conversational openings here and Ashley and the boy talked freely. James might be gangly of body, but his mind was sharp and clear. A moment ago, Ashley had been comparing his physique unfavourably with his nephew's; now, Tom One was on the nether end of a comparison of intellects. Ashley guessed that James' A grade and acceptance into Oxford would follow in natural succession though, naturally, much depended on how well the boy had been taught by earlier teachers. He asked various historical questions and was impressed with the quality of the answers: not just in the names and facts learnt, but in the ability to interpret evidence and to give a clear picture of events without losing sight of important details.

He was surprised when the hospital clock struck a quarter past seven. For a moment, they were both amused that they had talked for over half an hour without realising the passing of time; then James looked despondent and said, 'He's not coming, sir, is he?'

'It doesn't look like it, James. Perhaps he's forgotten.'

'He's never forgotten before, sir. And when I saw him yesterday, he was emphatic that I should get here on time today. He wanted me to bring an essay to mark before we got down to the proper lesson.'

It was clear that James was worried; it was dangerous to get behind with a programme of learning and revision so close to the examination.

'Is there some work you can be getting on with while you wait, James?'

110

'Not really sir – the whole point of today's lesson was that Mr Peachey would read my essay and then suggest work on anything I'd left out or got wrong. Then I'm supposed to do a re-write tomorrow – so if he doesn't show tonight, I lose tomorrow as well. Unless…'

Ashley had felt the last word coming. He was flattered and rather embarrassed.

'Unless I read your essay for you, James – is that right?'

James looked awkward, his body even more angular than before. 'Would you, sir? I'd be really grateful – and my mother will pay, sir, she pays Mr Peachey.'

The sentence had begun hesitantly and then blurted out all at once. Suddenly, Ashley felt an anger inside him that tightened his muscles and caused his cheeks to flame. Here was a boy, whose clothing and demeanour proclaimed his poverty, having to pay comfortable, self-satisfied Peachey for his lessons. What need had Peachey for the few pounds which would make so much difference to James and his family? What extra work did Mrs Oakley have to take on in order to give her son a chance in life? And how many hours of scrubbing floors or stacking shelves did it take to pay for an hour of Peachey's time?

Ashley gained control over his temper, not least because he could see that James was looking alarmed. The boy might even think that he had taken offence at the suggestion, which would be awful.

'James, I'd be more than happy to read your essay. And don't be silly – I wouldn't dream of taking any money.'

111

CHAPTER FOURTEEN

DEBRIEFS

At half past ten on Friday evening, Ashley and Green discussed the case so far. Ashley was back in bed and had been ready to fall asleep but Green had marched in, announcing cheerfully that Ashley's riding kit was, 'In shit order, sir,' and suggested that Ashley drank a final whisky while his boots were bulled and his breeches and hacking jacket were brushed down. Weakly, Ashley agreed: he worked his way steadily through a tumbler of Colin Clifford's single malt while Green, squatting in his eyrie on top of the chest of drawers, rubbed polish into Ashley's riding boots.

'So, sir, how does the old boy's disappearance fit into theory number one?'

'About as much as it fits in with any other theory, Lance Bombardier – which is to say, not very well at all. In theory number one…'

'That was my favourite, sir.' Green postponed a projectile of saliva to make his point, then shot it with extra force against a toecap. Ashley resisted the temptation to ask him whether he had read the Tantric Guide to boot polishing.

'It was mine too – but I think we'd have to come up with some impressive distortions to retain its viability. Peachey can't possibly have stolen the picture during the service, so we have to hypothesise a less likely time for the theft and a different explanation of Peter Bulmer's death.'

'So, theory number one goes down the pan, sir.'

'Well, let's not pull the flush too hastily, Lance Bombardier but probably, yes.'

112

Green took a rest from his task and gulped tea from a large mug. 'Where do you think the old boy's gone, sir?'

'Peachey? The obvious explanation is that he's run off to try and sell the picture – but that's a problematic theory as well. It's unlikely the picture is very valuable, so he won't make enough money to justify his efforts. If Peachey *is* the thief, I think it far more likely that he stole the picture to possess it.'

'So perhaps he's gone off to hide it, sir?'

Ashley nodded. 'That's a good suggestion – though it's stupid of him to take so long to do it. If he's not back by morning, all the police in Somerset will be looking for him – and, even if he does come back in the night, he's got some very awkward questions to face.'

They fell silent for a few minutes: Green returned to his methodical work and Ashley pondered the events of the evening.

James' essay had been very good for the first five pages, but had been spoiled by a hastily written and scrappy conclusion. It was a timed essay, it turned out, and James had only five minutes in which to write the final side and a half. This meant that Ashley had been able to offer plenty of advice and James had departed to spend an evening revising and expanding. Before taking his leave, he had tentatively asked the detective whether he would be willing to read the second version: 'If Mr Peachey isn't back, that is.' Ashley had agreed, hoping that he would be able to find the time to do so.

Shortly afterwards, Lance Bombardier Green had arrived on his needless mercy mission; they had called on Dr Holbrooke to find out if he knew anything of Douglas Peachey's whereabouts but it seemed that Peachey had departed without leaving any information. At a quarter to eight, the master was more inclined to serve claret than to worry, but he had promised to ring Ashley when Peachey returned. So far, no call had been taken; Ashley wondered whether the placid doctor had started to feel any concern.

Turning his mind to the future, Ashley contemplated the

morning ahead. The ride out to the old Fitzjames house was unlikely to be productive in any detecting way, but it promised to be enjoyable and energetic. Dr Holbrooke had pointed it out on Ashley's map and Green, with occasional calls on his mobile to ex-Sergeant Jones, had worked out a route across country, taking in some good galloping ground and hills from which panoramic views were to be had. Jones had guessed that the ride would take a couple of hours, plus the same back, so promised to provide saddle bags in which they could store some food. Ashley was just thinking that it all sounded very agreeable, when Green voiced a similar opinion.

'It should be fun tomorrow, sir, shouldn't it? Just like when the Troop goes off to summer camp.'

'I hope that doesn't mean that you're putting a couple of army ration packs in the saddlebags, Lance Bombardier.'

The soldier grinned over the instep of Ashley's boot. 'You could do worse than a rat-pack, sir. Bacon and beans in your mess tin, washed down with a mug of tea-flavoured bromide to keep your baser urges at bay. Not that it does, of course… But not to worry, sir, I'll knock up some sandwiches before we go.'

'A much better idea.' Privately, Ashley wondered what Green's idea of a good sandwich was. Fish paste and peanut butter? Marmite and lettuce? He resolved to eat a hearty breakfast before leaving, just in case.

Whisky, and the aroma of boot polish, proved a powerful soporific. A few minutes later, Ashley was only vaguely aware of Green jumping down from his perch and moving towards the wardrobe. The gentle scrubbing sound of a clothes brush accompanied him to sleep and he dreamt of Lance Bombardier Green grooming a horse with a toothbrush while the contented animal placidly ate its way through a plateful of jam and tuna sandwiches.

*　　*　　*　　*　　*

Dreams are in plentiful supply in Bruton. Rejuvenated matrons are locked in embrace with soldiers and policemen; Dr Holbrooke discovers his hospital deserted. Mary Compton's sitting room is stripped of its contents; Sergeant Archdale and Constable Telfer are baffled by the crime, the only clues to the thieves' identities being three grey wigs and a blue one in the cupboard under the sink. In the front bedroom of a squat and ugly cottage, Bismarck and Napoleon III play with multi-coloured marbles to decide the fate of Alsace-Lorraine. Losing the match, the French Emperor throws a petulant marble at the Prussian Chancellor: it bounces harmlessly off his *pickelhaube*.

James wakes: the silly dream has given him an idea for a final paragraph. He switches on a bedside lamp and jots down a few notes, which will serve to remind him in the morning. Returning the room to darkness, he lies on his back, one arm curled over his eyes to keep off the glare of the street lights, which easily penetrate the thin curtains.

Ashley's kindness has not gone unappreciated. James is deeply touched by his concern and assistance; moved, too, by that flash of anger which, though it was hard to understand, was clearly exercised on his behalf. He hopes there is a chance to present the redrafted essay tomorrow.

The dream returns. Douglas Peachey is wearing the *pickelhaube* now, scheming his way to European domination. Napoleon III doesn't stand a chance.

* * * * *

Constable Telfer is on a late shift at the police station, working overtime in order to finance a holiday with the latest in a sequence of Wincanton girls. Outside, colleagues are coping with closing time brawls and breathalysing drivers; behind the desk, all is quiet, for the moment.

Telfer is no detective, but he is intrigued by this latest case: a murder that might be an accident — or, rather, an accident that his superior thinks is a murder. And the theft: just as the death is only half a murder, so the theft is only half a picture. Why steal a fragment? He reflects on Sergeant Archdale's parting words: 'There's more to this than a canvas tart and a tumble down the stairs, young Telfer – but I haven't the faintest idea what it is.' Whatever it might be, Telfer hopes there will be a role for him; it beats sitting behind the desk and listening to ear-bashings from community support officers any day.

The telephone rings, just to hammer the point home.

* * * * *

In bed, Sister Barnfield is surrounded by the complete works of Delia, planning a menu. An army, she knows, marches on its stomach; and as far as this particular gastropod is concerned, Sister Barnfield has every intention of being the parade ground.

Oysters, alas, are out of season; garlic and asparagus not without danger. But surely you couldn't go wrong with pheasant (she has a brace in the freezer, left over from the last season) in cream and apples? Her eyes run hungrily down the list of ingredients and she instinctively doubles quantities of butter and cream. Cider seems a rather dull fluid; how about a crisp Riesling with a dash of brandy? Or, even better, a white Burgundy with a glassful of Calvados?

Not for the first time, Sister Barnfield's research brings on an attack of night starvation. There are cold new potatoes and mayonnaise in the fridge, maybe even some ham. With difficulty, she swivels her body through forty-five degrees and lowers two plump little feet to the floor.

Half a mile away, Lance Bombardier Green sleeps blissfully, oblivious to the culinary courtship which lies ahead.

His dreams are set in Yeovil.

CHAPTER FIFTEEN

A MORNING RIDE

Tom One reported to the medical officer at half past eight. Blue blotches now blended into the brown and yellow stains on his back, making him look – as Tom Two observed – like a mouldy *crème caramel*. From a medical point of view this seemed to be a good thing: the officer ran an icy and inquisitive finger down Tom's spine, then grunted in a positive manner.

'Seems all right. Lower your trousers – I need to take a look at your coccyx.'

Tom obeyed the order and submitted to the indignity, consoling himself with the thought that this would cost good money in Harley Street. The medical officer fondled around, finally convincing himself that there were no fractures. Cold hands and warm buttocks parted company.

'Okay – trousers back up. Have you had a shit this morning?'

'Yes, sir.'

'Did it hurt?'

'Only when I sneezed, sir.'

'Any blood?'

'No, sir.'

'What about your urine?'

Tom toyed with the idea of replying that it was fine as long as you spoke up and enunciated clearly, then reminded himself that the medical officer had no sense of humour. He contented himself with observing that his water was like vintage champagne, only without the bubbles.

'Good – your kidneys must be all right, then. You can get

117

dressed now. You're not on duty until Monday, is that correct?'

Tom answered as he buttoned up his shirt. 'Yes, sir – stable routines at six-thirty, and riding at ten.' He thrust his tails inside his trousers and adjusted his braces.

'Right then – I want you to report to me in between the two. Earlier if you have any pain; just inform the NCO on duty and come right over. I'll be here from seven onwards.'

'Very good, sir – thank you, sir.'

'That's okay, Gunner Noad. What are you up to this weekend? Nothing too strenuous, I hope.'

Tom adjusted his tie and pulled on his jacket. 'Actually, sir, I'm off to the Portobello Road this morning – my uncle's trying to trace a stolen picture.'

'Really?' For the first time, the medical officer regarded Tom as something other than a body to be examined. 'Have you been to the Portobello Market before, Gunner Noad?'

'No, sir.'

'Well, if you'll take my advice, you'll leave your cheque book and credit cards back at the barracks.' For a moment, the officer relaxed: 'Have fun, Tom – see you on Monday.'

'Yes, sir – and thanks for looking after me.'

'No problem, Gunner Noad.'

Tom Two was waiting by the barracks gate, chatting to the sentry on duty. He was wearing similar clothes to Tom One: a blazer and regimental tie, light chino trousers, and parade shoes. Not knowing where the morning task would lead, they had decided to opt for smartness. Moving with only a slight awkwardness, Tom joined his friend.

'All clear, One? Is Quasimodo allowed back into the community?'

'He is, but he's not going to be tugging on his bell rope for a while. Shall we get a taxi? Uncle George is paying our expenses, so we may as well.'

They walked a few hundred yards to the junction of a busy street and hailed a black cab. Sitting in the back, Tom Two pulled out his written notes and glanced down the list.

'Hey, One?'

'Yes?'

'I dare say this is a stupid question, but surely your Uncle could have got most of this information over the telephone. Why is he sending us to see this chap?'

Tom One grinned broadly; he knew the answer to Two's query. 'Apparently Mr Robbins won't do business over the telephone. Uncle George says he once had a very nasty experience when he mistook the voice of a chap from Scotland Yard for a buyer. So now he plays safe and insists on dealing with people face to face.'

'Sounds fair enough – like that time when shifty Scott was sneaking a call on the guardroom telephone, and forgot to dial nine for an outside number...'

'And got the adjutant instead of his girlfriend.'

The gunners savoured the memory. Whether or not Captain Raynham had complied with Scott's suggestion had never been established conclusively. It was certain, though, that he had fined the hapless gunner a day's pay for misuse of army property.

The cab drove along Oxford Street and the Bayswater Road, then turned right into Ladbrooke Terrace. The traffic here had reached a standstill, so the driver slid back the glass and suggested that the Toms should walk the short distance to the market: 'It'll take you two minutes by foot, and half an hour driving. Always like this on a Saturday morning, it is – bleedin' awful. Oh, thanks, mate – good on you.'

Neither of the soldiers had been to the Portobello Market before: turning into the road, they were amazed by the sight of stall after stall of antiques of every description and the thronging crowds of all ages and nationalities, milling around, admiring, haggling – and blocking progress. Forced to move at what Tom Two called 'mollusc miles per hour', they enjoyed examining the articles for sale as they inched their way ahead.

'Hey, look One – that silver cup has got Prince Albert's crest on it.'

119

'Yes – and it's also got a price tag of four hundred pounds.'

'Well, you did say your uncle was paying expenses…'

Another stall specialised in militaria. The Toms had fun digging around among piles of cap badges and shoulder insignia to find their own unit, and were amazed at the amount of money people would part with for items of kit which they were simply issued with.

'Ten quid for that? What a rip off!'

'And look over there – thirty for a set of buttons. You can get them in the PRI shop for half that. Have you seen the swords – and the First World War saddlebags?'

They were beginning to feel the magic of the market. No wonder the medical officer had advised Tom One to leave his cheque book and cards back at the barracks, and that Ashley had given strict instructions not to buy a picture from Mr Robbins. Reluctantly, they tore themselves away and continued their slow passage along the road.

*　*　*　*　*

Lance Bombardier Green crammed an already squashed and misshapen parcel of sandwiches into a more modern saddlebag. Then he forced two apples on top of them and latched the bag tightly shut. 'I'm afraid they won't look very pretty, sir – but it's the flavour that counts, isn't it?'

With some trepidation, Ashley agreed. Actually, the sandwiches had never been objects of beauty, even when freshly made: Green's technique with a bread knife was far from subtle. By the time he had filled the clumsy wedges with fried bacon and mushrooms, and wiped the top slices of bread around the pan to soak up the fat, Diana Clifford's kitchen had resembled a war zone. Crumbs and discarded rinds covered the table and the draining board; the oven was spattered with fat, projected from an overheated pan; and a negligent discharge from the ketchup bottle enhanced the impression that a minor atrocity had taken place. Overall, Ashley had been rather glad to quit the scene before Diana Clifford came down for breakfast.

They had been greeted at the stable by a cheerful volley of invective from ex-Sergeant Jones and were now on the verge of departure. Green walked to the other side of his horse and filled the corresponding saddlebag with a map, a compass, and two cans of beer. Then, gripping the pommel and cantle of his saddle, he took two or three preparatory jumps and vaulted into the seat. Feeling distinctly less athletic, Ashley made use of a mounting block while Jones held onto his stirrup to steady the saddle. A few adjustments later, they trotted out into a lane, followed by a parting obscenity from Jones, which was returned in kind by Green.

Their horses were pensioners from Prince Albert's Troop. Past pulling guns, they still had several years of active life ahead of them, and the adjutant had been glad to authorise their sale to a good stable. Less authorised, Ashley guessed, were the military bridle and saddle which Green's horse was wearing; these, he suspected, had fallen off the back of an army Land Rover at about the time Sergeant Jones had quitted the Troop. The Lance Bombardier, as military in attire as his horse, confirmed Ashley's suspicion.

'I think Jonesy had a fairly flexible attitude to army property, sir – there were quite a few empty pegs in the harness room after he left, and he took enough horse blankets to set up a refugee camp. Still, it beats riding in civilian tack, sir, once you're used to it.'

Ashley took his word for it. For himself, a rein in each hand and comfortable, flexible leather between himself and his horse seemed a better option in every way than Green's double bridle, with all the leads held in the left hand, and his uncompromising steel-framed, high-ridged saddle. There was no doubt, however, that Green looked far smarter on his horse than Ashley did – but that, after all, was his job.

Green stood up in his stirrups to peer over a high wall and was rewarded with a high-pitched scream.

'Sorry, Miss.' He saluted, then lowered himself back into the saddle and grinned at Ashley: 'Lovely day for topless sunbathing, isn't it, sir?'

They followed the lane for half a mile after which a right turn led onto a bridle path. Never having hacked out with Green before, Ashley had already guessed that the experience would be a vivid one; sure enough, the lance bombardier shot up the track at a full gallop, folding his body along the horse's neck whenever low branches attempted to decapitate him. Fallen trees and ditches existed to be jumped, spurs were there for encouragement, and his spare hand came in useful for holding his service cap on in moments of crisis. Ashley kept his head and heels down and hung on as best he could, reflecting that, if Green made love as energetically as he rode, Wendy from Warminster had missed out on a treat.

After a terrifying mile and a half, the bridle path opened out into fields, which they crossed at full pelt. Then, mercifully, Green had to consult the map; Ashley wiped himself down while the soldier checked his bearings.

'We follow this track here, sir.' He indicated some dots on the map which looked as though they crossed half a dozen ravines and a few raging torrents: 'But before we do that, Jonesy says there's a really good run up the hill just over there, with some fantastic views. Shall we make a race of it, sir?'

*　　*　　*　　*　　*

Mr Robbins had bags under his eyes large enough to put the family shopping in, and a lower lip that the Hapsburgs would have admired. He greeted the Toms at the door of his shop then led them upstairs to his office. This was a simple room, its peeling walls lined with shelves containing old catalogues and reference books. Pictures, in various states of repair, were stacked against the skirting boards and a well-thumbed legal guide lay open on the desk. In one corner an electric kettle sat amongst chipped, brown-stained mugs, packets of tea, powdered milk and sugar. The Toms exchanged glances: Lance Bombardier Green would have approved.

Mr Robbins indicated chairs for the two gunners, then flicked the switch on the kettle before easing his corpulent frame into a tightly fitting captain's chair.

'I thought you were American missionaries in those outfits, till I saw your ties. Artillery, are you?'

'That's right, Mr Robbins – Prince Albert's Troop.'

A hungry gleam appeared in the art dealer's eyes. 'Oh well, then, you'll want to see this.' Diving for the skirting board with unsuspected agility, he rummaged among a pile of mounted but unframed watercolours. 'Here – have a look. Victorian workmanship at its very best – one of a matching pair.'

An officer of Prince Albert's Troop sat astride his charger, obviously issuing orders to a mounted trumpeter, who stood poised ready to play. A dismounted gunner held on to the officer's bridle. It was a fine ensemble, beautifully painted and accurate in every detail. It was unsigned.

'It's fantastic, Mr Robbins – do you have any idea who painted it?'

The Hapsburg lip formed itself into a rubbery smile. 'Whoever you like: Orlando Norie, Richard Simkin, Caton Woodville... I've got samples of all their signatures – easiest thing in the world to transform it into the work of your favourite artist.'

Tom One began to understand his Uncle's advice. Nonetheless, forged or not, the picture was very fine and it would certainly add a touch of much-needed class to the bare walls of the Toms' accommodation. Tom Two asked, 'Did you say it was one of a pair, sir?'

Mr Robbins began to sense a deal. 'That's right – the other one shows a gun team at work. Lovely, it is too.'

'May we see it?'

'Sorry – the chap hasn't finished it yet – it'll be here next week. What do you say? Normally I'd ask eight hundred the pair, but since you've come from Mr Ashley – and since I've just given the game away about the artist – I'll knock it right down. Five hundred the two?'

'Sorry, Mr Robbins – we haven't got five hundred pounds between us.' Two sent a look in One's direction, which translated as, 'Not even if we play poker with Vernon and Sorrell for a whole week'.

'Four fifty? Four hundred, if you're not fussed about a signature. Can't say fairer than that, can I?'

The Toms stuck to their guns. With a sigh, Mr Robbins replaced the picture and poured boiling water onto three teabags. 'All right, lads – down to the real business. What does Mr Ashley want to know?'

By prior arrangement, Tom Two did the talking. He consulted his notes before replying.

'There's been a picture stolen, Mr Robbins…'

'Oh, how shocking.' The dealer sounded stoic and sanctimonious.

'It was by someone called Peter Lely.'

Mr Robbins showed instant interest. 'Very nice – someone's going to be very well off. In fact, several people are, by the time the chaps along the line have taken their cut. Carry on.'

The latex lip pursed in annoyance as Tom Two read out Ashley's description of the mutilated state of the picture. Two continued: 'So he asks two questions, Mr Robbins, and then a favour. First, he wonders how much the damaged painting is likely to be worth – as a stolen picture that is, not on the open market. Then…'

'Hang on a minute.' Mr Robbins wanted to deal with questions one at a time. He looked among his catalogues for inspiration while the Toms drank their tea. It tasted only slightly less appalling than Lance Bombardier Green's.

'In a way,' the dealer thought aloud, 'and with all respect to Mr Ashley, asking how much a thing might be worth is a silly question – because anything is worth just as much as some idiot is prepared to pay for it. Suppose you've got a rich, loony

American – and, thank God, there are plenty of them around this place every Saturday. Well, Mr RLA, as we'll call him, has made his packet and wants to become a connoisseur; perhaps he'll collect porcelain, perhaps it's stuffed rare birds – or perhaps it's portraits by Sir Peter Lely. They tend to stick to a genre, and if you've got something they want – well, you can ask the sky for it, and they'll cough up, without as much as a hint of a haggle. What's more, they won't be too fussed how you came by it.'

Tom One was beginning to look dazed, but Two got the idea: 'So if our RLA is a Lely loony, it could still be worth a lot, even in its damaged state?'

'That's right – especially if it completed a collection or filled up a gap of just the right size on his wall. Don't laugh – I once made fifty thousand pounds by having a picture cut down to just the right size. Beautiful job, the man did, and the RLA was none the wiser. But...' Mr Robbins' enthusiasm began to abate, 'I have to tell you that I don't know, offhand, of any rich yanks with a Lely fetish. And if *I* haven't heard of them, it means they're probably not in England.'

'So where does that leave us, sir?'

'At a guess, I'd say it leaves us with someone who doesn't know what he's doing. Here's your thief, fancies himself as knowing a bit about art, hears there's a Peter Lely in the area – and he pinches it. Then, of course, he's got to get it off his hands – and it's damaged and people are going to know it's stolen, so they're not going to pay the full price – and all the way from theft to final buyer, people are going to want to be paid for taking a risk. I don't reckon he'll have much joy of his painting, frankly. In fact, I wouldn't be in the least surprised if he didn't end up dumping it. It often happens – unless you've stolen for a specific customer, getting rid of work by a famous artist can be the very devil. Does that answer your question?'

Tom Two was scribbling away frantically; finally, he had everything down. 'I think so, Mr Robbins. The next question was this: it seems that someone called Samuel Cooper painted a miniature from the original portrait – is this known to exist? And how much would such a piece be worth?'

'Oh, now, that's a very nice question.' Mr Robbins' bags and jowls wobbled approval. 'And, of course, I don't really know the answer. Miniatures don't come my way very often – they're a very specialist field.' Once again, he busied himself with his catalogues, grunting as he reached for one on the highest shelf. 'What I do know, is that Samuel Cooper was the best miniaturist of his day – the equivalent of Nicholas Hilliard at the end of the sixteenth century. Look here…' he held out an open page: 'His miniature of the Duchess of Portsmouth fetched a hundred thousand pounds at Sotheby's five years ago. That's probably a quarter of a million today.'

Tom Two wrote down the details carefully. He didn't know all the circumstances of the crime in Bruton, but he knew that two hundred and fifty thousand pounds was enough to inspire theft – or murder.

'What about the other part of Mr Ashley's question, sir? Is the Cooper miniature known to exist?'

Robbins shrugged. 'You need an expert to tell you that. To be precise, you need Andy Esmond – or *Sir* Andrew, as we're supposed to call him now. He's the Director of the Albert Museum – and owner of most of the important private collection of miniatures in England. Reckoned to be worth in excess of six million quid and the whole damn lot would fit in a cat litter tray. Imagine what that would be like to a burglar, if he could shift them after he'd stolen them.'

Tom Two got the idea. 'So, these miniature things are serious money then, Mr Robbins?'

'The best are – but you ought to go and see Andy for yourself. He can tell you much more than I can.'

'And how do we do that, sir?'

'Nothing easier: he never goes home – hasn't spoken to his wife for years. He spends all his time at the museum – if you hang around by the display of miniatures, he'll find you. He's easy to recognise – his nostril hair is the longest in London.

He's known as Rapunzel in the trade, but don't tell him so.' Mr Robbins consulted his watch: 'You could go over this morning and catch him before lunch, if it's that important.'

'That's great – we'll do that. I think that's everything, sir, apart from the favour, and that's simply that you'll keep your eye open for the picture if it comes up on the market.'

'Consider it done, young man – I owe George Ashley about ten years of freedom, so I try to do what I can for him when he needs a helping hand. Where is he, by the way, in case I need to get in touch with him?'

Tom One, woken from his daze by the prospect of imminent departure, gave the answer: 'He's down in Somerset, Mr Robbins – at Bruton.'

Robbins froze, half risen from his chair. 'How very strange.'

'What's that, sir?'

The art dealer looked genuinely concerned. He struggled between his loyalty to colleagues and his debt to Ashley: after a moment or two, the latter prevailed. Robbins sat back down, stared from one Tom to the other, and said, quietly:

'Bob Simpson's been lying low in Bruton for the last few months. He's a bit of a spent force now, but in his day, Bob Simpson was the shiftiest art dealer in London.'

CHAPTER SIXTEEN

ANOTHER PICNIC

The woods had an almost ecclesiastical atmosphere: Ashley half expected the choir of King's School to appear between a pair of massive trees, bellowing out a pantheistic hymn. Instead of Gothic pillars, massive trunks supported an elaborate tracery of foliage, which fanned out above them. Occasional gaps in the greenery acted as a clerestory, admitting Apollonian shafts of light, so that the detective and the soldier were alternately dazzled and plunged into darkness as they guided their horses along.

They had slowed down to a steady walk since entering the wood, allowing the reins to run through their fingers and hang loosely around chestnut necks and closely cropped manes. For much of the time, the horses could simply follow a track; once in a while the riders used their calf muscles to indicate the correct direction. Ashley enjoyed the sensation of instant response beneath him, as powerful, experienced muscles adapted themselves to the instructions of the rider.

They reached a glade, and Green suggested that they should stop for lunch.

'It's on the early side, I know, sir, but the horses are nicely cooled down now, so it's a good time to rest them. Added to which, sir, we can chill our beer in that stream over there.'

It was a sensible and welcome plan. They dismounted, and Green, in scrupulous sequence, catered for the needs of the horses, his companion, and himself. In a few minutes, the horses were unsaddled and loosely tethered; they grazed comfortably and drank from the brook that was doubling as a fridge for the beer. Ashley, resting on one of the outspread brown saddle blankets, enjoyed the scene: the lighting effects could have been painted by any of the great landscape artists, but only Munnings could have captured the relationship between the soldier and his two horses.

Their race, naturally, had been won by Green, though Ashley's horse did its best to keep up, while Ashley himself had concentrated on staying alive. Ex-Sergeant Jones had promised spectacular views, but for a mile or more all Ashley could see was an enormous pair of chestnut buttocks, belonging to the horse in front, topped by a more compact, khaki version of the same, belonging to Lance Bombardier Green. Both were fine specimens of their type, but Ashley had been pleased that they weren't the last things he ever saw on earth.

At the top, Jones' assurances were shown to be well founded. It seemed as though half of Somerset and Dorset lay beneath them: to the south they could see as far as Shaftsbury, perched on top of its own hill; westwards, the Blackmore Vale stretched out endlessly; and in the north east, Alfred's Tower dominated a wooded skyline. As he contemplated the patchwork beneath him, Ashley wondered if a patrol of Lifeguards had stood on this spot in 1685, tracing the path that Monmouth and his rebels were taking across the county. Or had Arbella herself cantered up to the peak, in the hope of catching a glimpse of her hero and his forces? He suggested both possibilities to Green, who spoiled Ashley's vision by remarking that any Lifeguards would probably have been so busy doing what came naturally to them that a whole army could have marched past without being noticed.

For another hour, they rode around the countryside, racing each other when they could or hurtling themselves in single file along narrow tracks. Ashley began to enjoy the sheer thrill of riding with such a fearless companion, though the sense of his own mortality never fully left him and he had been grateful when they had reached the woods and were forced to relax their pace.

129

Green finished tending to the horses and wandered towards Ashley. In one hand, he carried the second saddle blanket; the other held a large, misshapen foil nugget; their sandwiches. The two apples were warming up nicely in the pockets of his breeches.

'There you go, sir – help yourself now, if you like, or you can wait for the beer to cool, which is what I'm going to do.' Green deposited the food, the blanket and his service cap next to Ashley. He hung his tunic on a convenient branch and coiled up his belt until it fitted inside his inverted cap. His tie and spurs were added to the pile and then he relaxed on his own blanket, opening the neck of his shirt and rolling up his sleeves. His tasks finished, he gave a satisfied sigh: 'This is the life, sir, isn't it?'

'Well, there were occasions when I thought it was going to be the death as well, Lance Bombardier, but on the whole I agree.'

The soldier gave one of his broader grins. 'You're doing very well, sir, for a civilian – if you were twenty years younger, I'd be trying to recruit you.'

Ashley tried to picture a younger version of himself in ceremonial uniform, sitting to attention astride his horse, but the vision failed to convince.

They lay on the ground for about fifteen minutes, chatting now and then, but mainly enjoying their rest in silence. Their blankets retained the warmth and scent of their horses and created an atmosphere that encouraged contemplation rather than discussion. Eventually, Green broke the silence by announcing that the beers would be chilled and – more importantly – safe to open. He checked the horses on his way to fetching the cans; on his return, both riders drank deeply. As well as making them thirsty, strenuous exercise also had the unexpected effect of making Green's sandwiches quite palatable and Ashley almost kept up with the lance bombardier in his consumption. The fat, soaked up from the frying pan, had solidified into a thick layer of dripping, which cemented the sandwiches together. It occurred to Ashley that if he wasn't killed in a spectacular riding accident, he would probably die of a heart attack as the result of Green's cholesterol cuisine.

When the last sandwich was finished, Green stretched himself out again, contented, resting his head on his hands.

'So, sir, I reckon we're about half an hour's plod from the old house. What are you hoping to find there?'

Ashley was still sitting, leaning back on his arms; he shrugged as well as his position would allow.

'To be honest, Lance Bombardier, not much. If the picture was simply stolen for its real or imagined value, this trip is probably a complete waste of time, even though it's been great fun so far. On the other hand, if it was taken for its intrinsic interest, then any insight we get into the world of Arbella Fitzjames could be useful.'

'So, if old man Peachey is our crook, sir, the trip could be worthwhile.'

'That's right. He's obsessed with the whole period, so it's worth finding out as much as we can.' Ashley reached over to his hacking jacket and took a photocopied sheet of paper from an inner pocket. He passed it over to Green. 'Have a look at this.'

Green sat up and studied the paper. It was taken from a nineteenth-century history of the county. Ashley provided a short summary.

'There's not likely to be much of the house left – after it was destroyed by fire, locals took a lot of the stone to build cottages and farm buildings. Judging from that though, we should still be able to pick our way around a plan of the ground floor.'

Green studied the first of two diagrams; it looked, he said, like a design for a Cluedo board. 'And what's this other picture, sir?' He pointed to a lithograph of a twin-towered structure.

'That, Lance Bombardier Green, is supposed to represent the triumphal arch which Arbella Fitzjames had built for the Duke of Monmouth. I think it must be drawn from a

131

description, because the arch was destroyed soon after the rebellion was quashed. It was only made of wood but, according to the book, the stone foundations can still be seen. I'd quite like to find them, just to get a proper idea of the arch's size – of course, they might be completely overgrown by now.'

'But if we don't go and have a look, we'll never find out, will we sir? When shall we set off again? I reckon the horses will want to be moving in about ten minutes.' Green handed back the paper and returned to his horizontal position.

'Ten minutes it is then, Lance Bombardier.' And Ashley also stretched himself out, relaxing his muscles and inhaling the powerful aroma of the horse blanket.

*   *   *   *   *

If the diagram of the old Fitzjames house looked like a Cluedo board, the plan of the Albert Museum represented an advanced version of the game. The Toms passed through gallery after gallery, hopelessly lost: the Egyptian Room should have been the display of British costumes, and the Japanese collection, according to Tom One's calculation, ought to have been Aztec. They lingered long enough in the Phoenician Gallery for Tom Two to observe that everybody loved a man in cuneiform; then turned left down a corridor and found, to their disgust, that they were back where they started. At this point they tore up the map and decided to follow their noses. In a surprisingly short space of time they were surrounded by paintings from the sixteenth and seventeenth centuries and a moment later they were staring into a glass cabinet containing dozens of miniature portraits.

'Wow! We're talking seriously short-sighted here.' Tom One bent as low as possible over the pictures, only to have his breath steam up the glass. 'How do you think they painted them? With a magnifying glass?'

To their untrained eyes, every detail seemed perfect. Minute jewels shone from necklaces as elaborate and fragile as

132

spider's webs; lace, like snowflakes under a microscope, seemed to have been painted by a brush that had only a single hair. On a succession of deep blue ovals, most no larger than two inches at their widest or longest, a whole series of faces and figures were delineated with a clarity and subtlety that defied the limitations of the medium. Inspired to an attempt at cultural analysis, Tom One remarked that the pictures were like nanotechnology with a paintbrush.

Tom Two tore himself away from a decorative example of late Tudor youth and moved along the display.

'Look – here's one by the artist your uncle mentioned.'

Tom One moved along the display to where Two was bending over a portrait by Samuel Cooper. At this end of the cabinet, the costumes were just as elaborate, but their wearers looked rather more comfortable in them – and significantly more available. A card beneath the portrait told them that the picture was of an unidentified lady at the court of Charles II.

'One of his mistresses, probably – he was a real old goat, according to my history teacher.'

'Was he the one who got his head chopped off?'

'Who – my history teacher?'

'No - Charles II, idiot. You know – the one that happened opposite Horse Guards. Probably when Major Benson was on duty as a young gunner.'

Tom Two shook his head. He toyed with the idea of telling the truth, but it seemed a shame to tarnish the brilliance of Tom One's ignorance.

'That was Mary Queen of Scots, One.'

'Oh.'

Two was contemplating padding out his lie with false detail, when Sir Andrew Esmond appeared, exactly as Mr Robbins had predicted. What the art dealer had failed to predict, was that the newly-honoured art historian was the same former national serviceman who had visited the Troop and spoken to them less than a week ago. Attracted by their interest in his favourite display, he recognised their ties; a second later, he recognised Tom Two's ears as well.

'And what brings two smart young horse gunners to my museum?'

The Toms instinctively braced their bodies and were told to relax: Sir Andrew preferred shaking hands to saluting and reminded them that he, too, had been a lowly gunner in his time. After an exchange of names, the curator asked if the Toms had arrived with a message from the commanding officer, or if they were visiting purely for pleasure?

'Neither, actually, sir.' Tom Two did the talking again: 'A Mr Robbins suggested we come here to see the miniatures and ask some advice.'

'Joshua Robbins?' The tone was suspicious. 'I hope you haven't bought a picture from him?'

The Toms exchanged a shifty glance: in the cloakroom on the ground floor, a bubble-wrapped officer and trumpeter awaited their collection. Two decided to move the conversation on. He told Sir Andrew of their mission and handed over his transcription of Ashley's instructions. The two gunners watched as the curator became increasingly animated: Tom One was sure he could see nostril hairs contracting with excitement.

'Arbella Fitzjames – my goodness, yes – I see, the miniature taken from the Lely portrait – the portrait stolen? I'm not sure it was known to have survived, even – I must check...'

He lowered the paper and looked at the Toms. 'This is more interesting than I think you realise. If you come to my office, I can check a few facts. You've already seen the Samuel Cooper in the cabinet, I presume?'

'That's right, sir.'

'I could waffle on for hours about how he worked and the techniques of miniature portraiture, but that's not what you're here to find out, is it?'

Tom One answered, hurriedly: 'Not really, sir.'

'Quite. Well just take it from me that Samuel Cooper was

the finest painter of miniatures in his day. You probably haven't heard of him before, simply because miniature painting is such a neglected form of art. It was quite standard, after a portrait had been painted, to commission a minute copy of it that you could wear – and, if you were rich, the person to ask was Samuel Cooper. A generation after him, enamels started to become fashionable, so he was really the last to paint in this style.' The curator dismissed enamels with a wave of his hand: they held no interest for him.

Sir Andrew led the way to his office, which was a gratifying clutter of books, pictures and correspondence, most of which seemed to be piled around a large tray marked "In". Even more gratifying was the bottle of dry sherry, from which three generous glasses were poured before the curator began his research.

'Now, if I remember rightly...' Sir Andrew ran a forefinger along a shelf of books: 'Yes – here we are!' He removed a large volume with a long and unmemorable title, and very small print inside. It reminded Tom One of the sort of book in the school library that one occasionally opened by accident and immediately replaced. There weren't even any pictures, which seemed odd for a book about art.

The curator flipped through the pages, tutting all the while, then admitted defeat and consulted the index.

'Ah! Of course! Page six hundred and seventy-two – here we are! It's a list of all Lely's paintings, known, lost and spurious. "Portrait of Arbella Fitzjames, known to have been painted in 1671." That's very late if we want a Cooper miniature from it. "Lely's account book records payment, 24th March 1670" – that must be Old Style, of course – "portrayed as the Classical figure of Arion astride a Dolphin, the dolphin being the Fitzjames emblem".'

Tom One decided it was a good time to lose concentration. Fortunately, Tom Two was taking notes almost as fast as Sir Andrew was speaking; the expert's voice accelerated and increased in pitch as he read, so that he seemed in danger of taking off. It occurred to Tom One that, if he did so, he could probably be hauled back to earth by hanging on to his nasal hair.

The narration reached a climax: "'The portrait is believed still to be in the Fitzjames family, though permission to view has not been granted for over a century." I bet it hasn't, if, as you say, it was slashed to pieces in the eighteen-hundreds… "see also, Cooper, Samuel".'

There followed another frantic turning of pages, during which Tom Two caught up with his notes.

'Cooper, Samuel – list of works – no – ah! Yes! "Paintings believed lost – miniature of Arbella Fitzjames, taken from a portrait by Sir Peter Lely, *circa* 1671. Mentioned in Court accounts of Charles the Second and attested to by John Aubrey and others, blah, blah, blah… Whereabouts unknown".'

Sir Andrew looked up from his book with the triumphant air of one who has been talking perfect sense and has thoroughly enlightened his audience. Tom Two's head was still in his notebook, so the curator was rewarded only with a blank stare from Tom One. He looked crestfallen and drank some sherry to console himself.

'Put simply, your uncle's information is all sound. It's exciting that the Lely still exists, even in a mutilated state. The speculation, naturally, is that if the portrait has survived, maybe the miniature has as well. That's not strictly logical, of course, but it's an instinctive reaction.'

Tom Two finished his writing and looked up. 'Suppose, sir, the old woman who cut up the painting just locked the miniature away somewhere?'

'Absolutely – nothing is easier to hide or lose than a miniature.'

Tom Two's ears were almost waggling with the intensity of thought. An alarming possibility occurred to Tom One that, one day, his friend's ears would start to sprout hair like Sir Andrew's and he would be mistaken for an aspidistra.

'So, sir, do you think the person who stole the picture

would have known about the miniature?'

When the curator replied, it was obvious that he was speaking from experience.

'There are two types of art thief: one hasn't the faintest idea about what he's stealing, but assumes that an old picture must be worth something; the other knows exactly what he's about. If your thief belongs to the first category, he won't even have heard of Samuel Cooper.

'But if he belongs to the second, he will know every detail.'

CHAPTER SEVENTEEN

DOCTOR HOLBROOKE'S DILEMMA

The master's study in the Fitzjames Hospital is yet another gloomy, oak-panelled room. Its natural light has always to be supplemented: there is a green banker's lamp on the desk, a standing lamp in a far corner, and a picture light above an oil painting of the founder. Bishop Fitzjames occupies the space between the chimney piece and the elaborate plaster moulding of the ceiling. He is a Victorian fake: a well-meaning artist has made him spiritual rather than corpulent; post-Tractarian, rather than pre-Tridentine.

Normally, the bishop is a genial companion when a sermon has to be written. Often, in a dull moment – and there are many dull moments in Dr Holbrooke's sermons – the master will lay down his pen and contemplate the deliberate archaisms in the artwork. There is real gold leaf stamped on the bishop's mitre and the jewels on his fingers and crozier stand out as little glassy humps on the surface of the oils. Perspective has deliberately been disregarded, so the bishop is distinctly two-dimensional and the woven carpet on which he stands appears to be upright rather than flat. The poor man could slide off it at any moment and end up in the grate below.

Today, however, the master has had enough of portraits, just as he has had enough of accidents, missing persons and the police. It is still just about possible to cling to the theory that Peter Bulmer's death was an accident, that Douglas Peachey has simply gone to stay with a friend overnight and forgotten to tell anyone, and that the only crime to have taken place is the theft of a picture, which will probably turn up at a car boot sale in the next couple of weeks. Publicly, Dr Holbrooke clings to this version of events, but he is aware that it grows more straw-like at every turn.

There is no rule stating that a resident must inform the master of any overnight absence from the hospital; nonetheless, it is a convention which is usually observed. Dr Holbrooke had received Ashley's news calmly enough the previous evening and feigned an urbane lack of concern – but, after the detective had left, he had let himself into Peachey's flat. There he found a scholar's muddle of notes and open books, of shoe boxes crammed with loose papers, both handwritten and photocopied. A map of Somerset was pinned down at its four corners with a butter dish, silver salt and pepper pots and a heavy crystal decanter: perhaps Peachey had eaten and drank as he studied. It was clear, at any rate, that he hadn't stolen Mary Compton's paperweight. Of Peachey himself, there had been no sign and, as far as the master could tell, no clue. The master had returned to his house, not yet worried, but with a sense of foreboding. Enquiries around the hospital had served only to ignite gossip and to fuel rumours.

This morning, he had telephoned the police station and reported Douglas Peachey missing. Constable Telfer, functioning on only five hours' sleep, had sat at the master's desk, taking methodical notes and writing down the contact details of Peachey's friends and relations. Of these, there were few – particularly friends. Telfer had suggested a further viewing of Peachey's accommodation, and the sight of the master and a uniformed policeman entering his front door had inspired the retired matrons to a frenzy of speculation; naturally, they were unable to keep this to themselves; and so all Bruton knew.

Having been anxious to get rid of Ashley last night, Dr Holbrooke now rather wishes the detective was at hand. He would surely have some plan of action; he might even have a task for the master to carry out, which would be better than this dreadful state of inactivity. But Ashley has gone off somewhere on a horse and nobody knows when he is due back.

Dr Holbrooke gives up on his sermon, abandoning the stress of religion for the consolation of administration. In his desk, there is a folder full of applications for places in the hospital. He has at least one vacancy to fill.

*   *   *   *   *

Mary Compton is writing a letter to Bombardier Burdett, thanking him and his fellow non-commissioned officers for their gift. In front of her, the book itself lies open, bringing back memories of her time with Prince Albert's Troop. Royal Salutes, ceremonial guards, occasional State Funerals and frequent grand dinners process through her mind. Then she delves beneath the surface glamour and recalls the daily life of the unit: the endless hard work and dedication of officers and men; the unfailing sense of humour of the British soldier – usually toned down in her presence; the overriding sense of purpose and duty which governed every aspect of the military life. She recalls individual soldiers: her husband's batman, who seemed to exist purely to pour gin and polish leather; the master farrier, who showed her how to beat a horseshoe into shape; and her wonderfully old-fashioned riding instructor, who insisted that she rode side-saddle at all times – unlike wicked Arbella, who had shocked society by straddling her dolphin.

Mary has every intention of spending her remaining years as usefully and actively as possible. Nonetheless, she knows that she will increasingly rely on memories like these; that she has reached an age where yesterday is more interesting than tomorrow. That is why she is upset by the loss of her portrait: not as a possession – she has just shed hundreds of those, and it cannot be many years before she is taken from the rest – but because she feels she has had a memory stolen from her. Arbella, immoral, ambitious and unrealistic, has been with her

140

for eighty years and now, in a mild form, Mary feels the symptoms of bereavement.

She turns another page of the book. Lance Bombardier Green is there once more, a saddle over his left arm, a bridle hanging from his right shoulder and a grin the size of a boomerang on his face. Around him, other soldiers untack their horses and begin the work of grooming. It is a sight she has seen many times: it occurs to her that she would like to see it again.

*   *   *   *   *

'I reckon this must be the Great Hall, sir – it's an enormous space.'

'I think you're right, Lance Bombardier. If so, the large gap in front of us would be the main entrance and we've probably just come through the kitchens and outhouses.'

The horses are once more on a long rein, sometimes walking a few yards here and there, on other occasions stooping their heads and grazing peacefully. Lance Bombardier Green has the ground plan of the house and a compass in his free right hand and is attempting to navigate his way around remnants of walls and the fragmentary remains of old pillars and hearths. The destructive work begun by fire and an acquisitive local population has been continued by nature, determined to reclaim the ground as her own. Shrubs grow where once people dined or danced and the roots of trees have displaced stones, causing the low walls to subside. Here and there, a complete arch survives, and Ashley and Green have to fold low over the necks of their horses to pass through; more often, the walls have disappeared altogether and the full extent of a chamber has to be guessed at. As with all ruins, the atmosphere is melancholy and forlorn: the horses seem to feel it and even Green has put away his smile for the last quarter of an hour.

'It's hard to imagine it ever having been a place where people lived, isn't it sir?'

'I know what you mean, Lance Bombardier. There are places – Waterloo, for example, or the Tower of London – where you really can visualise historical events taking place. You feel that they have a sense of immediacy about them, and that just being at the location puts you in touch with the people of long ago – but this isn't one of them. I'm afraid we've wasted our time.'

'We've had some fun in the process, though, sir, haven't we?' The smile reappears. 'And we haven't found her arch thing yet.'

'That's true, Lance Bombardier.' Green's unflagging optimism is infectious. 'Mind you, it's not on the ground plan, is it? What does the text say?'

Green consults the photocopied sheet. 'About a quarter of a mile in front of the house, it says, sir. So, if – as we think – this is the main entrance, we head in that direction, for about four minutes at the plod. Look, sir, do you see how the ground slopes away from the house and then rises again – that would make sense, wouldn't it? You'd want to build an arch on a bit of higher ground.'

The soldier's reasoning is sound and they walk their horses through the gap in the wall, and down the gentle slope, between trees too young for Arbella to have known them. Ashley wondered how the original approach to the house must have looked. Was the ground completely open, to make the building seem more impressive; or did an avenue of oaks, long since sold for their timber, once line the route?

Green asks a simple question which had not occurred to Ashley; 'Who do you think owns all this now, sir?'

'I don't know, Lance Bombardier. I don't think it can be the National Trust or English Heritage, because they'd surely have tidied it up a bit and put it to use one way or another. Presumably, it's long since passed out of the Fitzjames family. I dare say Mrs Compton will know – we can ask her when we get back.'

The ground begins to rise again. Uphill, the horses are less keen to maintain their pace, so both riders take up their reins once more and apply their calf muscles. Green posts himself as left lookout and directs Ashley's gaze to the right: 'With any luck sir, we'll spot one hump each at the same time, and that'll be it – but of course, it might have been off to one side.'

It was – and it is a good thing that Arbella built her arch to the left, because Ashley would never have seen the stone bases of the two towers. Green, trained in fieldcraft and used to detecting shapes and outlines disguised by the greens and browns of military camouflage, has no difficulty spotting them, about twenty yards from their path. Large stone squares, they rise about two feet out the ground. Today, they support only a matting of ivy and a few brave plants: once, they must have been the foundations of something far more spectacular. Between them, a vague, bushy undergrowth has accumulated.

'That's them, sir.' Green extends an arm and an outstretched palm, turning his horse on the forehand at the same time, so that both horse and rider indicate the direction.

'I think you're right, Lance Bombardier. Shall we dismount here and walk through?'

'Actually, sir, I think we can squeeze along on the horses – we'll have to keep our heads down, but it opens out quite nicely after a few yards, and it'll save us the trouble of tethering them again.'

Back bowed, Green leads the way. Ashley feels his horse testing each step carefully before placing any weight on a hoof. A low-lying branch hits his hard hat with a dull thud and then scrapes his back as he passes under. Green, more flexible, has already passed unscathed, flattening himself, like a cat passing underneath a fence. His service cap defies gravity, leading Ashley to speculate that it might be nailed on.

In the glade, the riders can sit upright once more. Before the trees grew, this must have been a fine place for a monument: the rising is only a small one, but the ground is already quite high, and Arbella's timber declaration of treason and love must have been a frighteningly public one. The foundations themselves are substantial, as if the ultimate intention had been to tear down the wooden structure and replace it with stone.

'You know what this reminds me of, sir?'

'Tell me, Lance Bombardier.'

'It's like a temporary camp, sir – a harbour area where a platoon has dug itself in, then cleared up afterwards and covered its traces. Do you see those leaves?'

Once more he indicates direction with an outstretched palm. Some of the vegetation between the foundations is dry, the greenery shrivelling. Looking more closely, they see the pale gleam of snapped stems and broken branches amongst the dark piles of artificially arranged wood. On shrubs around them, they begin to see corresponding pale ovals.

'Hang on to these, sir.' Green gives Ashley his reins and leaps off his horse. He examines the matted branches, selecting one that seems less entangled than the others. It comes away easily; he throws it aside and starts tugging on another. Gradually a second pile of branches accumulates as the original diminishes.

Somebody has dug a trench between the foundation stones. A line of raised soil, about five feet long and two feet wide, slowly reveals itself. When its extent is clear, Green abandons his work and returns to Ashley, wiping sweat from his face as he walks.

'It looks like we haven't wasted our time after all, sir.'

Neither have the rats. As Ashley and Green contemplate the oblong mound of earth, a head emerges from one of several small tunnels. Perhaps it has been disturbed by Green's efforts; or perhaps it is on its way to invite family and friends to the feast. Seeing horses and riders, it freezes for a moment, then the whole, fat, body emerges and scuttles around the perimeter of the soil heap. With difficulty, Ashley controls a nauseous, lurching sensation in his stomach.

'What do we do, sir? Find a shovel and dig?'

Ashley shakes his head. 'There's certainly a shovel waiting

to be found, Lance Bombardier, but it's not our job – we've already disturbed the site quite enough. Do you have your mobile with you?'

'Sorry, sir – I left it in the Land Rover.'

'In that case, what we do is consult the map and work out how to get to the nearest house…'

'And I gallop there like buggery and ring the police, is that right, sir?'

'That, Lance Bombardier, is exactly right.'

CHAPTER EIGHTEEN

AFTERNOON TEAS

The Toms decided that "necessary expenses" could include tea at the Minerva. In a generous moment, inspired by an exhilarating ride in the park and too much gin afterwards, Ashley had arranged for Tom One to be given family membership of his club. Since then, the detective had lived in dread of a military coup, in which his nephew's gun team invaded the bar, stabled their horses in the library and converted the committee rooms into stores for hay, ration packs and harnesses. This frightening scenario was accompanied by a chilling vision of panic-stricken clergymen and civil servants streaming down Decimus Burton's marble staircase and seeking refugee status in the Institute of Directors on the other side of Waterloo Place. In the process, senior bishops and elderly government mandarins would be trampled underfoot by more nimble colleagues.

Mercifully, the club's strict dress code and Tom One's irregularly active instinct for doing the right thing had prevented any such affront to the dignity of the Minerva or its members. The Toms would visit the bar on the rare occasions when they happened to be well dressed and at a loose end, and the coffee room came in handy when Margery Noad made one of her periodic swoops on the capital to denude a department store of supportive underwear and sensible shoes.

The two gunners sat in green armchairs on either side of a low table, systematically working their way through a large pot of tea and the club's entire supply of date and walnut cake. Among the debris of crumbs, napkins and sugar, they had spread out a dozen or so cards with reproductions of miniature artwork by Samuel Cooper, together with Tom Two's extensive notes on the artist and other jottings. Their other purchase stood propped against a chair leg, a mounted artillery officer peering opaquely through layers of bubble wrap; his trumpeter was just about visible, but the dismounted soldier was obliterated by a strip of brown parcel tape. Two was attempting to arrange the postcards in chronological order; a process made difficult by One's habit of randomly selecting a picture for admiration and then replacing it in an incorrect position. An archdeacon, seated some distance away, assumed that they were playing an obscure and intellectual card game and nodded approval before returning to his digestive slumbers.

'Who's the fat old bag in the vast frock?' Tom One indicated a discarded postcard, out of his reach. It was taken from an early Hilliard miniature and had been bought in error. Tom Two picked it up and read the information on the back.

'Margarite of Navarre, apparently. She was an important figure in the French Renaissance.'

'Wow!' Tom One was impressed: 'You mean she blew up bridges and sabotaged railway lines?'

'That's right, One – she once concealed an RAF pilot under that big skirt and walked him through a road block set up by the Germans.'

'Awesome...'

Tom Two restored the heroine to her place on the table, at the same time preventing his friend from further disruption of the sequence.

'No, One – the Countess of Pershore should be next to the Duchess of Grimsby, otherwise everything will get muddled.'

'Is the Duchess the one with an udder hanging out?'

'Yes – no, sorry, that's someone else. The Duchess is the one who's supposed to be dressed as Diana.'

'The one with the slice of melon on her head?'

'I think it's meant to symbolise the moon.'

'Oh.' Tom One leaned back in his chair and ate more cake.

'Did you understand all that stuff about symbols and imagery, then?'

'Bits of it. I wrote down everything Sir Andrew told us about Arion riding on a dolphin, but I couldn't keep up with him when he got excited. I reckon we've got more than enough for your uncle, though – he just wanted to know the basics about valuations and whether a miniature of that woman ever existed.' Tom Two gathered up the postcards carefully before his comrade could disrupt them again. 'We can post them from here, can't we?'

Tom One's mouth was too full to answer, so he pointed towards a writing desk nearby. Two wandered over, paused briefly to speculate whether Tom One's family card entitled him to filch club stationery, then crammed the postcards and his voluminous notes into the largest envelope he could find. Before sealing the package, he jotted a short covering note.

'Do I send your love?'

Tom One swallowed hard before answering: an unchewed date abseiled painfully down his oesophagus. 'Lots of it, together with a hint that we might have taken him at his word as far as expenses go. We can get a stamp from the porter's lodge and the postbox is just outside the bar.'

The suggestion of ideas was very powerful. The two soldiers glanced at each other and then at their watches.

'It's a bit early...'

'They do champagne by the glass...'

'And champagne is said to be good for bruised backs – especially if taken in sufficient quantity...'

They took the stairs at a more sedate pace than the stampede of members in Ashley's nightmare. A few minutes later, redeployed and recumbent, they admired the bubbles eternally rising to the surface of their drinks as they talked through the events of the day. Something jogged in Tom One's memory.

'I say, Two – what do you think about that dodgy art dealer who's moved down to where Uncle George is staying?'

* * * * *

Robert Simpson wears a cravat which exactly matches his pocket handkerchief; similarly, the jewelled pin which holds his neckwear in place coordinates perfectly with a glittering pair of cufflinks. His Italian leather shoes glisten as well, with a sheen deriving from the maker rather than from any manual labour on the part of the owner. Did he but know it, Simpson is talking his mother out of a happy retirement in the Fitzjames Hospital.

Dr Holbrooke is wishing that he had stuck to his sermon. He is repelled by the expensively vulgar fraud who is drinking his sherry and assaulting his ears with artificially elongated vowels. Simpson may have persuaded dozens of American clients that they were in the company of somebody at the upper end of the English class system, but Dr Holbrooke can spot a fake gentleman as quickly as Robert Simpson can spot a fake picture. And, talking of pictures, the master is distinctly uncomfortable with the hungry look which comes over the face of Simpson every time he glances at Bishop Fitzjames.

'Of course, to you and me, Padre, it's just a pretty piece of Victoriana – plenty more where it came from and we wouldn't expect to pay more than a tenner at a car boot sale or a couple of hundred at an antique fair. But you mark my words, Padre...'

Dr Holbrooke reflects that he is marking all right – a big cross through Mrs Simpson's application for an apartment in the hospital. As the unctuous Simpson recounts tales of West Coast Americans who have paid small fortunes for cheaply acquired pictures, the master resolves to count his spoons the moment his guest has departed.

'...of course, they pay as much for the history as for the look of it. If you can find a big name with some connection, that makes a difference as well. I sold an altarpiece – ugly thing – which had been in a church designed by Pugin. Well, that was good for an extra ten thou, Padre – dollars, of course, not pounds or guineas, unfortunately – though dear old Augustus

149

Welby Pugin himself had nothing to do with the picture. Probably never even saw it....'

With effort, Dr Holbrooke steers the conversation back to old Mrs Simpson.

'Of course, Padre. My apologies – I was getting carried away. Nonetheless, if you ever should need to sell the bishop, I can get you a very good deal. Yes, mother's dead set on a flat in the hospital. The house is too big for her now – it's a burden on her, and she gets upset when she can't keep everything as she likes it. I do what I can, but you know how it is, Padre...' Simpson makes a deprecating gesture with an over-manicured hand; a signet ring sparkles in the process.

Dr Holbrooke thinks he knows exactly how it is. This slimeball, having conned his mother into signing over Power of Attorney, is anxious to get her off the scene as quickly as possible. The house on Quaperlake Street must be worth the best part of half a million pounds, an inheritance which is regarded with the greedy eyes of one whose business has not been going too well lately. Once poor Mrs Simpson is shut up in the hospital, her son will be free to do as he pleases.

'Of course, Mr Simpson, there are many applicants for every vacancy in the hospital; this is simply a preliminary meeting...'

'Understood, Padre – absolutely.' Robert Simpson responds with the confidence of one who knows he has made a good impression.

* * * * *

'No answer,' Tom One returned to the bar, having wandered outside to use his mobile.

'What do you think he's up to?'

Tom shrugged. 'Could be anything. Anyway, he'll find out when he gets your notes, won't he?'

Tom Two contemplated the remains of his champagne. 'It's Saturday, though, isn't it? Even if there's a late collection

150

from the porter's lodge, he won't get them before Monday. Tuesday, probably.'

They had decided that Mr Robbins' information concerning Robert Simpson was important enough to pass on straight away. Denied the chance to do so, they felt an irritation which not even more champagne could drive away.

'We could get the porter to open up the box and give us the letter back – then we could get a courier to deliver it.'

'If it came to that, we could bribe Shifty Scott to drive it down in his Tin Lizzie.'

'Hey! That'd be great! Then we could go too!'

For a few minutes, they speculated on the possibility of a weekend's adventure in Somerset. An exciting vista of dead bodies and long lost masterpieces appeared before them and the prospect of brilliant solutions and heroic acts acted as a spur to ever more fanciful speculations. Common sense, unattractive and anticlimactic, asserted itself at about the same time as the champagne ran out; as Two pointed out, they could hardly just descend on Ashley's hosts without telephoning first, and if they could telephone, there was no need to drive down anyway.

Tom One nodded a dismal agreement. 'Besides, Scotty's probably well over the limit already – not to mention the fact that his motorised mess tin probably won't get as far as Somerset. I bet we'd have to push it for the last fifty miles.'

'At least. All the way from Baker Street, more likely. After all, there's no known record of it having been further than the kebab house. And the suspension's not been the same since he took Available Annie to the cinema. But it was a nice idea.'

Tom One tilted his flute in the vain hope of spotting a final droplet of champagne. 'Well, we'll just have to keep trying to ring Uncle George. Shall we head back to barracks and hang the picture?' He nodded towards the blurred figure by Tom Two's feet. Two had finally beaten Mr Robbins down to two hundred and fifty pounds: the art dealer had made pitiful pleas for his wife and starving children before pocketing Two's cheque triumphantly and promising to send on the second picture as soon as it was dry. Then he had hustled them out of the building before they had time to repent the deal. The Toms were left pleased with their picture, but uncertain whether they had a bargain or a turkey for their money; Mr Robbins' clients often felt that way.

*   *   *   *   *

As Sergeant Archdale had predicted, the inspector from Yeovil made a nuisance of himself. Within a minute of his arrival, the whole glade had been cordoned off with white tape; Ashley and Lance Bombardier Green were left stranded on the wrong side of the barrier, out of sight and earshot, while the police got on with their business. Fortunately, Sergeant Archdale, acting on his own initiative, sent Constable Telfer over to them with any new information. Also, Green discovered that a view of the glade could just about be gained if he stood up on his saddle and peered through a natural gap in the branches.

Ashley held the reins of Green's patient horse, amusing himself with the sight of the soldier's legs disappearing into the tree and the ludicrous sensation of holding a conversation with a pair of loquacious riding boots. He was vaguely reminded of a stained glass window he had seen in the parish church, in which Christ was taken up to heaven in a cloud, with just his feet protruding, objects of admiration to a crowd of confused but admiring disciples.

'They've just removed the last few bits of greenery, sir – the photographer's fiddling about with his camera. I wish they'd just get on and dig.'

'Be patient, Lance Bombardier – this is slow, thorough work. They might miss out on something important if they rush the job.'

'Point taken, sir. And here comes Telfer again – he's looking quite cheerful this time. Hang on tight – I'm coming back down.'

Green returned to a seated position by the simple process of opening his legs and allowing himself to descend into the saddle. His horse turned its neck and sent a reproachful glare in the direction of the soldier but made no other protest. A second later, Constable Telfer appeared, grinning.

'Latest news, is the inspector's seriously pissed off with life, sir. He thought he was on a wild goose chase and he'd be off duty by five o'clock – but it's definitely a grave, just like you said, and very new at that.'

'And at a guess, Constable, shallow rather than deep?'

'That's what they reckon, sir – it's just topsoil we can see, so Sergeant Archdale reckons we're only talking a few inches down. Anyway, if it had been any deeper, the rats wouldn't have got to it so soon.' Telfer abandoned his grin and gave an involuntary shudder; while exposing the grave, he had disturbed a pair of rats going about their business. 'The sergeant says you think it's Mr Peachey in there, sir.'

'Peachey's the odds on favourite, Constable Telfer; he must be involved in all this somehow.'

Green hypothesised an alternative theory: 'I suppose he couldn't have dug the grave, sir? And it's someone or something completely different in there?'

Ashley shrugged. 'It's just about possible, Lance Bombardier, though he was pretty unsteady on his legs...' Ashley noticed that he was already using the past tense to describe the historian. 'I'm not sure he could have managed it all by himself. We'll know one way or the other soon.'

Telfer confirmed this. 'Not more than half an hour, sir, the sergeant reckons. He wants to know if you'll be happy to come over and do an identification if necessary, sir – he could do it himself, but this way will annoy the inspector more.' Telfer's grin staged a second performance.

'In that case, Constable, it will be a pleasure.'

'Thank you, sir – I'll go and tell him, if you'll excuse me.'

Telfer returned to his duties, curving round a tree trunk and disappearing into the woods. Green shifted back in his saddle and raised a foot onto the pommel. 'I'll get back to lookout duty, sir – unless you want to have a go?'

It was a question expecting a negative answer. Ashley pictured himself teetering unsteadily on his horse's back and predicted disastrous consequences: 'And I saw how you got down again – I'm not sure I could manage it without sacrificing either dignity or manhood.'

Green outgrinned Constable Telfer. 'It's not too tricky once you know what to do, sir. As my first army instructor said, you either learn the knack, or you lose your knackers. Anyway, here goes.' He raised his other foot to the saddle, squatted for a second to gain his balance, then stood up.

The soldier gave a detailed commentary as Telfer and his colleagues patiently and carefully removed the soil from either end of the grave. Within ten minutes the policemen were concentrating their efforts on one end only. And in another quarter of an hour Lance Bombardier Green watched Ashley enter the glade and identify an exposed head, shattered, clotted and cheekless, as that of Douglas Peachey.

CHAPTER NINETEEN

POST MORTEM

There were questions for Ashley to answer and details to be explained. Lance Bombardier Green made good use of this time by planning a new return route, shorter and faster than the original. Once released by the inspector, they headed back, galloping whenever they could and maintaining a brisk trot at other times, only slowing down to a walk for the last half mile to allow their horses to cool down.

The rapid pace prevented the development of any real conversation. The pounding of urgent hoofs on grassy tracks and the metallic clopping of horseshoes on narrow lanes acted as an accompaniment to the muddled questions, theories and speculations which whirled around Ashley's mind. What was Peachey doing at the old Fitzjames house? How had he got there? What was the connection between a mutilated seventeenth-century portrait and a shallow grave in the middle of a wood? He explored various hypotheses, none of them satisfactory, and finally gave up the effort, allowing himself to be soothed by the rhythms of the powerful animal beneath him. Rising and sitting with the trot, or leaning forward to gallop, he lost himself to detection and involved himself instead in the timeless bond between horse and rider, his aching calves both imparting and absorbing energy as they curved themselves around the ribs and flank muscles of his chestnut mare.

As they neared the yard, Green let out his reins, took his feet out of the stirrups and broke the silence: 'So, what do you think, sir?'

Having no answer to give, Ashley returned the challenge:

'Give me your thoughts first, Lance Bombardier – you might have spotted something I've missed.'

The soldier released his reins altogether, placed his hands behind the saddle and leaned back. It was the relaxed pose of a rider who has complete confidence in his horse. Ashley contemplated imitation, but his vision of the manoeuvre also involved an immediate and painful descent to the ground, so he abandoned the idea. After a few relaxed and comfortable strides, Green spoke again.

'Well, sir, I didn't think much to that inspector. He reminded me of the sort of officer who plays everything by the book because it saves thinking for himself – we get them occasionally in the Troop and they're really boring to work for. Of course, you saw more of him than I did, but that was my impression.'

'Mine too.' Ashley nodded agreement. 'He'll be very thorough, and his report will be beautifully filed in triplicate, and he'll drive Sergeant Archdale up the wall with an insistence on correct procedure...'

'But he won't actually solve the case, sir, will he?'

Ashley shrugged; his horse interpreted the action as a half halt and twitched her ears, expecting further instructions. He ran a hand down her neck by way of apology. 'He might, Lance Bombardier, he just might. Once the police are mobilised, they have access to vast quantities of information and resources with which a private detective can't compete. If this is the sort of crime that can be solved by a painstaking sifting through evidence, then he'll get there in his own good time.'

'But you don't think it is like that, do you, sir?'

This time, Ashley managed to smile a response without disturbing the even pace of his mare.

'I rather hope it isn't, Lance Bombardier – it would be a bit of an anticlimax after the last few days, wouldn't it? Let's forget the inspector – what else did you notice?'

Green moved his left leg behind the girth and applied pressure with his right calf, guiding his horse around a corner.

'There was something funny about the grave itself, I thought, sir. I'm not exactly sure, because it only occurred to me after they'd cleared all the wood away – and by then we were on the wrong side of the mine tape. But from what I could see…' The soldier paused, trying to recall the sight of the partially disinterred corpse: 'Well, sir, he seemed a bit dwarf-like, if you see what I mean. Which, presumably, he wasn't in real life.'

Ashley too tried to picture the scene in his mind. He had relied on Green's descriptions before being summoned to identify the corpse; and by then, Peachey's body had been covered with a blanket. Ashley had concentrated on the battered skull rather than on the length of the grave. A full vision, therefore, eluded him.

'He certainly wasn't a dwarf, Lance Bombardier – about five feet ten, I should say, though he stooped of course. I respect your powers of observation, but I can't visualise your description. I dare say we can scrounge a sight of the police photographs from Sergeant Archdale.'

'Only if you think it's worth it, sir – it might be nothing, of course. Anyway, here we are at last.'

They rode into the stable yard, to be greeted in loud and fluent – if somewhat repetitive – Anglo Saxon. Ex-Sergeant Jones demanded to know what time Lance Bombardier Green called this, where the hell he had been for the last year or so, and whether he realised that he had kept everyone waiting for hours? Finally, he suggested that the next time Green wanted a free ride from his stable, he could go and perform an unnatural act upon himself instead. Without waiting for answers, the retired soldier then turned to Ashley, smiled politely and said, 'I hope you had a pleasant ride, sir?'

'Have a heart, Sarge.' Green swung his right leg over his horse's back, then appeared to hover in mid-air before completing his dismount. He continued talking as he ran up his stirrups and loosened the girth: 'We found a dead body.'

'Yeah, and I bet I know what you did with it, Green, you deviant.'

157

'Thanks, Sarge – as it happens, it was very unattractive.'

'Just as well, probably.' Jones turned to Ashley once more, holding his horse while the detective performed a less proficient dismount. 'Don't worry about your tack, sir – the lad will do it for you.'

"The lad" turned out to be a round-headed teenager with short blond hair, dirty clothes and dusty Wellingtons. He had clearly spent the afternoon mucking out, sweeping and grooming. White teeth gleamed a smile from a healthy, grubby face as he unbuckled the girth and lifted the saddle from the horse's back.

'It's Mr Ashley, sir, isn't it? I'm Stephen.'

Ashley made the link between the well-spoken urchin in front of him and the smart schoolboy who had eaten strawberries and cream at the Cliffords' picnic: 'You're Amelia's boyfriend, aren't you?'

Another white smile appeared over the top of the saddle: 'That was Thursday, sir – this is Saturday. Amelia's moved on since then, but it was fun while it lasted. Educational, too, in the nicest possible way.' Stephen added this afterthought as he took the reins over the horse's head and led her to her stall. On the other side of a wooden partition, Green was already untacking his mount. Ashley was about to follow, but Sergeant Jones suggested otherwise.

'He's crazy about horses and the army, sir,' Jones explained, 'So when I said I had a lance bomber from the Troop over today, he was on his bicycle like a shot. If we just leave them together, I'll get us some tea in the office.'

Ashley was happy to fall in with the plan; his whole body ached from the exertion of the day's exercise and tea, even of the type approved by the soldiers of Prince Albert's Troop, was a welcome suggestion.

Jones' office appeared to be furnished entirely from an army surplus shop; or more likely, Ashley guessed, from a horsebox full of equipment purloined from Prince Albert's barracks. Anything, it seemed, that had not actually been nailed down was considered fair game by the acquisitive NCO, from the metal desk, chairs and filing cabinet, to the enamel kettle and mugs which were arranged scruffily on a plastic tray. On the whole, the quartermaster had probably been quite relieved when Jones had shoplifted these last items from an unregarded shelf in the stores, together with the paraffin fueled hob, which was now being lit. Ashley amused himself with speculating as to the contents and décor of Jones' house. Were the curtains and furniture covers made from an old roll of camouflage material? Had he adapted a Clansman radio set and ground spike antenna so that he could listen to his favourite radio channel? And was the whole house wired with cable from a field telephone spool? A nine-by-nine canvas tent would undoubtedly serve as a gazebo for summer evening barbeques and guests would eat their sausages and burgers from a mismatching assortment of mess tins, enamel plates and crockery from the cookhouse.

'Here you go, sir.' The ex-sergeant brought Ashley back to reality with a steaming mug of some military strength brew. 'The others won't be long – the lad did all the stable routines while we were waiting for you, so it's just a quick sponge down for the horses and a bit of saddle soap on the leathers. I like to keep the place smart, but not four-o'clock-inspection smart, if you see what I mean, sir.'

Ashley understood. When his nephew groomed a horse for him, his attention to detail verged on the obsessive. Hoofs were picked out until every last fragment of dust or grit was eradicated, then oiled so that they gleamed even more than the coat, which shone from hundreds of strokes of the body brush. Tail and mane were combed, eyes, nose and dock carefully sponged. The process took a good half hour, at the end of which the horse sparkled and Tom looked filthy – and then there was still the bridle and saddle to polish to a quicksilver shine. It was easy to imagine that, after a decade or so of this, the retired soldier had welcomed a slight relaxation of standards.

159

Jones settled behind his desk and Ashley sank carefully and gratefully into a chair made of tubular metal and canvas.

'So, this body, sir – were you expecting to find it?'

'Not really, Sergeant Jones – I was just curious to see the place. I was aware that the dead person was fascinated by the history attached to it, and we knew, of course, that he had disappeared, so I suppose you could say I was responding to a hunch, but there was certainly nothing more specific than that.'

'And no idea who's done it, sir? Tell me to mind my own business if you don't want to answer – I shan't be offended.' Jones took a mouthful of tea, rejected it as being not sweet enough and added more sugar, stirring it in with the remains of a defunct ball-point pen.

'Too early to say.' Ashley responded truthfully, glossing over his ignorance. He was just toying with the possibility of trying some theories on Jones – who, for all his roughness, had a sharp mind – when Lance Bombardier Green and Stephen arrived, their tasks completed and their need for refreshment paramount. There followed a second clanking of enamel mugs and a re-boiling of the kettle, creating enough steam, it seemed, to power a small factory during the heyday of the industrial revolution. Green then devoted himself to the arcane rituals of the perfect brew; the high priest of army tea instructing his newest acolyte in the hermetic art of distilling the maximum caffeine and tannin from cheap and unpromising bags. Unaware of his impending Ordeal by Bromide, Stephen contentedly converted the contents of his mug into a supersaturated sugar solution, then sat cross-legged on the floor, content with being allowed to remain in the presence of so exalted a person as a serving and uniformed lance bombardier. Green, looking around for an appropriately elevated throne, vaulted onto the filing cabinet. It clanged emptily as his spur hit the drawer marked "Tax returns".

'So, Mr Ashley, sir – any flashes of inspiration while we were rubbing furniture polish and hoof oil into your horse?'

Green and his old sergeant were looking expectantly

towards Ashley. Stephen, fascinated in equal measure by murder and the military life, glanced rapidly from the lance bombardier to the detective. Ashley decided to play to the crowd and think aloud; after all, giving sound and shape to vague ideas might lead somewhere.

'All right, then – point number one. Peachey was either murdered where we found him, or he was killed elsewhere and brought to the wood for burial. The first possibility is the simplest, but that doesn't necessarily make it correct. Does anyone have any thoughts on that?'

There was a pause before Green suggested, 'Car tracks?' Stephen nodded a loyal agreement without being fully sure why. Ashley nodded as well.

'Whichever scenario is correct, there'll be tracks of one kind or another somewhere. Peachey was an old and frail man – he can't possibly have walked all the way into the wood. Either he or someone else must have driven him – dead or alive – to a convenient parking space and proceeded on foot from there.'

'If he was already dead, sir,' Jones interjected, 'and they had any distance to cover, they'll have left one hell of a trail. I used to lead a Casualty Evacuation course once a year, and I can tell you, moving a body is a big job – it leaves traces.'

'He's right, sir,' Green confirmed. 'I had to be the casualty a few years back – I got tangled up with everything.' He clicked his spurs by way of showing pleasure at the memory, before adding, irrelevantly: 'We faked up wounds with offal from the cookhouse, and the chef produced some home-made yogurt as a substitute for vomit.'

'No change there, then,' observed Jones, sardonically.

Ashley brought the conversation back on course. 'This is where the police will be at their best. They'll comb the whole area and work out every possible approach to that glade. If our hypothetical car left the road and if Peachey was already dead, then – as you've realised – they'll find the route easily.'

'And if the car didn't leave the road, sir? And the old man was still alive? You said that was the simplest solution just now.'

The questions were asked by Green; once more, Stephen nodded enthusiastically, before slurping his tea and looking inquisitively at Ashley over the top of his mug.

'All right – let's go for the simplest line and see where it leads us.' Ashley paused to organise some ideas before continuing: 'Peachey arrives in a car and parks it somewhere on a road, so as to leave as few tracks as possible. He makes his way on foot to the glade – and from what I saw of him, I should say about half a mile was the farthest he could attempt over ground like that. When he gets to the glade, he is murdered by some large heavy object crashing down on his skull and immediately – and hurriedly – buried. Any more thoughts?'

The others were now enjoying their role in the process of detection. Suggestions tumbled over each other in rapid sequence:

'He'd arranged to meet the murderer at that spot!'

'Then we're talking two trails and two cars…'

'Which means that Peachey's car will be found abandoned somewhere…'

'Unless the murderer himself walked and drove off afterwards.'

'Or there were two murderers – they arrived together, but left separately.'

'If there were two murderers, it could be that Peachey just disturbed them doing something dodgy, so they killed him.'

This last suggestion – Stephen's – was rejected by the two soldiers as involving too much coincidence. Jones started the ball rolling again by asking a question:

'If he had arranged to meet the murderer, why choose that place? There are plenty of easier rendezvous points in the world, even in Somerset.'

'Perhaps the murderer chose the place.'

'Yes! The murderer wanted to bump him off in some quiet spot, so he suggested they liaise there, knowing that the old boy was obsessed with the local history and would come along eagerly. How about that?' Jones looked around triumphantly, accepting the ovation which his genius merited. He gave a satisfied smile to Ashley: 'Problem solved, sir – now all you have to do is find the murderer.'

Ashley was amused: he rather hoped that Jones' solution would prove to be correct, so that the ex-sergeant could spend the rest of his life boasting about his brief but brilliant career as a detective's assistant. Privately, though, he had pieced together a different sequence of events, which he was anxious to think through carefully before discussing them. He rose from his chair and made the sort of appreciative remarks that precede departure. Lance Bombardier Green jumped off the filing cabinet, straightened his belt and service jacket, and reached for his cap.

'Shall we give Stephen a lift back to Bruton, sir? We've got plenty of room for him and his bike – assuming he doesn't mind bouncing about in the back of an army Land Rover with buggered suspension.'

Stephen beamed the smile of one who could think of no greater happiness. Ashley wondered if he would be quite so happy by the end of the journey, when the battered remains of his bicycle would probably have to be surgically extracted from his body.

About two miles into the journey, Stephen stuck his head through the canvas flap which divided the front and back of the Land Rover. Green had just driven at top speed along a pot-holed stretch of lane and, for an awful moment, Ashley thought that their passenger was going to be sick all over them. But Stephen's tense expression was due to concentration rather than to an upset stomach.

'I've been thinking about Mr Peachey, sir – I don't think he could drive.'

CHAPTER TWENTY

PEACHEY'S APARTMENT

The original plan for the evening had involved hot baths,
alcohol and a leisurely debriefing session in Colin Clifford's
study: like so many good plans, it had to be abandoned.
Returning to Old House, Ashley discovered his mobile choked
up with confusing but important text messages from Tom,
several more from a disturbed and querulous Dr Holbrooke,
and a polite voice message from Mary Compton, requesting
information. There was even a message for Lance Bombardier
Green, which came via the Old House telephone and Diana
Clifford: Sister Barnfield had accidentally cooked far too much
food and would be delighted if he would join her for an
informal dinner.

'With me for afters, by the sound of it, sir,' remarked the
soldier, apprehensively. 'Do you think I should go?'

Ashley responded brightly; it wasn't his body that was
under threat.

'Of course you should go, Lance Bombardier. Sister
Barnfield might be full of valuable information – and she'll
certainly know what's been going on during our absence.
What's more, if you wander over in your uniform, it's a fair bet
that she'll trill away even more sweetly than yesterday. Give me
ten minutes to talk to Tom and I'll wander over as far as the
hospital with you.'

Flattery did the trick; Green wandered over to a full-length
mirror, admired himself, and decided that his boots and tunic
were still smart enough after a day's riding. 'Moderately
gleaming on the outside, sir, sweaty and sticky underneath –

what woman could resist it? All right, I'll do it, but only if you promise to give me an emergency call in a couple of hours.'

'It's a deal, Lance Bombardier.' Ashley reached for his mobile.

*   *   *   *   *

'Hi, Uncle George – where've you been all day?' Tom One gave a "thumbs up" sign to Tom Two, scattering dominoes across the NAAFI table in the process; 'Oops, sorry, Two... Another body, you say? Wow!'

What little conversation there had been died down. The bar was thinly populated with those soldiers who were too hard up to afford a proper Saturday night out, and who were glad to have something of interest to listen to. Tom became aware of their attention; he rather enjoyed it, but this conversation was best handled in private.

'Keep talking, Uncle George – I'm listening, but I'm heading for the harness room where we can speak more easily.' Tom gestured to Two to follow and they wandered towards the exit, ignoring a large sign which said NO DRINKS TO BE TAKEN FROM THE BAR. Playing to his audience, Tom One gave an unnecessary gasp of astonishment and exclaimed, 'Really?' just before he went out of the door.

In the harness room, they found Vernon and Sorrell, their left arms up to the elbows in riding boots, stoically working off the final instalment of their debt. Their presence still counted as privacy as far as the Toms were concerned. A saddle lay ready for cleaning on the central frame and out of habit, Tom One vaulted on; he immediately regretted it as a spasm of pain shot up his spine.

'Ouch! No, don't worry, Uncle George – I just forgot that I was meant to be resting my back. Were you saying that the lance bomber helped you find the body? What happened to Wendy from Warminster?'

The other three soldiers pricked up their ears, but guessed

from Tom One's shrug that his Uncle's answer was tactfully vague. It need not have been; a second later, the lance bombardier's voice was loud enough for them all to hear:

'She was as frigid as a hairless polar bear in a snowstorm, Tom One... Sorry to interrupt you, sir...'

Ashley resumed his narrative; his voice being less carrying, Vernon and Sorrell turned back to their work. Tom Two passed round his glass and the three of them drank in rotation.

After a while, it was Tom's turn to talk. With some prompting from Two, he told his uncle of their research into the work of Peter Lely and Samuel Cooper, supplying a general summary of recent valuations and information from Mr Robbins' catalogues and Sir Anthony's more learned volumes.

'Sir Anthony said he's got digital pictures of some of the miniatures, Uncle George, so he'll e-mail them to you – he might even have done it already. I gave him your Hotmail address – I hope you don't mind. You won't get the other bits until the post arrives, of course, but I think we've given you all the important stuff.'

Tom Two frantically mouthed, 'Tell him about the dodgy dealer.' One responded with an impatient nod; he had just been coming to that. He waited for Ashley to finish jotting down some notes, then said: 'But there's another thing that might be even more useful, Uncle George – Mr Robbins says a really shifty dealer has just moved down to Bruton. His name's Robert Simpson... No, Mr Robbins says you probably wouldn't have heard of him, because he dealt mainly with Americans, flogging off old rubbish as serious art. Mr Robbins said you'd be amused if we said "West Coast" to you... Oh, I see...'

Neither of the Toms had understood the significance of this information: Tom One took time out from his telephone conversation to pass on Ashley's explanation, that most dealers considered West Coast Americans to be an easier touch than their more hard-headed Eastern countrymen.

'Well, anyway, Uncle George, he's lying low for a while after a few too many deals went end up – he's gone to Bruton because his mother's got a house there. Mr Robbins reckons everyone in Somerset should be nailing their pictures to the walls as a basic precaution, but he also said that he thinks Simpson is fairly stupid – he's spent so many years dealing in rubbish that he probably won't recognize the real thing when he sees it any more. I hope that's helpful, Uncle George.'

The others could tell from Tom's expression that it was; helpful enough for him to come clean about the accumulated expenses of the day, though not about the picture they had bought. Judging that his uncle was probably good for a little more financial gratitude, Tom painted a bleak picture of four impoverished soldiers spending a sorrowful evening in the harness room, down to their last tea bag, and huddled around a Hexi-burner for warmth. By the time he hung up, the gunner had negotiated a taxi to the cinema, four tickets for a particularly violent film and supper at a pizza house afterwards.

*   *   *   *   *

'And cheap at the price,' Ashley whispered to Green as the sound of adolescent whoops and cheers assaulted his left ear. He sent benign greetings to his nephew's comrades and returned the mobile to his pocket. 'That's the most promising lead we've had since this whole affair started.'

There was no need for him to pass on the details: at Ashley's invitation, Green had listened in to this last part of the call, pressing his ear against the diminutive mobile, so that he and the detective looked like Siamese twins, joined at the cranium.

'It sounds good, sir, doesn't it?'

'It does, Lance Bombardier – up till now, the trail has been colder than your description of Wendy from Warminster...'

'But the polar bear has started to grow her hair again, sir – is that right?'

'Well, she's put a cardigan on, at any rate.'

167

Ashley's good mood continued as he tugged off his boots and exchanged his breeches for trousers. He used the time to supply Green with a series of questions to put to his hostess.

'In the first place, we need to know everything she did and saw yesterday: if my assessment of Sister Barnfield is correct, she's a very nosey woman and keeps a close eye on the people in the hospital.'

Green agreed: 'Not to mention keeping a close eye on the crotch of any handsome young man who happens to pass her way, sir. But she couldn't have had anything to do with old Peachey's death, could she? She'd never have managed it.'

'Not by herself – and we don't want to hypothesise multiple killers unless we have to. All the same, it's worth remembering that she was very well placed to kill Peter Bulmer on Thursday.'

'And you're sending me there for dinner, sir?' Green made the observation in a reproachful voice: 'I could be murdered in my bed. Come to think of it, I could be murdered in *her* bed, which is even more worrying.'

'Only if she rolls over in the night, Lance Bombardier – it might be worth taking a snorkel with you, if you've got one in the back of the Land Rover.'

'That's right, sir, they're standard army issue to any soldier going on leave,' Green responded sarcastically, then added thoughtfully, 'I suppose I could prise her off with the car jack.'

'Well then, that's settled.' Ashley finished tying his shoelaces, ran a comb rapidly through his matted hair, and headed for the door. 'Two more things for you to find out, if you can. First, as I said earlier, we need to know what's happened while we've been away. Second, see what she knows of this Robert Simpson chap – if he's remotely good looking, she'll know all about him.'

'You're starting to make me jealous, sir.'

They let themselves out of Old House and headed towards the hospital.

* * * * *

'Are you really thinking of joining the army?' Amelia Clifford twirls a thoughtful index finger around Stephen's closely cropped hair. The soldier-to-be, aware that he has just become considerably more attractive, adjusts his head in Amelia's comfortable lap and responds casually, 'Probably – I might even leave school early to do it.'

'Really?' A pair of artificially phosphorescent eyes widen to maximum extent; 'That's so impressive.'

Stephen had been waylaid as he wheeled his bicycle around the perimeter of the cricket fields. Now, he and Amelia occupy a bench in front of the First Eleven pavilion: a spot well suited to romance and, indeed, often put to good use. A breeze wafts a potent mixture of horse sweat and pheromones into Amelia's nostrils.

'I'm sorry about last night, Stephen – I don't know why I went off with Duncan, he's really horrible.'

'He's really rich, too.' Judging from the small amount of money Duncan had spent on Amelia, he intends staying that way.

Amelia ignores the implications of Stephen's remark and continues her erotic phrenology. As she does so, she looks down the length of his body, stretched out on the bench, and imagines him dressed as she had seen Lance Bombardier Green that morning from her bedroom window. Stephen's Wellingtons transform themselves into military riding boots, polished and spurred; his dirty jeans are close-fitting khaki breeches. His tunic? Well, that would be undone, of course, with his belt and woollen tie lying tangled in his cap; his shirt loosened and open.

Stephen, unaware of the full extent of his metamorphosis, feels Amelia's free hand slip under his rugby shirt and rest on his stomach.

It is going to be another educational evening.

*   *   *   *   *

Constable Telfer was on sentry duty outside Peachey's flat. At a window opposite, Avril (the dummy of the moment) was similarly engaged on behalf of her colleagues. A second after Ashley and Green appeared, the faces and coiffeurs of all four matrons crowded into the narrow aperture. Irene clutched her cards tightly; they were far too good to be abandoned.

Telfer gave a friendly, unmilitary salute. 'Evening, sir – we thought you'd be rolling up soon. Sergeant Archdale is with Dr Holbrooke now, if you want to see him.'

'And the inspector?' Ashley raised a quizzical eyebrow and received a grin in response.

'Gone back to Yeovil to file his report, sir.'

'In triplicate?'

'At the very least, sir. He's left the sergeant in charge of things, so if you want a look round the Peachey palace, now's your chance – in fact, here he comes now.'

Archdale descended from the master's apartment, followed by a nervous Dr Holbrooke. The doctor's attitude towards Ashley seemed to be reproachful, with an implication that the detective should not have taken the day off to go riding when so many stressful things were going on in Bruton. Ashley was tempted to point out that, had he *not* gone riding, nothing would have happened at all: Sergeant Archdale made the observation instead, and the master nodded repentantly. The policeman then turned to Ashley.

'I suppose you'd like to have a look around the flat, sir – not that there's much to see, I'm afraid.'

'No portrait of Arbella Fitzjames rolled up inside the umbrella stand, then?' Ashley adopted a mock disappointment. Archdale gave an appreciative smile.

'Fat chance, sir – at a guess, I'd say the picture's wherever the murderer is. We had a good look, though, just in case.'

They crowded into the small apartment, causing a spasmodic twitching of floral curtains at the matrons' window. Telfer allowed himself to grin in the direction of the elderly ladies before closing the door firmly and resuming his guard

170

duty. Disappointed, Irene, Jasmine and Mavis returned to a hotly contested contract of four spades.

Peachey's sitting room was substantially as Dr Holbrooke had observed it the previous night, though the signs of careful searching were also visible; in particular, the butter dish, cruets and decanter had all been dusted for prints. Beneath them, the ordnance survey map of the area was grubbier than before.

'We thought the old boy might have been planning his trip out to the wood, Mr Ashley – and if anyone else was in on the plan, we might get some useful dabs. Too early yet to say whether we have, of course.'

Ashley nodded. 'Did you find his route into the forest?'

'We think, so, sir.' Archdale drew a pencil from his breast pocket and used it to indicate a spot on the map. 'We reckon he parked here, sir and then walked along this track...' The pencil hovered above a dotted line, then followed it for a quarter of an inch: 'And then cut across to the tower foundations. We found broken twigs and trampled greenery along the way.' Again, the pencil traced a short course above the map, coming to rest just south of the ruins of the mansion. Ashley decided to release Stephen's information; had the inspector been with them, he would have kept it to himself.

'I was told this afternoon that Peachey couldn't drive. I don't know if that's correct but, if it is, it's useful information – had you heard?'

Archdale appeared surprised and shook his head; Dr Holbrooke looked sheepish.

'I didn't think to mention that to the inspector, Sergeant Archdale – I was so bewildered at the time – but it's quite true. Or, at least, it's true for all practical purposes. Peachey probably still held a licence but he got rid of his car shortly after he moved into the hospital. To be precise, he accidentally drove it into the garden wall and wrote it off. As far as I know, he hasn't driven since. I'm sorry – if I'd realised that the information was important, I'd have passed it on when the inspector was talking about Douglas's movements.'

171

The police sergeant seemed amused rather than annoyed.

'Oh dear, sir, that's just scuppered the inspector's working hypothesis. We found the driving licence, you see, so he imagined that Peachey had driven himself there. Quite what he thought happened to the car afterwards, goodness only knows. Presumably, Mr Ashley, you've had a chance to think of something a bit better.'

Ashley had, but wanted a bit more privacy before he revealed it. He caught Green's eye and glanced sideways towards the door and then in the other direction at the master. Years of wriggling himself out of the presence of officers and senior NCOs had taught Green the art of quick thinking.

'Actually, sir, if you're going to have a long chat, I ought to be going – Sister Barnfield will be expecting me. You couldn't point me in the right direction, could you, Dr Holbrooke? I was told there was a connecting door between the hospital and the medical centre, but I don't know where it is.'

Dr Holbrooke gave a startled look on hearing his name, then acquiesced: 'Of course. In fact, if you'll excuse me, gentlemen, I'll make my own departure as well. My sermon, you understand...'

Ashley and Sergeant Archdale proved very understanding. Left to themselves, they sank into a pair of armchairs.

'May as well be comfortable, sir – in fact, while I was searching, I noticed that Peachey had a very well stocked drinks cupboard. I'm off duty as soon as I've finished here, so I don't mind stretching a point if you don't.'

Ashley certainly didn't mind; Archdale rose again, used a handkerchief to open a cupboard door and extracted an unopened bottle of whisky and two crystal tumblers. He held the latter up to the light, to make sure that no possible evidence was about to be obliterated: they were spotless. He poured generous measures.

'I'd take one to poor Telfer, only those old bags over the way would report it first thing in the morning.' Archdale handed a glass to Ashley, raised his own by way of drinking

Ashley's health, then lowered himself back into his seat. 'So, come on then, sir – what's your theory? Purely off the record, of course.'

'Thanks for that assurance, Sergeant: if my theory's flawed, I wouldn't want your inspector to be led astray by it – and if it's correct, I don't want him to take the credit.'

Archdale was sympathetic: 'I'm sorry he cold-shouldered you this afternoon, sir – it's the nature of the beast, I'm afraid. Mercifully, he stays behind his desk whenever possible.'

'Well let's do our best to *make* it possible over the next few days, then. Can I just ask a few questions first, Sergeant Archdale? There are one or two points on which you'll be more up to date than I am. In the first place, I assume you only found one route into that glade?'

'That's right, sir. We knew where you'd got in with your horses, of course – there was no mistaking that – and your lance bombardier guided us in through by the same access point, as you'll remember. Apart from that, we only found one way that looked as though it had been used.'

'That's good – two would have been trickier. Second question: a spade and/or a murder weapon – any sign of either? At a guess, I'd say it's possible that the two articles could be one and the same thing – that he bashed Peachey several times over the head with the flat of the spade and then used it to bury him.'

'It's a good guess, sir, and I wouldn't be at all surprised if it was correct, but we didn't find anything – which is stupid, if you ask me. The killer would have been more sensible just to wipe down the spade and chuck it into some thick bushes. Now, he's got to go to the trouble of disposing of it properly – not to mention the danger of leaving matching soil samples in the boot of his car. It could be his big mistake.'

Ashley nodded. 'It might very well be, Sergeant. Perhaps he got a bit of his own blood on it somehow and was forced to take it with him? And I suppose if he had a bin liner in the car, the soil needn't be a problem.'

The two detectives agreed that a good supply of sturdy bin liners was a vital part of any successful modern murder. If Crippen had used a few, the sergeant remarked, he'd probably have got away with it. 'Anyway, sir, your theory?'

'Well Sergeant, the simplest explanation of the facts, as we know them at present, is not that Peachey arranged to meet his killer there, but that they arrived together. Peachey worked out the route on his map and did the navigating, but he couldn't drive, and so got someone to take him there. That person then killed him, for reasons which we don't yet fully understand, hurriedly buried the body and made a rough attempt to conceal the grave, before returning to the car and driving off. Any other theory seems full of difficulties – we have to imagine more people, or miraculously disappearing cars, for a start.'

Archdale aided his concentration by wetting his index finger and passing it over the rim of his empty tumbler. A soft but penetrating note sounded for a few seconds. When the echo had died away, he said: 'Now you might arrange a rendezvous in a strange place, but there's not much sense in travelling there together. Which means that they went there with a specific purpose in mind, sir, doesn't it?'

Ashley's tumbler still had some whisky in it: it produced a slightly higher note. Before replying, he drained the glass.

'To be accurate, Sergeant, Peachey went there with a specific purpose – but his killer went there with *two*.'

CHAPTER TWENTY-ONE

NOCTURNE

Half past ten on Saturday evening. Dr Holbrooke has given up on his sermon and is rummaging through the published works of Dr Cleverley-Ford for something suitable to pass off as his own. Constable Telfer, relieved at last from his watch, stretches out in front of the television in his Wincanton flat, a can of beer in his hand. He has not bothered to change out of his uniform and his shirt and tunic, unbuttoned and casually open, are everything Amelia Clifford could have asked for.

In London, four soldiers noisily debate the wisdom of another round of drinks. In front of them, the skeletons of half a dozen enormous pizzas testify to huge appetites and the generosity of Ashley's expenses account. Vernon and Sorrell have arranged some of the crusts to look like the fossilized remains of an unspecified but primitive mammal; one whose extinction was, as Tom Two points out, inevitable.

Tom One's spine makes the final decision for them; as he turns to attract the attention of a waitress, another flame of pain sears his spine. The bill is settled and Tom, hobbling, is assisted to a taxi by his comrades. He climbs gingerly into the front passenger seat and the remaining three bundle into the back.

In the cottage adjoining his stables, ex-Sergeant Jones relaxes in his sitting room with cheap whisky and the latest issue of *Horse and Hound*. Ashley would be disappointed with the retired soldier's accommodation: the curtains and rugs, which were bought with the house, are of good quality and hard-wearing; the log fire is serviced by means of clandestine visits to Forestry Commission land; the military prints on the walls are well-framed and mounted and the furniture, old without yet being antique, is solid and respectable. Jones looks up from his magazine and surveys his territory with satisfaction; it had been a good day's work, that time he had parked the horsebox behind the Officers' Mess and visited some little-used upstairs rooms.

Back at Bruton, Ashley has finally enjoyed that long-postponed bath and sits robed and relaxed on his bed, surrounded by his notes and rough jottings. It has been a busy evening; in turns, entertaining, emotional and frustrating. Too much has happened for Ashley to reflect on all of it, so he sips his drink – more expensive than Sergeant Jones' – and allows his mind to wander where it will.

James.

How could he have behaved so thoughtlessly to this vulnerable boy?

He has, at least, redeemed himself by subsequent care and kindness, but the memory of a stupid moment of insensitivity haunts him.

Leaving Peachey's flat with Sergeant Archdale, he had been in a good mood. Their breach of regulations had acted as a bond between the two; they had taken another glass each and indulged in anecdotes and reminiscences. Outside, they had paused to chat with Constable Telfer, who had given an amusing account of the matrons' bridge-party-cum-spy-ring. And then James had appeared.

Better dressed than yesterday, he had arrived through the Town Gate of the hospital and headed round the path towards them. He had paused at the sight of a uniformed policeman and then glanced rapidly from Telfer to Ashley, from Ashley to Archdale and then back to Ashley. Then he had continued walking, but more slowly, until he was with them.

'He really has disappeared, sir, hasn't he? It's serious, isn't it?'

Had James been elderly, or female, Ashley would have made him sit – would have prepared him in some way for the dreadful reply. Instead, unthinkingly, he had simply said: 'We found his body this afternoon, James.'

The colour had disappeared from James' face in an instant; again, his eyes shot backwards and forwards between Ashley and the two policemen. And then he began to sway.

Ashley and Telfer caught him in time. He did not actually faint, but clung on to them; without energy or will of his own, he had to rely on them for guidance and stability. They had led him to the bench where, only twenty-four hours previously, he and Ashley had passed such a pleasant hour; now, Ashley cursed himself for his callous behaviour. Archdale had rushed to fetch a drink from Peachey's flat – brandy, not whisky, and who cared about the fingerprints or regulations this time? After a short while, James had started the process of recovery.

'I'm sorry, Mr Ashley – that was really stupid of me.'

'No, James – *I'm* sorry. It was all my fault.'

'Yesterday, sir, I just thought – well, that there was some mistake. I came along tonight, the same as usual, thinking everything would be all right. I've got the essay, even.'

It had been in his hand. Now crumpled and wet, the shapeless pages looked forlorn; ink had smudged where he had gripped most tightly. Pathetically, he had tried to smooth out the creases and succeeded only in tearing one page and spilling some brandy on another. The alcohol rushed through the natural capillaries of the paper, mixing with the ink; black letters faded to brown as blue fronds extended from the carefully shaped curves and strokes.

For a moment, Ashley had thought that James would cry, shedding tears of frustration and confusion. When the boy had managed to control himself, the detective had almost felt like weeping on his behalf. He had taken the essay from James' hand, folded it away and promised to make sense of it somehow. Then he had bidden farewell to the two policemen and walked James back to Old House, where Diana Clifford had given him food and another drink and promised to drive him home later.

The essay is lying on the bed now; dry, but still crumpled. Looking at it, Ashley revisits his embarrassment. He has had no time yet to read it; visiting Dr Holbrooke and Mary Compton had taken up the next hour.

And then he had tracked down Robert Simpson.

* * * * *

Enveloped in silk pyjamas and a quilted dressing gown, his feet cosy in embroidered slippers, Robert Simpson enjoys a final cream liqueur before retiring. His review of the day is smug and self-congratulatory. And why not? He has charmed Dr Holbrooke, who will doubtless be writing in the next few days to invite old Mrs Simpson to take up residence in the Fitzjames Hospital – that genteel lobster pot, whence there is no escape: at least, not in this world. His mother's future will be cheap and untroublesome; the sale of the house in Quaperlake Street will release more than enough capital to enable him to resume his art business and buy a few luxuries besides. More, the contents of the house will act as his stock for a few months. San Francisco and Berkeley might have wised up to his Victorian daubs, but there are other places...

Following the thought through, he wanders over to a set of mahogany bookshelves and searches for an atlas, eventually finding a leather-bound volume that had belonged to his grandfather. It was printed in the early nineteen-hundreds, so the political map of Europe is surprisingly up to date.

Turning to North America, Simpson traces a pudgy finger down the west coast. Washington and Oregon are unknown territory: there will be money in Seattle, but will there be the unquestioning enthusiasm for art which is so vital to his trade? The town names of Oregon sound unpromising. A carefully tended nail comes to rest on California; too bad that San Francisco is a no-go area for a while. But Santa Rosa? Santa Barbara? All the other Sans and Santas? Religious art nearly always goes down well in towns with Catholic names.

But, in the short term, who needed to go abroad to flog off second-rate art? Simpson replaces the atlas and tops up the thick brown fluid in his glass. Then he sits back and contemplates, with deep satisfaction, his conversation with George Ashley.

It was one of those happy coincidences which occasionally bring riches with them. Simpson had been sitting in a quiet corner of the Blue Ball Inn. Over the last month or two, he had adopted the comfortable window seat as his own and the attractive girl behind the bar was usually ready at about half past six to mix his gin and Dubonnet without being asked. On the days when his mother's pension was paid into the bank, he would usually buy one for her as well – it brought a little sophistication into her life, and a little flirtation into his. Today was not a pension day, but he was celebrating his visit to the Fitzjames Hospital, so an extra gin and Dubonnet it was.

Ashley had entered the bar, looked around and then given a smile of recognition.

'It's Robert Simpson, isn't it? I think Joshua Robbins once introduced us when I was buying a picture at his gallery.'

For the life of him, Simpson couldn't place Ashley, but anyone who called Robbins' dirty little shop a gallery and then actually bought a picture from it was welcome company. He had stood and extended a hand.

'Of course – I thought you looked familiar as you entered the bar. Eighteenth-century English School, wasn't it?' Eighteenth-century English was one of Robbins' specialities: he had a very good man turning them out to order.

'That's right – how very clever of you to remember.'

After that, a third gin and Dubonnet was called for. Ashley had tried to order a pint instead, but Simpson knew when a potential customer ought to be buttered up with something classy.

They had got on, Simpson decided, like a house on fire. And after Ashley had left, Simpson had gone for a little walk.

∗   ∗   ∗   ∗   ∗

'We do get on well, don't we? And you must call me Christine: "Sister" is so formal.'

'Thanks, Sis – er, Christine. And you can call me "Lance", if you like…'

Sister Barnfield is looking blurred around the edges, which is probably no bad thing. Indeed, if Lance Bombardier Green tries to focus on the end of his nose, she looks almost slender: on the other hand, there are two of her, which is not so good. Green tries to eliminate one by closing his left eye, but the illusion terminates abruptly and a single nurse, larger than ever, re-organises herself in front of him.

It was the first glass of Calvados that had undone him. Unused to spirits, he had examined the bottle as Sister Barnfield lit candles and arranged doilies on the table.

'Try some, Lance Bombardier Green – it's awfully good.'

So he had poured himself a full wine glass, taken a huge gulp, and felt his oesophagus burst into flames. A few splutters later, working on the sound principle that the second glass of anything is never as bad as the first, he had poured another. By the end of *that*, it had been quite tricky removing his belt and jacket, and Sister Barnfield had had to help him. She had slipped his braces over his shoulders at the same time, though he had retained his spurs, arguing that his ankles would feel chilly without them.

But it has been a fine meal and the sister has been warbling out information all evening, so his mission is accomplished – if only he can remember everything when he gets back.

They retire to a necessarily sturdy sofa. As the squashy fabric envelops him and the room appears alternately to leer and retreat, Green reflects that there are worse ways of spending an evening – perhaps a night, even. After all, no one need ever know…

A hand, pink and soft, rests on a khaki knee: 'And now, Lance, I've got some really good news. Guess what?'

180

Different possibilities stagger through Green's mind. Tickets for two on a world cruise? Laughing gas and a leather play suit? The cavalry, riding over the hill to rescue him? No, come to think of it, that would be out of the frying pan and into the fire... He beams blearily by way of reply.

The nurse's continuation almost sobers him up.

'Peter Bulmer has left me all his money. A quarter of a million pounds.'

The telephone rings.

*   *   *   *   *

Community Support Officer Sharon Flavell is feeling cross, tired and unappreciated. The day before yesterday, her suggestion that the death of Peter Bulmer was just a tragic accident had been received with gratitude by Dr Holbrooke and with full approval by the inspector to whom she had submitted her report. Now, that report is worthless, her theory as shattered as the skulls of the two victims, and she has been summoned without ceremony to stand watch over the apartments of the dead men. Questions concerning her relief have been answered in a vague and non-committal manner and successive attempts to ring the desk at Wincanton Police Station have been met with a pre-recorded message.

Sharon resolves to take revenge by finding objections to any new version of events; assuming, that is, that anyone chooses to confide in her. In the meantime, she has been brusque with the matrons and taken a small satisfaction in sending them scuttling back to their flats, under the clear impression that any infringement of the curfew will involve handcuffs and a night behind bars. She had tried a similar approach with Mary Compton, who infuriated her by remaining calm and courteous and then bringing her a thermos flask and some cake. It had to be admitted that they were welcome, but the perceived loss of dignity and authority rankled.

Still, the conversation with that art dealer had been enjoyable – what was his name? Robert Simpson, that was it – taking a short cut through the hospital on his way home. He had chatted cheerfully, shared her drink and then pulled out a hip flask: Sharon had refused his offer, of course; but, in the end, he had been very persuasive and the small nip of gin and Dubonnet had warmed her whole body. She had, Sharon felt, shown just the right amount of reluctance before accepting his invitation to a drink next time she was off duty.

The suavity of Simpson is in stark contrast to the half-dressed soldier who now staggers across the quadrangle. His tunic is unbuttoned, his cap is askew and his braces hang around his legs like baby reins.

'E'ening Mish.' Lance Bombardier Green attempts a casual salute by way of showing good manners and pokes himself in the eye. He zigzags his way to the school gate and an offstage yelp and scuffle testify to the difficulty of negotiating the far side of the bridge when wearing spurs.

Soldiers, Sharon reflects, are just like policemen: sexist, brainless and usually drunk. Freemasons too, probably.

CHAPTER TWENTY-TWO

ARBELLA AGAIN

Lance Bombardier Green restored himself to near-sobriety with an enormous mug of tea, even more rusty and electric looking than usual. He guarded against a hangover by swallowing the painkillers that Sister Barnfield had given him the previous morning. They might or might not work: one pill was very much like another, as far as Green was concerned.

'Thanks for your call, sir – I was all set to board the hovercraft when you rang. In fact,' his expression managed to combine shame and amusement in equal measure, 'it was just a question of whether we were going to have a short trip to the Isle of Wight, or sail all the way to France, if you see what I mean, sir.'

Ashley did see what he meant, and tried very hard not to think about it.

They sat in Ashley's room, the detective on his bed and the soldier disarrayed in the chair, his legs hooked over one of the arms and his boots dangling in mid-air. Every so often, he attempted to click his spurs together but they steadfastly refused to meet and a dull leathery thud was all he could manage.

Ashley consulted his notes.

'So, as well as inheriting the bulk of Peter Bulmer's estate, the good sister has no satisfactory alibi for any of the times when Douglas Peachey might usefully have been done away with?'

'That's right, sir – she says she was just cooking or watching television in the medical centre. It's pretty lonely for her in the holidays. But – like you said, sir – she couldn't have done away with old Peachey by herself, could she? And why would she want to?'

Ashley shrugged and topped up his whisky. 'Why indeed? Perhaps, in his devious way, Peachey had found out that she was going to inherit Bulmer's money and had tried to blackmail her somehow.'

'You mean, he worked out that she could have killed Bulmer, sir?' Green yawned, stretching his body horizontally across the chair; Sister Barnfield's pills were beginning to take effect.

'Well, that wouldn't take too much working out, Lance Bombardier – but Peachey would probably have been more subtle and manipulative than that. He'd have hinted at scandal rather than murder, I should think – which would avoid any burden of proof. Sister Barnfield, guilty or not of killing Bulmer, realises she is in for a lot of trouble from Peachey and decides to get him off the scene as quickly as possible.'

But how? Had Sister Barnfield dialed Directory Enquiries and asked for the number of a good assassin? Had she once extracted a thorn from a gangster's paw, and been promised a return of the favour any time she needed it? As Ashley flitted from one entertaining and ridiculous theory to another, Green made a final, soporific, observation.

'And I don't see how that picture fits into anything, sir, if it's just a question of Sister Barnfield and a load of money.'

This was all too true, Ashley reflected. There was nothing to suggest that the person who inherited the money had any interest in the picture; on the other hand, the two people who were most likely to want the portrait were already dead. What about Robert Simpson? He would happily lay his hands on both the money and the portrait if he could, but had he been given any real opportunity?

'At least, Lance Bombardier, we can't complain that we have nothing to go on – since our conference last night, we've gained another body, an extra suspect or two, and some intriguing motives. At this rate, half Bruton will have been wiped out by the middle of next week and anybody left alive will be implicated.'

By way of reply, the soldier snored loudly, his head having tilted back as he fell asleep. Ashley rose from his bed, crossed over to the sprawling body and attempted to wake it; but the combination of Sister Barnfield's pills and too much Calvados was a powerful one. Accepting defeat, Ashley wedged a pillow between Green's head and the corner of the chair, then draped a spare blanket over the whole, ungainly ensemble. The lance bombardier's head stuck out at one end and his boots at the other: a picture which remained with Ashley after he had climbed into bed and turned out the light. In a disturbing dream, a magician entered the room and sawed Green in half but then failed to reassemble him. The two pieces of the soldier's bisected body slid down into the depths of the chair; the magician rearranged the blanket, then vanished, leaving a body which gave the appearance of being about four feet tall.

Then the body turned into Douglas Peachey.

* * * * *

Several hours later, Ashley was woken by another loud snore. This time, it came from the floor rather than the chair; as the detective's eyes became accustomed to the gloom, he made out a large, woolly lump on the bedside rug, rising and falling in time with a series of grunts. In a minute or two more, his pupils now widened to their fullest extent, he noticed various items of uniform randomly scattered over the floorboards, like snakes and ladders in a children's game. Throw a six, he thought irrelevantly, and you climb up the braces to the next level – but a five will have you sliding all the way down a boot and back to the beginning.

It didn't take much detecting effort to realize that Green, racked with cramp, had woken and transferred himself to a less uncomfortable position. In the process, he had discarded his

185

uniform, releasing the scents of the day into the atmosphere of the bedroom, which now smelt of Sister Barnfield's kitchen, Sergeant Jones' stable and Green's own feet and armpits. On the bedside table, a bowl of Diana Clifford's *pot pourri* was overpowered, inadequate to the struggle; Ashley briefly wondered whether the limp rose petals and pine cones could be revived with the remains of his whisky, and then decided that the simpler option of burying his head under the sheets would probably be more effective. As he wriggled down, the bed creaked and the military wheezing ceased abruptly.

'Are you awake, sir?' Green's idea of a stage whisper easily penetrated the counterpane. Ashley considered a direct denial, then gave a muffled affirmative and resurfaced.

'Yes, Lance Bombardier, I'm awake. Any idea what time it is?'

'A bit after six o'clock, I reckon, sir. Shall I make some tea?'

'Not just yet. Maybe in a year or so.'

'Point taken, sir. Thanks for the pillow and blanket by the way – they made a big difference. When I woke up, I didn't fancy trying to find my way round the boarding house in the dark, so I just dossed down here – I hope you don't mind?'

'Not at all, Lance Bombardier – I like my bedrooms to smell of a mixture of Calvados and codpiece.'

'Sorry, sir.' Like all Green's apologies, this one betrayed no hint of remorse. 'If it's any consolation, sir, I reckon the pong is even worse down here.'

Ashley contemplated this possibility from the alpine purity of his mattress. A brief, satisfying vision of Green choking in a cloud of methane and sulphur cheered him up enormously. He sat up and found his watch on the bedside table. Green's estimate of the time had been reasonably accurate; a thin corona of light around the curtains further testified to the coming day.

'You're welcome to make use of my shower if you want to, Lance Bombardier. There are plenty of clean towels in there and you can borrow my dressing gown.'

'All right, sir – I get the hint.' Green rose from his blanket, revealing a lean, taut physique and a pair of boxer shorts in regimental colours. On his way to the bathroom, he gathered up his scattered clothes and boots and deposited them outside the bedroom door: 'There, sir, you'd never know I'd been here, would you?'

Green's shower involved bawdy songs, a good deal of splashing and one high-pitched squeal when the water suddenly turned cold. Fifteen minutes later, smelling of lavender and enveloped in Ashley's dressing gown, he was back in the armchair, sniffing himself thoughtfully.

'I'm not sure I didn't prefer my original smell, sir.'

'There we part company, Lance Bombardier – though I have to admit that Mrs Clifford's guest soap is rather overpowering. The effect wears off fairly quickly, though.'

'That's good, sir – if I went back to the barracks smelling like this, the lads would suggest I got a transfer to the Household Cavalry.'

Ashley suggested that the Life Guards would welcome Green with open arms and received a snort by way of reply.

'Open legs, more like, sir. Anyway – are you ready for that tea now?'

Ashley was; but before he could reply, Amelia Clifford knocked on the door and entered. Apparently psychic, she carried a tray with a teapot and two mugs of tea. A turquoise silk dressing gown rustled as the mugs were delivered to their destinations.

'Mummy heard your voices and said you'd probably like some tea,' Amelia explained, 'and Stephen's downstairs – he needs to see Lance Bombardier Green. Shall I send him up?'

Ashley wondered whether he had accidentally bedded down in the waiting room of a railway station. In a few moments, Stephen, nursing his own mug, was squatting comfortably on Green's discarded pillow and blanket; Amelia, who saw no reason to miss out on the fun, placed herself on the arm of the lance bombardier's chair, displaying an ankle

187

bracelet at one end and a cleavage to challenge the longest plumb line at the other. All this so early in the morning, Ashley felt, was a bit much for the system. He sipped his tea defensively.

Stephen, it seemed, was on his way to the stable once more – hence the disgustingly early hour. Inspired by the standards set by the army, he wore his best riding kit: a pair of military breeches, from the back of Sergeant Jones' horsebox, was combined with a check shirt and a crew neck sweater. An elderly but serviceable pair of leather riding boots, which had belonged to his grandfather, completed the outfit. Green nodded a grudging approval: 'Not bad for a civvy.'

Stephen beamed. 'Thanks, Lance – Mr Jones said he'd pinch some more stuff in my size the next time he goes to a reunion.'

'He'll have a job – the quartermaster's wised up to him now. He locks the stores on Old Boy days. Bolts them too, in case Jonesy's managed to sneak his own key. Don't worry though – when you've joined up they'll issue you with all the kit you could ever want, plus a fair bit you'd rather not have.'

Ashley knew all too well that soldiers and recruits could bang on endlessly about uniforms and equipment. He decided to intervene before the conversation got out of hand; otherwise, he might never get his bedroom to himself.

'Presumably, Stephen, you called with a specific reason?'

Reluctantly, Stephen extracted himself from a fantasy involving combat jackets, boots and ceremonial tunics. 'That's right, sir – though it's a really boring one. I left some holiday work in my room by accident and I came to collect it on my way to the stable – there was a light on in Mrs Clifford's kitchen, so I knew someone would be up. But it's my room that Lance Bombardier Green is using, so Mrs Clifford says I'm not to go in there without permission.'

'No problem.' Green swallowed half a mug of tea in a single gulp and stood up. 'I was heading down there myself in a second. Come on – let's go.'

Followed by Amelia Clifford, the two left the room, leaving Ashley to contemplate the bliss of solitude. He debated the merits of a leisurely soak in the tub, a bracing shower or another hour's sleep, finally concluding that the gold and silver medals went to the snooze and the bath respectively. After that, a descent to a plateful of eggs and bacon would be in order.

He snuggled down into the welcoming sheets and was drifting pleasantly into a sensual oblivion when there was another knock on the door and Stephen's round head intruded itself into the room.

'Sorry to disturb you again, Mr Ashley, but Lance Bombardier Green thinks you ought to come down as well.'

The head disappeared without further explanation. Swearing to himself, Ashley threw back the blankets and forced himself out of bed. A brief search for his dressing gown was followed by the annoying remembrance that he had lent it to Green, who had obviously filched his slippers at the same time. Barefoot and with his hacking jacket draped over his pyjamas, Ashley trod gingerly through the housemaster's private quarters and into the boys' side of the house.

What he saw in Green's room made him swear again – loudly this time.

Leering down from the wall and smiling, as it seemed, at the confusion she had caused, was Arbella Fitzjames.

CHAPTER TWENTY-THREE

ARBELLA UNFRAMED

'Bloody hell!'

'I thought you'd say something like that, sir.' Green looked from Arbella to Ashley and then back to the portrait. 'It is the one you've been looking for, isn't it?'

Ashley reminded himself that Green was now seeing the picture for the first time. 'It's her all right, Lance Bombardier. What on earth is she doing here?'

There was no answer to be given; Green and Stephen gave an impression of hopeful contestants in a synchronized shrugging competition. Ashley revised his question: 'All right, that was a stupid one to ask. Just tell me how you found her.' He looked at Stephen; 'I assume you had no idea she was here?'

'None, sir.' Stephen's confusion was genuine. 'We all came in here a few minutes ago, and while I was getting my books together, Lance Bombardier Green poked fun at my posters.'

'I thought they had an unnatural air of innocence about them, sir,' contributed Green, indicating the pictures of aeroplanes and sports cars which covered the rest of the walls: 'Not a naked woman in sight.'

Stephen resumed his narrative: 'So I told him, sir, that they were only there in case my mother visited the room on Corpus day and that the real posters were underneath. I took one down to prove it – and there was the picture. Almost as dirty as the one I was expecting to see, actually.'

It was a fair comment: Mary Compton's great-grandmother had drawn her Plimsoll line of purity somewhere between the breasts and the shoulders before slashing Arbella down to size;

nonetheless, puckering and lascivious, the courtesan still had the power to excite. Disappointingly, the unframed canvas revealed no more of the clumsy inscription than Ashley had noticed when he first saw it. It was, he decided, another detecting dead end.

'She must have been one hell of a slapper, sir,' Green, broke into his thoughts, cheerfully and anachronistically. 'Do we take her back to Mrs Compton?'

Ashley shook his head. 'Not yet, Lance Bombardier – the police will want to have a look at the picture where it is and then they'll probably take it away and examine it for prints. We can wander over and tell her that it's been found, though, which will please her.'

'But not you, Mr Ashley?' Amelia's suggestion was a perceptive one. Ashley sat himself on a hard chair and examined the picture in silence. Following his example, the others arranged themselves around the room and stared in the direction of Arbella. After a while, Ashley summarised his thoughts.

'No – I suppose I'm not very pleased. It's good to have the picture back, of course, but this isn't at all where I'd expected to find it. I was hoping it would turn up on the London market. I've got a colleague in the business looking out for it, so we might well have been led to the murderer that way.'

'And as it is, we've just been led up another garden path, sir, is that right?'

'That's entirely correct, Lance Bombardier – up the garden path, through the vegetable patch and right into the compost heap.'

*   *   *   *   *

The large mound of manure that the Toms are contemplating has the fertilization power of several hundred compost heaps. Teetering on top of it, Gunners Vernon and Sorrell pitchfork the morning's yield of straw and dung into position: a process which involves equal amounts of sweat and swearing. The Toms, off duty and in scruffy civilian clothes, lean against a redundant wheelbarrow, offering unwanted advice and dodging the occasional faecal missile. They are waiting for Vernon and Sorrell to finish their task so that the four of them can breakfast together.

'And I hope they remember to wash their hands first,' Tom Two adopts a sanctimonious tone. 'Otherwise, the chef's bubble and squeak is going to acquire a new flavour.'

'Well that could only be an improvement. Anyway, stick enough brown sauce on and nobody would be able to tell.' The thought of food turns an ignition key in Tom One's stomach: 'Are they nearly finished, do you think? I'm starving.'

'Me too. Here comes Shifty Scott with another barrow load – let's ask him.'

Gunner Scott brings the glad news that this is, in fact, the final instalment. Instead of emptying the barrow and wheeling it back into the stable he grabs a third pitchfork and sends projectiles of manure to the top of the heap, where Vernon and Sorrell prod and stamp them into position. When the pile has taken on the orderly shape of a Babylonian ziggurat, they abandon their pitchforks gratefully and leap to the ground.

'And the next time the Troop's horses decide to stage an inter-section sponsored shitting competition, they can do it when I'm on leave,' Sorrell observes, bitterly; there is general agreement that the horses have surpassed themselves during the night and that equine constipation has much to recommend it.

A few minutes and a good deal of soap later, four capacious mouths are being steadily filled with eggs, bacon and limitless rounds of toast. Every so often, the necessity of breathing asserts itself and disjointed, shrapnel-like fragments of conversation ricochet across the table. Finally, when the pile of toast has been reduced to a few cold and crusty fragments, the soldiers top up their mugs and get down to more extended talking.

'So, One, are you doing any more detecting stuff today?'

'Not that I know of – I think mission's accomplished at our end.'

'It was good, though, wasn't it?' Tom Two has enjoyed his scholarly tasks. 'It's a shame it's over, really.'

Vernon and Sorrell agree: the pleasure of free wine and pizza is not one that dulls with repetition.

'Any plans for the day, then?' Sorrell asks this with the resigned voice of one whose time will be spent feeding, grooming and sweeping. The Toms exchange glances, each hoping that the other will have a bright idea. Nothing suggests itself, however, beyond the simple task of driving an illegal nail into the wall of their room and hanging their picture – which will take all of five minutes. Their comrades have yet to see the military watercolour, which is still in its protective covering, and so, since they have half an hour before they need to be back in the stables, the four clear their table and head in the direction of the accommodation block.

'Is it a good picture?' asks Vernon, as they climb the stairs to the third floor.

'Probably not by your standards, Keith – there are no nude women or motorbikes in it.'

'Dull – any thugs with dark glasses and machine guns?'

'Sorry, no. But there's an awfully good horse and three soldiers.'

Sorrell sniffs. 'We can see those for free any day, just by looking out of the window. I bet checkout girls don't have pictures of tills on the wall.'

Tom Two remarks, snobbishly, that he is pleased to be ignorant on this matter: 'Besides, if a checkout girl wants to look at a picture, she probably has to put it on the ceiling.'

'It would fall on her.'

'Not if she held it in place with her feet.'

They reach the Toms' room before the banter can descend further and Tom One ceremonially unwraps the picture. Admiration for the accuracy of the artwork, pride in their unit and – somehow – a good deal of personal vanity, take the place of previous objections.

'Wow!' Sorrell clarifies his exclamation by stating that it is the best picture he has ever seen.

'And just how many pictures *have* you seen, Sorrell?' enquires Tom Two suspiciously.

'About three...'

*   *   *   *   *

'Well, sir, I don't know much about art...' Constable Telfer went on to complete the sentence in the usual way.

Stephen's room was even more crowded than Ashley's had been earlier. Two policemen, Colin and Diana Clifford and the earlier four occupants were all squeezed in, making room for themselves as best they could. Colin and Green leaned against a desk; Amelia occupied the bedside table and her mother sat on the chair formerly occupied by Ashley. Stephen, who seemed happiest in lowly positions, squatted on the floor once more, making cheerful remarks to any kneecap that would listen.

It was about half past eight; Archdale and Telfer had just arrived, the sergeant making the wry observation that any traces the thief might have left behind would have been nicely obliterated in the last hour or so. Ashley took the collective guilt upon himself: 'Apologies, Sergeant Archdale, I should have known better – it was very early in the morning.'

'As I can see, sir.' Archdale, amused rather than cross, observed the selection of dressing gowns, pyjamas and other nocturnal garments around him. What with all the speculating and theorising, telephoning the police and ringing Sergeant Jones to tell him that Stephen would be late, nobody had thought about getting changed. Ashley still had his hacking jacket draped around his shoulders; he had managed to recover his slippers from Green, who had pulled on a pair of combat socks by way of replacement.

194

Archdale made two sensible suggestions. The first was that the criminal was unlikely to have left any important clues behind him; he ('or she,' the sergeant added, carefully) had been very thorough in Mary Compton's flat, so the same situation was likely here. His second was that he should see each of them individually in Colin Clifford's study. If he started with Stephen, who was already dressed, the others could use the time to smarten themselves up…

'Very tactful, I must say,' said Green petulantly, when he and Ashley were back in the detective's bedroom. The whole party had been ejected from Stephen's room and Green, homeless again, was dressing himself in front of the wardrobe mirror while Ashley was in the bath. Conversation was yelled through the open door.

'Well, naturally, Lance Bombardier, a soldier of Prince Albert's Troop is smart enough for anyone at any hour of the day or night. We lower life forms, however, need a bit of cosmetic assistance from time to time.' Ashley applied the assistance to an outstretched leg and lathered himself. A powerful lavender aroma wound its way towards Green.

'Be thorough, sir – the police might want to do a full body search.'

'Piss off, Lance Bombardier.'

'Only joking, sir. Seriously, though, what sort of things do you think they'll want to know?'

Ashley soaped between his toes, marshalling his thoughts.

'They'll want to know how the picture was brought in for a start. There are plenty of entrances to Old House – official or otherwise – and if they can find out which one was used, it might tell them something about our suspect. Sister Barnfield, for example, couldn't have climbed through the pantry window like you did the other day.'

'Not without taking the window frame with her at any rate, sir.'

'Precisely. On the other hand, she is probably aware that the Cliffords rarely bother to lock their back door. She might even know the codes to the combination locks on the boys' entrances, in case of a medical emergency.'

'And Stephen's room is just around the corner from one of them, in case you weren't aware of it, sir.'

'I wasn't – thank you for pointing it out. If you've finished with my dressing gown, by the way, I'm almost ready for it.'

'Right you are, sir.' Green backed towards the bathroom and handed the robe around the door. 'You'll find I've kept it nice and warm for you…'

By the time Ashley had finished shaving, Green was ready to depart for his interview. He pulled on a respectable civilian jacket, which had been borrowed from Bombardier Burdett – other items of his luggage having been similarly scrounged from his fellow junior NCOs. Clothes trafficking among the men of Prince Albert's Troop was a well-established custom: so far, as Green proudly observed, the jacket had played a minor role in the seduction of at least five girls by three different soldiers. Ashley climbed into a lightweight tweed suit, more worn but less experienced than Green's outfit; in another few minutes, it was his turn to see Sergeant Archdale. Green offered Stephen a lift to the stable; the Cliffords were preparing Sunday luncheon and Constable Telfer was exploring the perimeter of Old House, examining the various entrances and exits.

'And he's got his work cut out, Mr Ashley,' the sergeant noted with amusement. 'The boys have been playing Escape from Colditz down every drainpipe and fire stair for years. Young Telfer got very excited at a set of footprints on the pantry window, but your lance bombardier says that was him.'

'Yes – sorry about that, Sergeant. If he'd tried the kitchen door first, he'd have found the Cliffords had forgotten to lock it. Colin can be quite absent-minded sometimes.'

'Though not last night, fortunately.' Archdale was pleased to be able to eliminate one source of access. 'Anyway, Mr Ashley, what's your take on the situation? Our thief realised the picture was becoming way too hot and got rid of it pronto?'

Ashley nodded. 'It's the obvious solution, Sergeant. I can't say I blame him – or her.' He echoed the carefully inclusive language that the policeman had used earlier, 'But it's annoying for us, of course.'

Archdale weighed up the pros and cons of the situation. 'I grant you, Mr Ashley, that we'd both rather the thief had hung onto it for a while, but I'd prefer to find it this way than have it dumped in a dustbin – at least it hasn't been damaged, apart from the holes for the drawing pins. Then there's the consideration that the inspector is seriously pissed off, which is never a bad thing.' He smiled widely: disturbing the inspector's Sunday morning lie-in with the news that his latest theory was in tatters had been a joyful experience.

'I hope that doesn't mean he's on his way over, Sergeant?'

Archdale shook his head: 'Don't worry, sir – he's sulking back at Yeovil. I'll have to call him if anything important turns up; otherwise he's left me and Telfer to get on with things.'

This, they both agreed, was very satisfactory. They chatted about art and art thieves for a while; Ashley gave Archdale the details of the Toms' research in London and the sergeant confirmed the contents of Peter Bulmer's will, which had been forwarded to the police by the dead man's solicitor. Finally, the sergeant glanced at his watch.

'And at a guess, sir, it'll be about chucking out time at the Fitzjames Chapel. What do you say to wandering over and giving Mrs Compton the good news?'

It sounded a good idea to Ashley. They left Old House by one of the boys' doors, where they found Telfer peering at the combination lock.

Hello, Sarge, hello Mr Ashley – it's just like the lad said. Pretty much anyone with any brains could have worked out the code – have a look.'

Beneath the round handle of the door, five numbered buttons provided an apparently inexhaustible series of possible combinations to any would-be intruder. The problem was, as Telfer pointed out, that the odd numbered buttons were quite worn down, while the even ones were untouched. They even had their original coating of black paint on them, whereas the others were shining metallically. This made life significantly easier for the code-breaker.

'Have a go, sir, and you'll see what I mean.'

Ashley pressed the three worn buttons in various orders. At the third attempt, there was a clicking sound and he was able to turn the handle. It would be the work of only a few minutes to enter the boarding house, find the nearest room and conceal the portrait under a poster.

'Though for the life of me, I can't think why anybody would want to.' Archdale pulled the door shut again as he spoke.

Telfer suggested a plausible explanation for the picture's hiding place: 'Do you think it was some sort of joke, Sarge?'

The sergeant considered the possibility. 'Maybe – or perhaps it was thought to be a safe place for a few days. The school doesn't return until next Sunday, so our thief might have thought he was being rather clever. He – or she,' Archdale reverted to his former careful language, 'wasn't to know that the room he'd chosen was being occupied by a detective's assistant and that the boy who normally slept in it would return for his homework. And if that's the scenario, our criminal is in for a nasty surprise – which can only be a good thing.'

In the circumstances, they decided to leave Telfer on guard. He positioned himself authoritatively outside the door to Stephen's room and adopted an expression which Ashley had seen many times on the faces of the sentries at his nephew's barracks: it indicated determination and a total evacuation of the brains.

CHAPTER TWENTY-FOUR

A SNAP AMBUSH

The sounds of an organ voluntary, arthritic and haphazard, greet Ashley and the sergeant as they enter the quadrangle of the Fitzjames Hospital. At the door of his chapel, Dr Holbrooke is receiving congratulations on the unexpected excellence of his sermon with no visible signs of gratitude. Standing in clumps on the grass or arranged on benches, elderly and fragile inhabitants are exchanging news, comparing the latest aches and pains and enjoying the mid-morning sun.

Mary Compton has yet to emerge from the chapel. By way of alternative entertainment, Ashley observes Robert Simpson, unctuously attending to the needs of an ancient and bewildered female. It seems that old Mrs Simpson is staking her claim on a hospital apartment – or, rather, having it staked out on her behalf.

'Mr Ashley! What an unexpected pleasure!' Simpson abandons his mother and strides across the lawn, his outstretched hand twinkling with the jewellery appropriate to Sunday devotions. Ashley endures contact with the moist and fleshly palm, calculating that sweat and hand cream have been transferred to him in about equal quantities. He does his best to wipe it on his trouser leg as he introduces Simpson to Sergeant Archdale, transforming the policeman into an old university friend with an interest in art. Archdale blinks once or twice and then gets into character. His first line is inspired.

'That's right, Mr Simpson. Er – portraits mainly.'

Simpson nods knowingly. 'Very sensible, sir. There's many a good portrait picked up cheaply because nobody can identify the sitter. With a bit of detective work, you can put a name to it – and instantly you've got something of value. Very lucrative, that can be...'

Ashley's mind wanders briefly as he envisages Simpson scouring Californian telephone directories for good names to pin to pictures before selling them at inflated prices to credulous customers, hungry for ancestors. He brings himself sharply back to reality in response to an alarmed glance from Archdale: having assumed that Fuseli was a type of pasta, the policeman is getting out of his depth. Fortunately, Simpson is treating the error as a huge joke.

'Oh, very droll, sir – very droll indeed. And Constable, of course, started his career as a policeman...'

It is time to intervene, Ashley decides quickly.

'As a matter of fact, Mr Simpson, we were going to get in touch with you about a portrait. Archdale here has just come across one and we'd value your professional opinion.'

There is a soft squelching sound as Simpson rubs his palms together. In an instant, he plots a low valuation, a quick purchase ('just to take it off your hands, sir') and a resale in America at a vast profit. It is, after all, quite clear that these two idiots couldn't tell the difference between a Van Gogh and a *vin rouge*. He chuckles inwardly at his own joke before adopting his most helpful and sincere voice.

'Well, gentlemen, if it's not too far away, lead me to it. The mater's as happy as can be here for an hour or so, meeting people and making new friends.' He glances in the direction of his mother, still standing alone, staring into the distance. She is shored up by her walking frame but seems likely to crumble at any moment. Deciding that one more dead pensioner will make little difference, and that Mary Compton can probably wait a little longer for her news, Ashley leads the way back to Old House.

*　　*　　*　　*　　*

'I'm going for a ride in the park.'

Tom Two, sitting cross-legged on his bed, looks up from his equestrian magazine; Tom One is already rummaging around in his locker, throwing breeches and other items of kit onto his bed.

'Don't be stupid, One – the doctor's put you off exercise until tomorrow. You might mess your back up all over again.'

'I'll be fine – I only want to plod around.' A green and cherry stable belt curves across the room like a rainbow with only two colours. 'Besides, if getting back on is going to be a fiasco, I'd rather find out by myself than in front of everybody else.'

'Fair enough. Do you want a hand with grooming and tacking up?'

'Thanks, Two – I was hoping you'd offer.'

Tom Two untwines his legs and pulls a set of green coveralls over his civilian clothes. Laboriously, he laces himself into a pair of army boots while Tom One buttons himself into a khaki shirt and rolls up the sleeves. A few moments later, grunting in reaction to the strain on his spine, Tom One pulls on his riding boots and buckles up his spurs. Tom Two watches the process with interest and raises an eyebrow.

'Not so much as a twinge,' Tom One lies. He pauses to admire himself in the mirror: 'You'd never know there was a cripple lurking beneath the kit.'

A riding helmet and a service cap are removed from hooks by the door, and the pair clatter down the stairs of their accommodation block. Tom Two puts on and adjusts his service cap as they emerge onto the parade ground; Tom One cradles his hard hat in his left arm.

Apart from a distant sentry, the barracks are deserted. Soldiers are either away for the weekend or, their morning routines complete, occupied elsewhere. Sorrell and Vernon have taken a bus into central London in pursuit of adventure and entertainment: a doomed expedition, since they have only ten pounds between them.

The Toms stop off at the harness room to collect a saddle and bridle, then make their way to the stable block, where Tom One's horse is munching his way placidly through a ball of hay. The animal submits with a good nature to Tom Two's hoof pick, making only a token effort to squash his new groom against the partition. The gunner ducks down with practised ease, climbs between the horse's legs and emerges on the other side, unscathed.

'Does he always do that?'

'Only if he likes you – you're in favour.'

The favour continues. The horse nuzzles up to Tom Two as he runs a brush along its neck: a large quantity of saliva transfers itself to the gunner's hair and right ear, and hot equine breath blows contentedly into his face. Expressing a hope that the horse would be less intimate when he was grooming the other end, Tom Two gets on steadily with his task, while Tom One makes encouraging remarks from his seat on a bale of straw.

'You've missed a bit.'

'Ingrate.' Tom Two refines the description with an expletive.

A few minutes later, a sparkling horse is led out onto the parade ground, its saddle and bridle flashing in the sunlight. Tom One contemplates the possibility of vaulting into the saddle, before taking his friend's advice and heading for the mounting block. He casts a furtive look around the square to make sure that he is unobserved, then climbs the steps and swings himself gingerly into position. He winces as his coccyx comes into contact with the cantle.

'Are you sure this is a good idea, One?' Tom Two guides his comrade's right leg to the front of the saddle while he adjusts the girth.

'No, I'm not sure – but at least I know what I'm in for tomorrow.' The girth tightened, Tom One brings his leg back into position. 'Thanks for looking after me, Two – I owe you a pint.'

'Make it a gallon and we're talking business. If you're not back in a couple of hours, I'll come looking for you.'

'Don't worry – I'll be back.'

Tom One gathers up the reins and squeezes with his calves; his horse walks towards the barracks gate at a dignified pace. Saluting the Officers' Mess and exchanging a greeting with the sentry on duty, Tom One turns onto the road and passes out of sight. Tom Two retrieves his grooming kit from the stable block, then heads in the direction of soap, water and an afternoon snooze.

*   *   *   *   *

As Tom One guides his horse through the streets of North London, Ashley and his companions emerge from the gates of the Fitzjames Hospital and walk across the bridge into the grounds of the King's School. Simpson has embarked on a self-congratulatory and tedious monologue concerning the sketchbook of a minor Victorian artist, which he had bought cheaply and then dismembered, selling off the individual drawings at a vast profit. He fails to mention that the process had involved forging Benjamin Robert Haydon's signature several hundred times, but the detectives are quite capable of working that bit out for themselves.

As they wander towards Old House, Ashley recalls a conversation with his nephew. As part of his basic army training, Tom had taken part in several military exercises: the ingredients of these always seemed to be patrols, weapon cleaning, quantities of camouflage cream and an unpleasant folding shovel, about which the less said the better. One such day in the field had been devoted to a ploy which Tom called a "snap ambush". The memory of his nephew's voice cuts through Simpson's triumphant droning.

'…It was great, Uncle George – there we were, just part of a routine patrol, when the rear man spotted the enemy following us at a distance. So we let them follow, pretending not to notice, until we came to a good wooded spot – then we turned into the trees, doubled back on ourselves and blasted them to bits.'

As it had turned out, the supposed enemy was the commanding officer, who had been none too pleased to be shot at, and who was particularly annoyed when a thunderflash erupted under his rear axle and a gas canister landed in his lap, filling his Land Rover with septic green fumes. This, as far as Tom was concerned, had just added to the fun.

It seems to Ashley that he has just set his own snap ambush. Simpson, untactical and unsuspecting, strolls along the perimeter of an imaginary copse, oblivious to any dangers: indeed, believing himself to be the predator. With Ashley and Archdale representing what Tom had called the "main killing group" and with Constable Telfer ready in position to cut off any retreat, the trap is set as efficiently as if it had been planned all along. In a few moments time, the detectives will unleash the full force of their intellectual firepower.

He finds the thought pleasantly sadistic.

* * * * *

Two cameras whirr electronically as Tom and his horse pass through the park gates. He is used to being photographed by tourists but usually he is in the company of other soldiers – his section, or Tom Two, Sorrell and Vernon. Today, the attention is all his own and he enjoys it to the full, casually saluting the pair of expensive, elderly Americans who have just added him to their sight-seeing collection.

'Morning, ladies.'

'Good morning, officer.' Instant promotion and digital immortality seem quite a good deal to Tom, so he allows the couple to take a few more pictures before continuing to the riding track, leaving them poring over the computerised displays at the back of their cameras. It occurs to him that modern technology would put an artist like Samuel Cooper completely out of business. Why pay a fortune for a miniature when a photograph is so easily available?

The sequel to this thought is disturbing, as Tom considers that perhaps he is just as obsolete as the exquisite portraits he had admired yesterday; what have horses, ceremonial swords and gold-braided uniforms to do with modern warfare? Perhaps he should climb inside a display cabinet as well, or allow himself to be collected by a rich enthusiast?

The gunner knows of only one way to shed depressing thoughts. Deciding that his back can look after itself for ten minutes, he spurs his horse into a canter and charges along the track. The American ladies, delighted at the thought of an action shot, point their cameras and take pictures of a dust cloud in which the hazy outline of Tom and his horse is vaguely discernable.

Along a tree-lined avenue and around the lake; past numberless flowerbeds, until a great expanse of open grass field lies before him and he can gallop flat out without endangering any civilians. As his horse charges across the park, he feels as powerful as any armoured vehicle; after all, who needs to be modern, when the bond between man and horse is timeless? When tanks and giant guns become outmoded and nations have learned to destroy each other by computer, there will still be people like Tom, healthy and muscular, astride their horses, representing the best of all that nature has to offer. Keeping his seat out of the saddle, to spare his spine any unnecessary jolting, with his head held high and his back arched inwards, Tom draws an imaginary sword and, with a wild yell, hurls himself at the forces of a hypothetical, brutal and mechanical enemy.

They scatter before him.

*   *   *   *   *

Ashley is having disturbing thoughts as well. If Simpson has the least idea of what awaits him in Old House, why does he seem so unconcerned? Is he acting brilliantly? Or does the theft of a seventeenth-century portrait really have nothing to do with the most crooked dealer in the area? The problem with ambushes, as his nephew could have told him, is that once you have set them, all you can do is wait and see what happens.

Ignoring the Cliffords' private door, Ashley enters the boarding house through the entrance nearest to Stephen's room, punching the newly learned code into the combination lock. As he now knows, Stephen's room is just around the corner: judging from the sound of a rustling skirt, Amelia Clifford is there as well. Ashley deduces that her instincts remain polygamous despite her renewed devotion to Stephen. He wipes his feet loudly and unnecessarily, banging the door shut and waiting for the soft, rapid pad of retreating feet before proceeding. The party turns to the right and finds Constable Telfer as they had left him, though blushing and with his tie at an angle.

Maliciously, Ashley turns to face Simpson and is pleased to note the art dealer's eyes flashing frantically from the uniformed policeman to Ashley and then to the exit: a passage which is blocked by Sergeant Archdale.

'I'm sorry, Mr Simpson – I should have warned you. We suspect the picture might be stolen, so we've put a police guard over it.'

'Er – so I see.' Simpson gulps, giving a convincing impression of a ham actor in a bad play. Ashley half expects him to run an index finger around his collar; the art dealer manages to resist this but his hands glisten with fresh moisture as he plays with his rings and he now looks redder than Constable Telfer. 'And – um – what makes you think it might have been stolen?'

'It was reported missing two days ago.' Archdale's stern voice suddenly sounds like that of a policeman rather than an inept amateur. 'That's right, isn't it, Telfer?'

Telfer has no idea what is going on, but he knows how to respond: 'That's right, Sergeant.'

Simpson renews his panic-stricken sideways glancing. The

rifles of the killing group are blazing away and there is no escape. Ashley opens the door to Stephen's room and formally introduces Simpson to Arbella Fitzjames.

He resists the temptation to ask if they have already met.

*   *   *   *   *

Tom is on the journey home. His gallop across the open grass has left him aching but content. Were he in the country, he would imitate Lance Bombardier Green, loosen his reins and take his feet out of the stirrups. In London, however, standards of smartness must be maintained and he walks his horse with ceremonial precision. His lower left arm and reins form a continuous line, which bisects another joining his heels, hips and shoulders; the geometry of the mounted soldier producing the perfect consonance of an inaudible *musica humana*. He passes the park War Memorial, turning his head to the right and saluting; another tourist captures him on camera.

He is about to return through the park gates when a voice calls from a distance. His first instinct is to ignore it – he has featured in enough pictures for one morning. The calling, however, becomes more urgent so, unwilling to twist his neck, Tom halts his horse and turns on the forehand. To his surprise, he sees Sir Andrew Esmond jogging in his direction, waving a handful of paper and looking like the White Rabbit, complete with pocket watch, but with nostril hair rather than whiskers. As he draws closer, panting and wheezing, Tom half expects to be addressed as "Mary Anne". Instead, and anticlimactically, Sir Andrew greets him by his proper name.

'I thought it might be you, Gunner Noad – I was on my way to the barracks to find you.'

'Really, sir? Is there anything I can do for you?'

'Well, I hope it's the other way around. I've been doing a bit of research. Have a look at this: it's from Elias Ashmole's journal. 1687, old style, which means 1688 to you and me.'

He holds up the crumpled roll of paper. Tom leans across

207

and retrieves it with his free right hand. He unfolds it and his eyes boggle at the first paragraph:

Feb 20ᵗʰ Being hard press'd at stool yester e'en I purged myself this morning and have been troubled with a looseness all this day, whereon I regret the strength of the dose, which was great.

'Er – I'm not sure I understand, sir?'

Sir Andrew, who has been studying Tom's face for signs of excitement and enlightenment, gives a start.

'Oh, sorry – I should have said that you can skip the bits about the bowel movements. That was Elias Ashmole all over.'

Judging by the next few lines, "all over" is an accurate description. Tom guesses that poor Mrs Ashmole, if she existed, spent a good deal of her time opening windows and wielding a mop. His eyes scan down the page until a familiar surname catches his eye; he reads aloud, so that Sir Andrew will know he has found the right passage.

'*Came to me this morning Sir Robert Fitzjames...*'

'Cousin to Arbella,' Sir Andrew clarifies. 'Her only surviving relative on that side of the family, so presumably her heir; not that she had much to leave by the time she had squandered everything and the house had burnt down.'

'I see, sir,' Tom continues, '*...requesting that I draw up his chart, he being in readiness to travel to Somerset to take possession of his new estate...*'

There follows an incomprehensible diagram. Tom's eyes boggle as he tries to make sense of what looks like a picture of the back of an envelope with strange hieroglyphs scattered over it. 'I'm afraid I'm lost again, sir.'

Sir Andrew retrieves the paper, glances at it briefly and then returns it.

'It's an astrological calculation. A funny thing – and I'm not sure I understand it either. Still, it's fascinating, isn't it? I'll talk you through the rest if you've got half an hour to spare.'

Alarmed by the prospect, Tom looks down at his horse,

who is getting impatient, and threatening to do an impression of Elias Ashmole all over a park bench: 'I probably ought to be getting the horse back, sir.' He adds, in the hope of a negative response, 'But I could offer you tea and a bite to eat at the barracks, sir, if you don't mind slumming it?'

To his horror, Sir Andrew accepts.

CHAPTER TWENTY-FIVE

ASTROLOGERS AND HISTORIANS

Ashley sat in Colin Clifford's study, irritable and unsociable. The day, he decided, had been a failure. In terms of the snakes and ladders game he had visualised earlier, he had indeed slid all the way down the riding boot and back to square one. Torn his trousers on the spur, too, probably...

In the first place, it was quite clear that Robert Simpson had never seen the portrait of Arbella Fitzjames before that morning. He claimed, even, not to have known of its existence, and this insistence had also rung true. He had given a surprisingly good summary of the picture's condition before departing, eyeing the policemen and Ashley warily. The only achievement, it seemed, of Ashley's stupid manoeuvre, was that the art dealer was now on his guard.

Then, after luncheon, Tom had telephoned with a disjointed and incomprehensible account of his meeting with Sir Andrew. Tom Two had done his best to organise the curator's enthusiastic but batty ramblings into a coherent sequence, but even he had given up after a while. Over strong tea, chips and an unidentifiable pie, Sir Andrew had acknowledged that the diary entry probably had nothing to do with Ashley's case: 'But it's quite remarkable, isn't it? I knew you'd both be interested.' Tom had described more lucidly the sense of relief that both soldiers had felt when they had finally managed to frog-march Sir Andrew to the tube station and deposit him on the first train that came along, regardless of direction and destination. Just in case it was of any importance, the gunner had then buttered up Bombardier Burdett, and the

NCO had let himself into the adjutant's outer office and faxed the pages of Ashmole's diary to Ashley. They lay on a small table in front of him, as meaningless to Ashley as they were to his nephew.

Colin Clifford looked up from his desk, deciding that it was time to end the grumpy silence. 'Who was Elias Ashmole, George? Anything to do with the Ashmolean Museum?'

Ashley nodded. 'Everything to do with it. He was a scientist and astrologer in the days when there wasn't much difference between the two. He was an early member of the Royal Society and left vast amounts of writings, many of them concerned with his bowel movements.'

'Sounds delightful...'

'Indeed. I remember one of my university tutors telling me that Ashmole had the best documented backside in history – but that's the first extract I've ever seen from his diary.'

Ashley passed the pages to Colin. After the astrological diagram, Ashmole had given his opinion that Fitzjames would find nothing of any value in Somerset. An entry from a month later testified to the accuracy of his prediction. Both Ashley and Clifford were sceptical enough to be unimpressed.

Colin finished reading. 'Of course, the person who would have known all about this was Douglas Peachey.'

Ashley grimaced: 'Don't remind me. I'm still furious with myself for not interviewing him while I could.' He stood and headed for the window. Staring out over the lawn where the Old House drinks party had taken place, he gave a bleak summary of the case so far.

'So, a portrait is stolen – but the only person known to have seen it and to have recognised it as being by a famous painter is dead. The person most likely to want it from the point of view of the obsessive collector is also dead, and is found in a location which suggests the picture has a significance – but what that might be is, as yet, unclear. The picture then turns up in a ridiculous place and the only known art crook in the area is either a fantastic actor – which I doubt – or demonstrates by his manner that he knows nothing about the case. Finally, the lady who is inheriting all the money has, as far as we know, no interest in art and was unlikely to be able to murder Douglas Peachey without assistance.'

He turned away from the window and flopped back into the armchair. 'Every new event raises plenty of questions, but fails to supply a single answer. I'm stumped. I find it hard to believe that Sister Barnfield has *anything* to do with the affair, even though she's an obvious suspect; and I find it just as hard to believe that Robert Simpson has *nothing* to do with it, despite the fact that we didn't get anywhere with him this morning. As for anybody else – who knows?'

'Will a warm, unlimed gin help?' Colin opened a desk drawer and pulled out glasses and bottles, which he kept there for emergencies. Ashley looked at his watch: it was half past three. For the first time that day, he grinned.

'Probably not, but it will cheer me up. Thanks, Colin – and cheers.'

They drank in silence for a while. Colin returned to his work and Ashley amused himself by drawing up the most ridiculous theory possible: Sister Barnfield, the leader of a coven of witches (consisting of herself and the four retired matrons) had murdered Peter Bulmer, intending to eat him at the next astrologically significant opportunity. Disturbed in her task by an unknown art thief, she had kidnapped the intruder and was holding him in her cellar, fattening him up for the feast. Douglas Peachey, meanwhile, had been ritually sacrificed by the retired matrons, whom he had taken by surprise as they danced naked round the glade in the forest.

Colin Clifford walked across the study to refill Ashley's glass and read over his shoulder. He laughed.

'From what I know of the people, George, it sounds a probable theory.'

Ashley rolled his paper into a ball and threw it into the wastepaper basket: it had served its purpose. A moment later, the extracts from Elias Ashmole's diary followed it: there was

212

no point in hanging on to irrelevant material.

Halfway down his second glass, he felt more inclined to take a positive view of things: after all, now that the police had moved in on the case, the murders were none of his business. He could claim the credit of the discovery of the second body and he had played his part in the recovery of Mary Compton's picture: as for the rest – well, that was the problem of Sergeant Archdale and his team. Ashley could simply walk away from it all whenever he wanted to.

Colin Clifford saw the flaw in his reasoning: 'Except that you're a first-rate Nosey Parker, George, and you won't be able to rest until the case is over. And rather than leaving it to the police, you see it as a race between you and them.'

Ashley was forced to recognise the truth of the analysis. He liked Sergeant Archdale, but he definitely wanted to get to the solution first, especially after the fiasco of the snap ambush that morning.

'You're right, of course, Colin. As far as the race goes, though, I don't think there's anything more to be done today.'

'Then why not telephone James and go through that essay with him? You said yourself that you owe it to him.'

*   *   *   *   *

The day had been much more enjoyable for Lance Bombardier Green and Stephen. Arriving at the stable, they had been put to work by ex-Sergeant Jones and had helped him construct a cross-country jumping lane in a nearby field. They had roped and hammered together six sets of logs and trestles, then hauled them into position, a hedge on one side and carefully arranged jumping poles on the other, so that lazy or awkward horses were unable to duck a fence by swerving to the left or right. Then the three of them had test-driven the course: they saddled up Jones' three best jumping horses, cantered into the field and took the fences in succession. Green, last in line, watched Jones fly over the third fence as Stephen took the second and his own

213

horse curved above the first with a good six inches to spare. The pattern repeated itself continually: when Jones had cleared the last fence, he simply charged around the perimeter of the field and started the process once more. They stopped only when the horses were steaming with sweat and their shirts were drenched and sticking to their bodies.

Back in the stable yard, they hosed down the horses, deliberately spraying each other occasionally, to cool off. Then, deciding that the saddles and bridles could wait until another day, they draped their shirts over the fence of the outdoor school to dry and retired to the office for tea. Wet riding boots were removed and thrown into a corner, and Jones distributed green army towels. Judging from their smell and texture they had last been washed some time before he stole them from the barracks; still, they did the job and the stale smell of old towel blended in with the aroma of three tired horsemen.

Their first mug of tea, like Ashley's gin, was consumed in silence. Half way through the second, Jones belched loudly, by way of expressing contentment, and conversation began.

'So yesterday you found a body, today you found a portrait?'

'That's right, Sarge – and considering the woman in the picture has been dead for three hundred years, she was looking a sight more attractive than the body, I can tell you. Stephen found her,' Green added, scrupulously giving the credit where it was due. Stephen beamed, as pleased as if he had just been awarded a medal.

'Is your Mr Ashley chuffed?'

'Not really – it's messed up all his theories.'

'Ah, well.' Jones, who had never had a theory in his life, was inclined to be stoical. He took another mouthful of tea in the satisfied manner of one who lives for the moment. 'So, come on then, fill me in on the latest details.'

Alternately – and haphazardly – Green and Stephen served up slices of information. Green sent Stephen out to check the horses before he gave an unexpurgated version of his time with

214

Sister Barnfield, expressing the opinion that a quarter of a million pounds was the nearest the nurse would ever come to being worth her weight in gold.

Jones whistled at the thought. 'Big lady, is she?'

'If she ever moves to London, she'll live in Wapping, Sarge. And if she marries, they'll need to hire two marquees – one for the reception and one for her frock.'

'Don't you knock the larger-boned lady, Green – there's a lot of fun to be had on a bouncy castle.' Jones stroked his chin thoughtfully; he kept Sunday as a day of rest by not shaving, so sharp bristles rasped against his fingers. 'You know, with a quarter of a million pounds, I could turn this stable into something out of a Gucci catalogue... You couldn't arrange an introduction, could you?'

*   *   *   *   *

The re-worked essay left Napoleon III in enemy hands, the Empress Eugenie fleeing from the Paris mob and Bismarck rubbing his hands with glee at the acquisition of new territory and increased power. James had done his work thoroughly: the facts were in a logical sequence and their interpretation showed insight and originality. The expanded conclusion was now worthy of the previous half dozen sides. Impressed, Ashley handed it back to its owner.

'Beyond congratulations, James, I've little to say. I think any A-level examiner will be delighted to read anything half as good as that. I've marked a couple of points in, but they're only about grammar and style – not about the content.'

James was embarrassed and grateful in equal measure. He covered up the former by sipping from the glass of claret that Ashley had poured for him. 'Thanks, sir, that's really good of you.'

'It's a pleasure, James.' Ashley replied truthfully. His mind had been taken away from the irritations of the day and he had enjoyed being able to help somebody who had known all too little support so far in life. While James analysed the handful of comments in the margin, Ashley took time to study the face and character in front of him.

He had noticed the painful thinness and awkward posture of the boy on their first meeting. Sitting in the second armchair of Colin Clifford's study, James' arms and legs contorted themselves to fit into furniture designed for more normal proportions: he looked like a long-legged insect trying to fold away its limbs. What was new to Ashley was the fire and determination that he could see in James' eyes. Before, they had sat side by side on the bench outside Peachey's apartment; now that the boy was sitting opposite him, Ashley saw an inner strength which he had not suspected. He recalled the toughness that underlay the surface vulnerability of Gunner Sorrell. Both Sorrell and James had had a rotten start to their lives: both were determined to escape their origins, Sorrell through joining the army, James through education and university. The resemblance between the two ended there but, in their different ways, the soldier and the student inspired first compassion and then respect.

Ashley became aware that he was being studied as well: James had finished reading his comments and now the dark, piercing eyes were focused on the detective. Ashley gave a slight shudder, realising how uncomfortable it was to be on the receiving end of an interrogative stare. He brought himself back to the matter in hand.

'So, that's about all I can do for you on the Franco-Prussian war, James. I'm on firmer ground with your other period – the English Reformation.'

They talked at length: the paranoia of the Tudors concerning the succession to the throne; the doubting vacillations of Cranmer; the ruthlessness of Cromwell and the unlikelihood of any honest man ending up with his head still on his shoulders. All these were considered in a rambling conversation which allowed itself to explore interesting digressions as they occurred or to switch direction as a new theme suggested itself. Above all these, and intruding into every aspect of the discussion, the figure of Henry the Eighth manipulated his way through the first half of the sixteenth century, raising and destroying his servants as it suited his purposes.

As the dialogue began to wind down, Ashley guessed that the awkward shuffling of James' limbs was in preparation for a request for an essay title. It occurred to him that what James needed was not another essay – he was going to sail through that part of the examination with ease. He needed less time crouched over his desk, not more. The boy would probably not thank him for the suggestion that he should spend a day at Jones' stable, mucking out and learning the first principles of riding, yet it would have done him the world of good.

By the time the request came, Ashley had thought of a more acceptable course.

'No James, I'm not going to set you any work – I'm going to do something far more practical than that.

'I'm going to take you to Glastonbury Abbey.'

CHAPTER TWENTY-SIX

MONKS AND MONARCHS

Nobody was in the mood for any detective work on Sunday evening. Shortly after James had taken his leave, Green's Land Rover spluttered up to the entrance of Old House; as if a victim of an efficient military operation, Ashley found himself bundled into the back and driven off at vast speed in the direction of a country pub. He and Stephen anchored themselves in position as best they could, while equestrian kit, a tool box and a couple of pairs of army boots bounced around dangerously.

'It's my fault, sir.' Stephen deflected the toolbox, which was sliding dangerously towards his kneecap. 'We've got to find a pub where they don't know I'm only seventeen. The lance bomber did suggest that Mr Jones might like to go in the back instead of you, but you can probably imagine what he said, sir.'

The pub, it seemed, lay across several ploughed fields, two or three barely fordable streams and at the end of a pock-marked track, with holes, bumps and an erratic camber. The army boots tap-danced their way through the journey and the tool box provided a regular shuttle service from one end of the vehicle to the other.

But the beer was good and the company entertaining. They sat in a garden, watching the sun become larger and redder, until it seemed to sink under its own weight beneath the tree line of the old Fitzjames estate. They talked horses and murders, school and army, London and the West Country. After a while, Green and Jones began to revisit episodes from their lives with Prince Albert's Troop, firing Stephen with enthusiasm and making Ashley feel like one who had missed out on the action on St Crispian's Day. Finally, Green switched to coffee for the last couple of rounds and drove them home through the night. In the back of the Land Rover, the army boots took on the form of poltergeists, flying through the darkness and attacking the passengers at every opportunity. The toolbox, taking advantage of reflexes dulled by several pints of beer, yapped at their ankles like a terrier. An old bridle detached itself from its hook and attempted to entangle their legs.

*   *   *   *   *

After a few unpleasantly realistic dreams, involving kidnapping and brutality, Ashley had slept deeply and at length. He woke late the next morning and enjoyed the unusual sensation of having his bedroom to himself and an uninterrupted period of quiet contemplation. At about half past nine, he descended to the kitchen, where he found James waiting for him and where Diana Clifford informed him that Lance Bombardier Green had gone to the stable with Stephen; he had taken his mobile with him and would return the moment Ashley needed him.

Ashley greeted James and pondered Diana Clifford's news. It had been his intention to ask Green to drive to Glastonbury, but it seemed selfish to ask the soldier to return just to carry out an errand which had nothing to do with the murders. Thinking aloud, he mumbled something about taking a cab, at which James interrupted him.

'Transport isn't a problem, sir, if you have a driving licence – I've got a provisional one, so we can go in my mother's car.'

And so they had squeezed into a shabby Ford Fiesta, James once more giving an impression of a long-legged beetle as he folded himself into the driving seat and drove the seventeen miles to Glastonbury, mainly in the wrong gear. When the exhaust pipe gave a convincing impression of a death rattle, Ashley concluded that Lance Bombardier Green must have a long-lost twin brother who eked out a living as a driving

219

instructor in Somerset. Leaving the car sprawled across two bays in the abbey car park, Ashley managed to pay for both the parking and the entrance tickets to the abbey while James painfully extracted himself from the car.

The visit was worth a dozen formal lessons. They stood at the west end of the fragmented building and realised that what had seemed to be the walls of a substantial nave was no more than a pair of chapels: a prelude to a structure of the most immense dimensions. Slowly, like the fragmented remains of a mediaeval procession, they passed up the centre aisle of the nave, noting the diamond slabs that marked the former positions of massive pillars. Ashley tried to wind back time, as he had so often attempted when solving cases. He imagined the pillars growing out of their markers, then heavy, semicircular Romanesque arches curving across from column to column and from side to side, sprouting tracery high above them, replacing the warm blue sky with dull, grey stone. He recalled an afternoon when the cathedral architect at Durham had taken him above the vaulting and he had stood on a wooden walkway looking down at the ugly, lumpen expanse of the vaulting from the wrong side: ridiculously terrified that the extra few stone of his weight would cause the structure to collapse and send him plunging towards the stone slabs on the nave floor. He smiled at the irrationalism of long ago, then reflected that, at some point, the vaulting at Glastonbury must have done just that. Piles of rubble seemed to appear before him; clouds of dust, thick and choking, enveloped his imagination, and the echo of the monumental avalanche pounded against his eardrums. Jerusalem was desolate: the heathen had come into the Lord's inheritance.

The vision receded; they passed through the remains of the great central crossing and into the choir, then headed steadily towards the High Altar, skirting around the site of Arthur's supposed tomb. Ashley reminded himself that this would have been an uphill journey; there would have been steps up to the choir, then more to the altar itself, so that a priest, turning to face the assembled monks and pilgrims, would have had a panoramic view of the whole vast expanse of the abbey.

There was an east chapel, finished barely in time for the Reformation; there were the outlines of cloisters, a chapter house and all the living quarters of the monks. From these grounds, they could see the Tor, the volcanic plug that must once have seemed to rise out of the water of the undrained levels as if by supernatural force. At the top stood the tower, witness to both the abbey's greatness and its downfall. It seemed to Ashley that he was one of a vast crowd, watching from below as the last abbot was dragged up the Tor and hanged from the top of the tower. Then, when he was cut down, his head had been struck from his body and displayed on the abbey gate, his body had been quartered and distributed around the country: a brutal crime, which dared time to obscure it.

James took up the theme.

'The whole building is a corpse, isn't it, sir? These isolated arches are just so many odd bits of bones.'

Ashley nodded. 'And like those fragments you see in museums, this was once alive. You can trace its growth in the patterns of the architecture.'

Mentally, Ashley continued the metaphor: individual monks and pilgrims became blood cells, their processions and activities the circulation of the body; the chapter house was the brain; the chanting of the services a respiratory system.

The thought of this life destroyed was profoundly melancholic: this building had been no Peter Bulmer or Douglas Peachey, decayed and almost ready to die of its own accord; it had been in the fullness of its late Middle Age, active, experienced and wise. Like the last abbot, it had deserved a better fate.

* * * * *

'I feel ready to die.'

'Shifty Scott's got some equine liniment in his room – do you want me to rub some into you?'

Tom One's reply combined a negative and an expletive. He lay supine on his bed, his arms draped over the sides and his boots and spurs hanging over the end. Having decided that any pain was better than a day's inactivity, Tom had mucked out and groomed his horse, then shuffled gingerly to the doctor and insisted that he was well.

'Are you sure, Gunner Noad?'

'Absolutely, sir – and anyway, I'm bored of being off duties.'

'Fair enough – I'll put you back on for a couple of days and see how it goes.'

Tom had thanked the officer, walked away as smartly as he could, then resumed hobbling once the door to the surgery was closed. He knew he hadn't fooled anyone, but he had got what he wanted. Tom Two reminded him of this as he lay back groaning, occasionally clicking his spurs softly, as a sign of life.

'You insisted on it, One.'

'I know – but that was before Sergeant Miller reverted to type and gave us a real bastard of a lesson. Rising trot without stirrups is bad enough at the best of times.'

'Tell me about it: my thighs are still pulsating. It's taking all my powers of concentration just to keep my knees together.'

'Just like Available Annie.'

'Thanks for that thought, One.'

In spite of their moans, the two gunners were content. They were both pleased to have survived a taxing lesson and they had half an hour of free time before the midday meal. Tom Two steadied a wobbling leg for long enough to flick the switch of an electric kettle with the toe of his boot and they gulped down strong tea, working their way through a packet of biscuits as they did so. Tom One rolled onto his stomach and propped himself up with his elbows in order to drink.

Two paused to contemplate a dunked and sagging biscuit,

then snapped his jaw around it before it collapsed into his mug. 'I say, One?'

'Yes?' Tom One had made his own lunge too late and was now occupied in fishing a forlorn biscuit from his tea with the aid of a boot hook.

'I was thinking about that astrologer chap.'

'Amyas Arsehole?'

'That's the one. Do you think that predictions in those days were self-fulfilling?'

'How do you mean?' Tom One flicked soggy bits of biscuit into the waste bin.

'Well, in those days, they believed in it, didn't they? It's not like Shifty Scott reading those rubbishy horoscopes in the *News of the World*, is it?'

'I don't know – that one about him "holding love in the palm of his hand" seemed pretty accurate to me.'

'Well, all right – but what I'm getting at, is that this Fitzjames chap must have gone to the astrologer in the same way that you've been to the doctor. He pays him good money and gets what he believes to be a serious dollop of good advice.'

'So?' Tom One retrieved another drowned biscuit from his tea.

'So, our man now goes down to the West Country *expecting* to be disappointed – which means he probably doesn't try very hard to find anything. Do you see what I mean?'

Tom One nodded and sucked soggy biscuit off the end of his boot hook. 'I think so. Do you reckon it's important?'

Tom Two shrugged. 'Probably not. At any rate, not important enough to ring your uncle.' Tom Two looked at his watch: 'And certainly not as important as lunch. If we go down now, we'll be first in the queue.'

* * * * *

Ashley and James had luncheon in the Sedgemoor Inn at Westonzoyland. Their original intention had been to return to

223

Bruton but the morning had been enjoyable and neither teacher nor pupil wished to bring the exercise to a close. On a whim, Ashley suggested to James that they drive out to the site of the battle of Sedgemoor.

'I know it's not part of your course, but after everything that's come up in the last few days, I'd quite like to see it.'

'Me too, sir – Mr Peachey was always talking about taking me there one day, but we never got around to it. It's not far at all.'

Westonzoyland appeared to have recovered from the shock of hosting a battle in its back garden by sleeping for the next three hundred years. A slow-spoken girl took their order with laborious precision, mouthing the words as she wrote them down phonetically. On her wrist, a charm bracelet rattled sympathetically.

This served to jog Ashley's memory. When the girl had shuffled off to the kitchen, he asked James: 'Was Mr Peachey interested in astrology?'

James considered his answer before replying, sipping a soft drink pensively.

'I think, sir, he was interested in it as an important part of seventeenth-century life. He thought it was all a load of nonsense, of course, but he talked several times of the hold astrologers could have over people – he liked that sort of thing, as you can probably imagine.'

Ashley could. He pictured Peachey in the role of *magus*, flogging off bogus predictions and persuading the weak minded that it was their destiny to do his dirty work for him. James continued: 'I remember him saying that after the fire of London, everyone was consulting astrologers to see if they could find buried treasure – and he reckoned the only people who got rich quickly were the astrologers themselves. Why do you ask, sir?'

Ashley shrugged. 'It was just something that Mr Clifford and I were looking at yesterday – an extract from a seventeenth-century diary. It contained an astrological diagram which didn't make any sense to me, but we thought it could have meant something to Mr Peachey.'

'It might have done, sir, but I don't think his knowledge could have been very detailed – otherwise he'd have banged on about it at every opportunity.'

This sounded like an astute piece of character analysis. Ashley nodded and the conversation drifted in other directions.

After luncheon, they strolled around the village, uncertain how to find the battlefield. At the church, James recalled one of his former teacher's digressions.

'I remember Mr Peachey saying all the captured rebels were held in here, sir – hundreds of them. They had to disinfect the building with frankincense afterwards.'

'Well, then, James – let's go in and have a look.'

Unlike Glastonbury, the church seemed to have got over its traumatic past: maybe the incense had worked, or perhaps three centuries of services had successfully overlaid the misery and squalor of a few summer days in 1685. They found a collection of leaflets on a table in the south aisle: one of them was a short guide to the battle itself, so they bought it and followed its directions along footpaths and back roads until they came to the scene of the Duke of Monmouth's defeat. They traced the course of the Bussex Rhine, now no more than a stream, but once a huge drain, large enough to block the rebels' progress. The forces of King James had been ranged on the other side and had been free to fire their cannon and muskets into the rebel lines with deadly effect. Moving away from the water, Ashley and James headed for higher ground and found themselves on the rising where the Life Guards had waited, ready to launch their decisive attack. In the distance, they viewed a long hedge line and speculated that behind it lay the road along which the rebels had trudged through the dark.

'They were trying to surprise the King's forces by attacking at night, sir, but a musket went off and alerted them. There's still a lot of debate about whether it was fired on purpose.'

Ashley gave a wry smile. 'Let me guess – Mr Peachey

225

favoured the conspiracy angle and maintained that it was deliberate.'

James grinned in return. 'You're half right, sir – he always wanted to see conspiracies wherever he could. But in this case, he reckoned it was an accident – he said you couldn't hope to get an untrained army through the dark without something going wrong.'

And so, thought Ashley, the rebels had been forced into a chaotic and hopeless offensive. How many had died at the edge of the very stream he had walked along a few minutes ago, their pitchforks and crude weapons smashed to pieces by the cannonballs of the Royalist army? Monmouth, Ashley knew, had fled the field: did he consider seeking refuge with Arbella Fitzjames? Did he even know the way? Whatever his intentions, he had been captured and taken to London and to the scaffold; with him had gone the hopes of Arbella and thousands of West Country peasants who had been caught up in his cause.

The leaflet from the church was short and vague as far as the strategy of the battle was concerned. It seemed that Colonel Oglethorpe – he who had stationed himself in the Fitzjames Hospital on his way west – had overslept and missed most of the action: this seemed appropriate conduct for one who was part of Bruton's history. They spent another half hour walking the scene, trying to work out the course of the battle; then, reluctantly, decided that it was time to return home.

CHAPTER TWENTY-SEVEN

THE STAIRS AGAIN

Half past five. Robert Simpson prepares to wander to the Blue Ball for a much-needed drink. As he adjusts his cravat in the looking glass, his eyes scan the reflection of the room behind him. He almost expects the two policemen to enter and to feel the heavy hand of Constable Telfer on his shoulder. Turning around, he surveys his threatened territory: surely there is nothing to worry about? Every drawer has been explored, every document studied, every computer file scanned. The house is clean; cleaner than his immaculate fingernails or his permanently shining slip-on shoes.

Even so, he is on edge. He reminds himself to be extra cheerful at the bar, conspicuously jovial, lest the barmaid should detect any anxiety. There will be gins and Dubonnet all round, although it is not pension day. Above all, he reminds himself, *act naturally.*

He is not sure he can remember how to do that.

*   *   *   *   *

Arbella Fitzjames is lying on her back, flirting with half a dozen policemen. It is impossible to dust her for prints, so two experts are examining her minutely with magnifying glasses. A third stands by, ready with a soft brush and a pair of tweezers. Judging by the expression on the courtesan's face, she is enjoying the experience enormously.

Impervious to her wiles, the inspector paces the room sulkily. He has no interest in art and this particular example has no right to be here: she should be in the basement of a crooked dealer, or rolled up in the wardrobe of a murderer. Evidence come by this easily is no evidence at all.

Archdale and Telfer lean back on a filing cabinet, secretly enjoying the discomfort of their superior. True, they are up against the same brick wall as him but, ultimately, it is he who carries the responsibility. Archdale sneaks a look at his watch, then angles it so that Telfer can see the dial. Half an hour until they can go off duty.

A magnifying glass reaches the top right hand of the picture. An expert looks up.

'I think I've found something.'

*   *   *   *   *

Lance Bombardier Green and Stephen have not found anything. Anticlimactically, they walk their horses gently back to the stable yard. Like Ashley and James, they had followed their instincts during the afternoon; and their instincts had taken them to the glade in the wood where Douglas Peachey lay buried.

They had had the wood to themselves: the police, satisfied that everything possible had been found, had abandoned it, though the grave itself was still fenced off with tape. They had moved their horses as close as possible to the barrier, uncertain as to whether crossing it would constitute a criminal act. The grave had been refilled, but the brushwood was left where it had been scattered and the dark brown hump could be seen in its entirety.

'It's not very big, is it, Lance? Was he curled up in it, or something?'

'No idea, Steve – I couldn't see from where I was. I noticed it was a short grave though. About four feet, do you reckon?'

'Thereabouts – that's really weird.'

Then Green had shown Stephen his former vantage point. More confident than Ashley, Stephen had insisted on standing up on his saddle to experience the same view, and the two had leaned side by side against a branch, peering through the leaves.

'What's that other tape, Lance?' Stephen had pointed through the greenery at a line of tape which began about ten yards from the grave.

'No idea – let's go and have a look.'

Once again, Green had lowered himself into the saddle by opening his legs and then gripping with his knees as they came into contact with the horse. His descent was smooth and his landing controlled. Stephen, attempting the same, descended with the speed of a guillotine blade and spent the next two minutes speechless with agony.

'Bad luck, Steve – if I'd realised you were going to try that, I'd have warned you. If it's any consolation, I don't think your horse enjoyed it much, either. I'll show you how to do it properly some time…'

They had moved round to the other tape and guessed that it marked the presumed route of Peachey and his companion. The path had every appearance of being well-trodden: grass was flattened and twigs on bushes were broken. Since every flat-footed policeman in Wincanton seemed to have taken a walk along it, there was no reason not to follow it themselves. They had pressed their bodies down against the necks of their horses to avoid low branches, which meant that they had been able to study the ground efficiently. If the path had ever concealed secrets, it had revealed them to the police: after ten minutes, they reached a narrow road without making any discovery or increasing their knowledge of how the crime might have been committed. With a sense of disappointment, they had turned their horses in the direction of the stable.

And now they are entering the yard and halting in front of the harness room. Just to show off, Green dismounts by backward somersault, hooking his left leg over the horse's neck, sliding part of the way down to the ground, then flipping his feet over his head, so that he lands on the near side of his horse and in the position of attention.

'Wow!' Stephen is in raptures: 'Can you show me how to do that, Lance?'

'Maybe – sometime.' The lance bombardier nonchalantly runs up his stirrups and loosens the girth. Recruits, he reflects, are like women – sometimes it is worth keeping them waiting...

*   *   *   *   *

Ex-Sergeant Jones hears the return of the riders as he smooths down an awkward patch of hair with some hoof oil. For once, the retired soldier is grooming himself rather than a horse, though the process is worryingly similar. Standing on an army towel in front of the bathroom sink, he has given himself a quick up-and-down with an ancient green flannel, picked out the fluff from between his toes and removed the grime from underneath his fingernails. This last task has been achieved with a dandy brush from the stable: it looks like one of the giant's props from a production of *Jack and the Beanstalk*.

He stands back to admire the effect: not bad, he decides, for the far side of forty – the muscles are good, the chest is hairy, and the hoof oil has had the added effect of obliterating a few grey strands just above the forehead. He cups his hands over his face, breathes out heavily and recoils from the blistering gust of halitosis. Making a mental note to gargle on some diluted Jeyes Fluid when he goes down to the stables, he retires to his bedroom to dress.

When he has finished untacking and grooming his horse, Lance Bombardier Green is going to introduce his old sergeant to a quarter of a million pounds.

*   *   *   *   *

Dr Holbrooke stares bleakly out of the latticed window of his study, every bit as anxious as Robert Simpson. Prayer has not helped him, nor have study and administration.

Alcohol has helped a little.

He takes another sip of sherry and contemplates life in the hospital courtyard. Sister Barnfield, tottering unsteadily, heads towards the door that leads through to the sanatorium. Arranged all around her, like sandbags stabilising a hot air balloon, carrier bags stretch and wobble, filled to capacity with good things from the supermarket. She pauses to look furtively at Peter Bulmer's apartment, then stares in the opposite direction towards Douglas Peachey's before resuming her progress.

The doors are unguarded now. Like the burial site in the wood, the police have found all they require. Before long, presumably, Dr Holbrooke will be authorised to begin the task of clearing the flats and preparing them for new occupants: authorised, too, to prepare for the funerals.

He sighs, turns to refill his glass, then resumes his watch. Sister Barnfield has disappeared. Instead, three matrons head for Jasmine's door, eager for a pre-prandial rubber of bridge and a dissection of the day's events. It is nearly a week since they visited the hairdresser and their elaborate waves and curls are distinctly sagging. Even from this distance, grey roots are beginning to peer through the sky-blue haze on top of Avril. A rare and welcome smile appears on Dr Holbrooke's face as he pictures Avril in a fortnight's time, her hair limp and bi-tonal, looking like a blue budgerigar grappling with a metal scouring pad.

He wonders how the surviving matrons will make up a bridge foursome if one of them is the next to be murdered.

*   *   *   *   *

Had Dr Holbrooke lingered for another minute, he would have seen the matrons replaced in the quadrangle by Ashley and James. As Jasmine's door shut – with a creak that came from a hinge, but which might easily have been from one of the matrons – the detective and his pupil entered through the High Street gate.

231

They were still seeking to prolong their day. For Ashley, it had been a time away from the frustrations of contradictory clues and dubious fragments of evidence. He had no wish to return to Old House and the accumulated messages he would doubtless find waiting for him. Besides that, he was enjoying revisiting his degree subject and he took pleasure in the company of his earnest and intelligent companion.

The day had been almost romantic: Ashley shrank from the word and the idea, but could find no better way of explaining his feelings to himself. For a day, he had taken James out of his studious prison and away from the penurious surroundings of his everyday life; he had seen him responding with enthusiasm to the historic scenes about him and, as they explored the abbey and the battlefield, he had felt the youth begin to relax. Probably for the first time in his life, James was slightly sunburnt; his nose, his ears and the back of his neck were pink and glowing. The frown of concentration had disappeared from his face, replaced by a smile that came from the eyes as well as the lips.

Transformations take more than a day. Ashley knew this and knew, too, that James had an exam to pass and would return to his desk in the morning. Nonetheless, he had made a difference: perhaps he had even changed the direction of James' life. What was certain, was that having brought pleasure to somebody else, he had been repaid in full measure.

And so he had suggested that they explore Bruton as they had done Glastonbury. They had walked along the remains of the old monastic walls and entered the church to see what scars the Reformation had left on a building still functioning. There were nonsensical holes in the wall and steps that led to nowhere as evidence of a substantial Rood screen, dismantled by the protestants. About six feet off the ground, empty niches must once have been occupied by statues; in the clerestory – in light, and inaccessible – the saints were still triumphant. They had passed time, trying to guess the identity of the statues from the heraldry of their symbols of sanctity. St Peter, with his crossed keys, was straightforward enough; the statue with the sword might be St James, St Thomas or any one of the holy and decapitated. Around and among them, like a playful shoal, the Fitzjames dolphins swam and gambolled, living up to their reputation as harbingers of social love.

And now they were in the Fitzjames Hospital, examining an institution that had managed to avoid the grasp of the avaricious monarch. Indeed, apart from the present murders, the hospital's biggest drama must have been the night that Colonel Oglethorpe had stationed himself here with his cavalry: and since the colonel's idea of a well-fought campaign seemed to have involved a solid eight hours' sleep, the crisis must have been of the most diminutive kind.

They entered the wood-panelled room where the colonel had held his council of war. James sat in the most ornate chair – presumably the very one that Oglethorpe had occupied – and improvised a pre-battle speech which dwelt on bedtimes and instructions for his early morning chocolate. It wasn't particularly funny but, coming from James, it was remarkable. Ashley laughed dutifully, as convincingly as he could.

Outside once more, they spotted carved dolphins until they lost count and then paused to admire the bust of Bishop Fitzjames.

'Do you think it's a true likeness, sir?'

'If it is, James, the bishop must have suffered from wind: he looks as though he was trying to suppress a particularly bad attack when the sculptor captured him. We'll get a better look at him if we climb up to Mrs Compton's balcony.'

Aloft, their view was clearer. They could see the faint remnants of the original pigments, worn down by more than four hundred years of rain and irreverent pigeons. The bishop looked as though he had applied his make-up in more restrained quantities than the retired matrons, but without their skill. The ornaments on his roundel now revealed themselves as a dozen or more tiny dolphins, chasing each other's tails.

Dolphins.

Arbella Fitzjames shocking the court by appearing as Arion, straddling a dolphin.

A portrait and a miniature, by the greatest artists of the day.

An obsession by a local historian.

And, throughout history, the manipulation of the weak by the strong.

Ashley gasped. It was as though one of the army boots in the back of the lance bombardier's Land Rover had sprung to life and kicked him in the stomach. His diaphragm began to pulsate spasmodically; he gasped for air, but all he could do was choke.

James, in a panic, reached out towards him.

And the next second, Ashley cascaded down the stairs.

* * * * *

His spine slams against the militant right angles of the steps; a hand attempts to grasp a banister and is wrenched out of alignment. Despairing, he sees his legs arch above his face and knows that the sickening sensation of a somersault is imminent.

Inside his brain, an imperative voice shouts: 'Keep your head up – your head, *up*!'

If he can just do that, he will survive: whatever the damage to his body, his mind will be intact. What are a few broken bones, so long as the intellect lives on?

The somersault complete, his shoulder blades strike the lowest step: in spite of his efforts, his neck jerks violently.

With tremendous force, his skull smashes against a flagstone.

CHAPTER TWENTY-EIGHT

LIMBO

At first, he registers his existence in shades of blue: a dark, Prussian blue for the night; a piercing, cobalt blue for the day. Everything else is formless, and void.

Then there are blurred sounds: vowels without consonants, tones without articulation.

And, through all, pain: the stronger the perception, the more intense the suffering, so that the temptation is to shrink from any awareness and retreat into an insensate vacuum. But he must not.

Once, indeed, he had felt the pain recede: it had retreated from his body, caressing him as it ebbed away, leaving him with an overwhelming feeling of relief. As he relaxed, it seemed that he could defy gravity, for his body had shed its heaviness and a great burden had passed from him.

Then a yell had slashed through the low, buzzing voices – Tom's yell; he knew that, somehow. In an instant, an incoherent, insistent barking – the clatter of urgent feet – the slamming, it seemed as of a hundred fists against his chest. Through the chaos, his first recognised words: 'Fight it – fight!'

He had fought; and the pain had returned, feeding off him and clawing him, worse than before.

A few days? A week?

He feels a hand wrapping itself around his fingers, gripping them tightly so that he has another, welcome, pain to distract him from the fire in his head. He wants to respond, but cannot transmit the instructions, cannot even remember the order to give to make his fingers return the pressure.

235

For a second, the hold is released and then once more fingers slide between his, interlocking and strong. Thumbs overlap and palms press together.

Only Tom has ever held his hand like that: the child Tom, crossing a busy road; the boy, in an aeroplane, thrilled yet frightened by the take-off; the young man on his first leave from army training, at first greeting his uncle formally, then impulsively flinging an arm around his shoulder and, with his free hand, clenching Ashley's fingers in the old way.

There is a primitive power in the contact with another human being. Ashley, passive and weak, feels the strength of his nephew and draws upon it. Struggling against the electric clamouring of his brain and screaming inwardly, he impels a message to the muscles in his hand.

And then there is another yell – of joy. There are footsteps again but they are eager, not urgent; voices are laughing, not shouting.

Ashley can do no more; the effort has exhausted him.

*　　*　　*　　*　　*

It was sod's law, Ashley felt, that when he did finally emerge from his state of unconsciousness, it should be the middle of the night. By rights, he should be surrounded by those he loved (and his sister), a clergyman or two and a posse of smug-looking medics. An off-stage orchestra would begin to play and the credits would roll…

As it was, his only companions were the sound of rain on the window pane and a vague smell of urine: still, any sensation was better than none.

His head ached and his eyeballs stung if he tried to move them, so he simply lay back and contemplated the ceiling, dimly illuminated by the hospital's night lighting. It was a boring ceiling, even by institutional standards but, as far as Ashley was concerned, it was as lovely as a fresco by Michelangelo.

He was not hungry, but his throat was dry. He found

himself with a sudden, unnatural craving for a chipped pint mug full of Lance Bombardier Green's tea. He had a vision of Green, booted and spurred, barging his way through a crowd of doctors and nurses ('Let me through – I'm a soldier.') in order to administer a steaming mug of his orange panacea.

Ashley laughed – and instantly regretted it.

*   *   *   *   *

Six hours later, Green really was there, really was booted and spurred and really did have an enormous mug of tea, though he was keeping it to himself. He and Tom One had been summoned from their horses by an urgent message; they had leapt into a Land Rover and had been racing towards the barrack gates, when the adjutant had leaned out of his office window, flagged them down, and flung them the keys to his Aston Martin.

'A hundred and twenty it did, Mr Ashley – no problem. I could have gone even faster, only Tom One looked as though he was about to puke all over Captain Raynham's nice leather upholstery.'

Green was doing most of the talking, in between munching grapes. Tom One, precariously balanced on a few spare inches by Ashley's side, just held his uncle's hand in the old way and blinked rather more frequently than usual. Ashley, too weak to say much, was now sitting, propped up by numerous pillows and a diagonal metal frame; this left plenty of room at the end of the bed for the lance bombardier, who was squatting, cross-legged on the sheets, to the horror of any nurse who put her head round the door.

'I don't know what they're fussed about, sir,' he said, as another nurse retreated. 'I wiped my boots as I came in – not that a dollop of horse poo on the sheets ever did anyone any harm. And that smear of polish will come out in the wash. Do you want one of these grapes, by the way, sir? They're jolly good.'

237

Ashley slowly shook his head by way of declining. Green examined the bunch, realized that he had eaten half of it and replaced the remaining grapes in their bowl, carefully arranging them so that the bare stalks were out of sight. He slurped his tea and rinsed it around his mouth to wash away the unnatural flavour of fresh fruit.

'It was James who rang for the ambulance for you, sir – but you probably realised that. Sister Barnfield says he's been to see you every day.'

Ashley felt his stomach buckle; the emotion was difficult to analyse. To put off thinking about it, he forced himself to speak: 'What news of the case?'

'Not much, sir.' Green rested his mug on the sheets, ensuring that the washing machine would have to cope with a virulent orange stain as well as boot polish. 'The day that you went arse over apex, Sergeant Archdale called about something they'd discovered to do with the picture, but I'm not sure what it was.'

Tom gave a start and sprang to life.

'I know about that – or at least, Two does, because he wrote it all down. The police got in touch with Sir Andrew and asked him to go down and have a look at it. He often does that sort of thing, apparently. The picture had been cut down.'

Green flipped his service cap in the air, dismissively. 'That's old news.'

'No, Lance – I mean, even more, and recently. I'm not sure of the details, but Sir Andrew rang us when he got back from Somerset. He was very excited – but then he always is.' Tom's information tailed off and he returned to his state of tender, gauche silence.

'Mean anything to you, sir?' Green retrieved his cap and began spinning it round his index finger.

Ashley nodded. He managed a few more husky words. 'I think so: I'll know soon. Anything else?'

'Not that I know of, sir – we spent Tuesday fussing about you, of course, and then my leave came to an end. I don't think much can have happened, because there's been nothing in the papers – not even the posh ones in the Officers' Mess – and Telfer said he'd give me a call if anything interesting came up: which he hasn't, except to say that Sergeant Jones and Sister Barnfield are flying to Italy next month for a holiday – if they can find an aeroplane in the Sister's size. Telfer reckons we'll be able to tell when they've landed, because it will be on the news that the leaning tower of Pisa has fallen over.'

That seemed to be it as far as Bruton news went. Green had some gossip from the barracks concerning Gunner Scott's discovery, in the shower, of the latest instalment of the Available Annie Memorial Rash. His ailment, described in colourful detail, made Ashley feel that he had got off quite lightly with concussion.

The gathering lapsed into the awkward torpor that precedes departure: Ashley was enormously glad that his nephew and the lance bombardier had visited but now he wanted to rest; Green, in turn, was pleased to see Ashley on the mend but keen to put the adjutant's sports car to the test once more. Tom would happily have stayed where he was for hours, but when Green bounced off the bed – landing, naturally, in the position of attention – it was time for them both to go.

When they departed, they left, in addition to boot polish and corrosive tea on the sheets, a vase of flowers in regimental colours and an overpowering smell of horse. This was, at least, an improvement on the earlier smell of urine. Ashley sank back down and dozed, dreaming of a cavalry charge; it was led by Green, who was standing up on his saddle. Tom rode to the right of his uncle, deflecting the sabre blows of the enemy. Less effectively, Gunner Scott rode on his left, scratching his groin and supporting a dropping lance.

Green and Tom stopped off in Bruton on their way back to London; mainly to spread the news of Ashley's return to consciousness and partly to show off the Aston Martin. As a result, there was a steady flow of visitors throughout the day: Colin and Diana Clifford brought more fruit and chatted aimlessly while Amelia flirted unsuccessfully with a male nurse; Dr Holbrooke popped in for a miserable fifteen minutes on his way to the geriatric ward; and Stephen arrived in time to top up the equestrian odours, which had been in danger of fading away. He proved himself a soldier in the making by eating the rest of the grapes and leaving straw on the end of the bed. While he was there, a nurse looked round the door to tell Ashley that Sergeant Archdale and Constable Telfer would look in after they came off duty that evening. She flashed a disapproving glare at Stephen before retiring.

Finally, James arrived. He stood awkwardly, clutching the rail at the end of the bed; not speaking, just staring. His eyes showed none of their former fire; they were anxious, and tired.

It was clear that Ashley was going to have to begin. He might as well get the most awkward question out of the way first. His voice sounded unfamiliar, low-pitched and hesitant.

'Did you push me, James?'

Slowly, the head shook from side to side. 'No, sir – I won't say I didn't think of it because, for a split second, I did. But you took a step back, and – well, you know the rest, sir.'

For a moment, Ashley relived the horror of his fall. He felt afresh the pain in his head and body; above all, he recalled the fear and desperation. He forced himself to return to the present.

'Sit down James – and tell me everything.'

James pulled up a plastic chair and sank into it. At first, he just carried on staring at Ashley; then his eyes sank towards the floor and he began his story.

'It all started when Peter Bulmer went to help Mrs Compton hang her pictures. He knew straight away that the portrait was by a famous artist and Mrs Compton told him about it being Arbella Fitzjames and being cut down because it was indecent and all that sort of thing.

'Well, Mr Bulmer came straight over to tell Mr Peachey. I was there at the time, having a lesson, sir, and I don't think I've ever seen Mr Peachey so excited – not just about the picture, but about the scruffy bit that had been added on to it. Did you know about that, sir?'

'Only what I could see when the picture was still in its frame, James. You cut the rest off before you returned the picture, didn't you?'

James raised his head once more to look at Ashley. 'I had to, sir – it was either that, or destroying the whole thing. I rubbed dirt into the cut edge to try and cover it up – but it sounds as though I didn't fool you, sir.'

In spite of himself, Ashley smiled: 'Wrong, James – you fooled me all right and Sergeant Archdale, which is by no means easy. But the police got in touch with an expert and he noticed. Go back to your story.'

James looked away from Ashley again. This time he stared at a patch of wall.

'Well, sir, Mr Bulmer said he thought that there was more of the odd bit behind the frame. Mr Peachey was desperate to see the picture, so Mr Bulmer suggested that they should go up together – but Mr Peachey wouldn't do that in any circumstances. I think he'd already started to contemplate stealing it, so he wanted to keep well away from it in the meantime. You can imagine how devious he was, sir.'

'I can, James. There's a type of person who can never do things in a straightforward manner when there's a more complicated way of getting them done. From what I saw of Douglas Peachey, I'd say that was him all over.'

'You're right, sir. He said Mrs Compton would never agree to have the portrait taken out of its frame – though there's no way he could have known that for certain. He thought up a plan – or rather two plans, one for Mr Bulmer and one for me.

'Mr Bulmer was to pretend to be ill and miss the Corpus Procession and Service. Once everybody else had left, he would let me into the hospital and we would go up to Mrs Compton's flat. Mr Bulmer still had a key that he'd forgotten to hand back. Once we were there, we were to see if the picture could easily be taken out of its frame; if it could, Mr Bulmer was to draw a quick copy of the concealed section and then put everything back as it was before, so that nobody would know we'd been there. That was the plan for Mr Bulmer, sir.'

'And the other plan, James? The one that ended up with Peter Bulmer dead at the bottom of the stairs?'

James expelled a lungful of air and sat for a while, teeth and fists clenched. Then he resumed his story.

'Once Mr Bulmer had left, sir, Mr Peachey came out with plan two. He didn't say anything about murder, of course – he was far too clever for that.

'In the first place, he thought that Mr Bulmer would lose his bottle and, secondly, he needed a plan in case the frame wouldn't come off easily. In either case I was to take charge – and to smash the frame, if necessary.'

'And if Peter objected?'

'That's what I asked, sir. Mr Peachey said that just by being in Mrs Compton's flat, Mr Bulmer would have put himself into a lot of hot water. I could safely tell him that I was going to break the frame anyway because he would be too scared to go to the police.'

'And if he continued to object?'

'That's what I asked Mr Peachey, sir. He said – I can see him now, as if he was looking at me – "You're an intelligent boy, James: you will think of something."'

Ashley felt sick. That rancid, evil old man had ensnared his colleague and his pupil and all for a picture that he could have seen if he had just climbed the stairs and knocked on the door. He pictured the scene in Mary Compton's sitting room: Bulmer, hesitant and scared, refusing to damage the frame; James, possessed and urgent, looking about him for some way...

'The paperweight?'

James' eyes flashed briefly into focus and then looked away again. 'Yes, sir. I didn't stop to think about it – if I had, I wouldn't have done it. I know that, sir, because...'

He stopped. Ashley knew what the continuation would

have been: James had nearly pushed *him* down the stairs, but he had held himself back.

'I understand, James. Just go on.'

'He wasn't dead, sir. But I knew I had to cover my tracks and the only way I could think of to do that was to finish him off. I dragged him out of the flat and down the stairs. Then – then I smashed his head against the paving stone until I heard the skull crack open.'

James was struggling to control himself. He put his face into his hands, like a child convinced that blindness brings with it invisibility. After a minute or so, he looked up again.

'It felt really strange once he was dead, sir. Peaceful, almost.'

James seemed to be displaying the same macabre calmness that he had felt after the murder. Apparently untroubled, he told the rest of the story of that day: how he had returned to the flat and smashed the picture frame; rolled up the canvas and placed it, as instructed, in one of the cardboard tubes Douglas Peachey kept for storing his maps; how he had wiped down the newly varnished steps and walked up them again in Peter Bulmer's shoes; put the duster back in the cupboard under the sink and, for no particular reason, the broken fragments of frame as well. To complete his task, he had locked the front door, slid down the banister and left the Fitzjames Hospital via the gate that led to the school. He had thrown the key and the paperweight into the river as he crossed the bridge.

Ashley pictured it all as James described it. Pictured, too, the gloating Peachey as he returned to his apartment and gained his first sight of Arbella Fitzjames. It was hard to imagine the historian feeling the least remorse for the death of his colleague; for Peachey, the end would almost certainly have justified the means.

'Now tell me about the rest of the picture, James. What was it that led you to the foundations of Arbella's arch?'

'It was surprisingly simple, sir. The hidden part of the picture was an arch with a Latin inscription underneath. It was

243

very badly painted – Mr Peachey reckoned Arbella had done it herself.

'You've got to remember, sir, that Mr Peachey knew everything about that period – and I really mean *everything*. He had all the book references to Arbella and all the circumstances of her life at his fingertips: I don't just mean that he had copies of the books and knew where to look things up – he really *knew* them. It was almost as if he knew her, as well. He'd heard of the portrait long before he'd seen it.'

Ashley digested this information. A few final fragments of mosaic tessellated into position.

'So he'd heard of the miniature by Samuel Cooper as well.' It was a statement, not a question.

James nodded. 'You're there, sir. I'm not a Latinist, so I didn't understand the writing on the picture, but Mr Peachey translated it for me: 'The dolphin and my heart lie under the arch.'

'He reckoned she knew she was dying, sir, and wanted to make some sort of dramatic gesture. The next day, after my mum had gone to work, we drove out in my car and got digging – or at least, *I* got digging.

'About four feet down, we found a box. And in the box...'

James sat up and put his hand in his pocket. He drew out a carefully folded handkerchief, which he passed to Ashley. Carefully, the detective opened out the cloth, then stared, amazed, at the minute perfection of Arbella triumphant.

She was utterly naked, save for a gauze veil, which wafted inadequately about her thighs and waist. The dolphin between her legs hovered, mid-leap, above the sea, its wet skin glistening and reflecting an invisible source of light. With one hand, Arbella gripped its dorsal fin; the other rested casually on the dolphin's tail, so that her torso was twisted, and her opulent breasts displayed to their full advantage.

It was no wonder that a Victorian Fitzjames had mutilated the Lely portrait: Arbella was pure seventeenth-century pornography. Three hundred years under ground had preserved her colours and she straddled the centuries as effortlessly and as shamelessly as she rode her dolphin.

Ashley forced himself to replace the miniature in the handkerchief. It would have been impossible to concentrate on James' narrative if the picture had remained in view.

'And then you killed Douglas Peachey.'

For a second, James' eyes flared defiantly. His jaw hardened and he glared at Ashley, as if daring him to condemn the act.

'I hated him, sir. He was just using me, like he had used Peter Bulmer: he'd turned me into a killer and he'd really enjoyed it – he thought he had total power over me.

'When he saw the picture, he completely forgot about me – I wasn't important any more. He just went on and on about *his* great discovery, *his* triumph and *his* treasure.

'I was already standing behind him with the spade. Killing him was easy – and the hole to put him in was already dug.'

Ashley remembered Green's observation of the shortness of the grave. He pictured Peachey's body, chevron-shaped, with his backside deep in the ground and his legs sticking up. It was difficult to feel any sorrow for him.

'I had to drive back by myself.' James smiled, ironically: 'It's strange, but that was the bit that scared me the most. I cleaned up the spade and put it back in the tool shed; then I had a shower and changed my clothes – and you know the next bit, sir.'

'You turned up for your history lesson as if nothing had happened. I was completely taken in, James.'

'I'm sorry, sir – I didn't mean to use you. I really did value those lessons, especially the day we went out together. I was so happy that day – partly because I thought I'd never be found out, but not just because of that. And then on the balcony, I suddenly realised that you knew I'd done it, and that it was all over.'

Ashley had to test him one last time, though he hated himself for it.

'Unless I died too?'

James was vehement: 'No, sir! I've already told you I didn't – I know it crossed my mind, but I couldn't have done it. You've got to believe me – you know I've been here every day since, and I've brought the picture with me each time, so that I could tell you the whole story when you recovered. If you don't believe me, I'll…'

It was a threat without substance. Instead of finishing the sentence, James erupted with the suppressed emotions of the last week. Howling, he slammed his face into one of the pillows that supported Ashley's back and stayed there, bawling and shaking.

Ashley rested a hand on the juddering shoulders. He felt as if he were a priest, but he was powerless to absolve.

Outside the room, there were footsteps and voices.

Archdale and Telfer were going to be on duty for longer than they realised.

CHAPTER TWENTY-NINE

ARBELLA RESTORED

She hangs in her old position on Mary Compton's wall, arrogant and inviting. By her side, there is a second portion of canvas, re-stretched and framed to match. It shows Arbella's rough attempt to paint her arch; beneath that, there is the continuation of the writing from the main picture. The inscription can now be read in full: *Delphinonem et cor meum sub arcam.*

Sir Andrew Esmond had undertaken the restoration. He had found a genuine seventeenth-century frame to fit the main portrait, then copied the pattern for the smaller fragment. He has also bought the Samuel Cooper miniature from Mary Compton; the price is undisclosed, but by the time the matrons disseminate the news, all Bruton will believe it to be half a million pounds. More accurately, it is known that this money, in addition to the funds acquired on the sale of her property, will fund a second scholarship at the school – for the son or daughter of a non-commissioned officer of Prince Albert's Troop. Several times over the last few days, Ashley has tried to picture a scale model of Lance Bombardier Green in the King's School uniform: the vision is strangely unconvincing. Easier to imagine is the pleasure Mary will gain from her return to the barracks next week, when the Toms will be part of another guard of honour.

Two parties are running simultaneously in Mary Compton's flat. With her in the sitting room, assembled around Arbella, Ashley, Sir Andrew, Doctor Holbrooke and two thirds of the Clifford family make polite conversation and sip claret from the master's cellar. The other Clifford is working her way through the soldiers in Mary Compton's kitchen while Stephen looks on indulgently. This second party is significantly more lively.

Sir Andrew, travelling down with Arbella in the front passenger seat of his Jaguar, found room for the Toms in the back. Lance Bombardier Green, in return for a polished saddle and an illegally accurate racing tip, has once more wheeled the Aston Martin out of the adjutant; he has driven a terrified Ashley to Bruton at the speed of a rocket.

Green flits between the two parties, acting as butler to the first and Master of Ceremonies at the second. By way of giving the wife of a former commanding officer a thrill, he has put himself and the Toms in service dress; a decision which has had the pleasing side effects of making Amelia Clifford swoon with delight and of inspiring Stephen to make the formal announcement that he will be signing up for the army as soon as possible.

'Which means when his mummy lets him, sir.' Green tops up Ashley's glass, flashing a sideways glance at the famous photograph of himself saluting the Queen. The Troop book lies open on a low table and the soldier has been doing his best to rival Arbella for attention. 'It's all going very nicely isn't it, sir?'

'Very nicely, Lance Bombardier: especially in the kitchen, by the sound of it. How have you all managed to squeeze in?'

'It's no problem, sir. Amelia's very happy to sit on any lap that's available – and most of them are. Stephen's sitting on the floor, Tom One's on the pedal bin and Tom Two's on the washing machine. We put it on the spin cycle and he's as happy as a tapeworm in an officer's charger. More wine, Mrs Compton, ma'am?'

Green moves around the sitting room, dispensing claret and lowering the tone of the conversation.

Perhaps it is the wine, perhaps it is an after-effect of his concussion: Ashley's head begins to throb. The sound of voices in one room and laughter in the other becomes painful; discreetly, he leaves the flat and leans against the balcony rail, gulping in fresh air gratefully, while hammers pound inside his brains.

The balcony is a place of memories. In bewildering succession, he sees Peter Bulmer lying at the foot of the stairs, James running up the steps in Bulmer's shoes, then returning, sliding down the banister, the portrait rolled under his arm; suddenly, sky and wood alternate before his eyes as he seems to fall afresh, re-encountering terror, experiencing again the immanent presence of death.

He has to sit, and to sit where he cannot fall. Slowly, shaking, he descends the stairs, then lowers himself down to rest on one of the lower steps, his feet on the flagstone that had cracked his skull.

He contemplates a brilliant mind, corrupted and entangled by the schemes of a wicked man; an inexperienced youth manipulated into committing the worst of crimes. If only James had never met Peachey; if only he, Ashley, could have been his guide; if only…

If only.

Above him, the door to Mary Compton's apartment opens. The sound of partying briefly rings around the quadrangle; as the door shuts, the laughter is sealed inside.

Without turning around, Ashley knows that it is his nephew. Tom steps down with the care that spurs and leather soles require, his boots heavy on the varnished stairs. He sits next to his uncle; a polished, khaki-clad, welcome presence. Their fingers interlock; Ashley feels conflicting emotions surging within him, inexpressible and frightening.

'I understand, Uncle George. At least – I think I do.'

Tom's shoulder is strong and reassuring. Ashley leans against it, allowing the raised metal lettering on the epaulet to dig into his cheek. In his nephew, he knows he has someone he can love without condition; trust without apprehension of any disappointment. In the midst of complexities, this simplicity is worth clinging to. Gradually, the pain in his head recedes and he feels at peace.

'Thanks, Tom. You've really helped.'

They stand, allowing their hands to separate. They climb half way up the stairs, then, impulsively, and risking their balance, they embrace each other. For a minute, they stand there, their bodies still and unbreathing, their eyes closed, their temples obliquely touching.

And then, smiling reassuringly at each other, they return to Mary Compton's flat, where the party is in full flow, and where everyone is happy.

THE END

Printed in Poland
by Amazon Fulfillment
Poland Sp. z o.o., Wrocław